A lone Nephilhim sighted down its forearm…

Grant's Sin Eater launched into his grasp, his finger hooking the trigger on the draw. The lightning reflex movement enabled the former Magistrate to pump a 240-grain bullet into the Annunaki's skull, an explosion of released pressure blossoming its head, leathery hide peeled back to resemble grisly flower petals. The dying drone's ASP blast missed Are5 by yards, destructive energy dissipating into the night sky.

"Great shot!" Are5 complimented.

"Nice improvisation," Grant returned.

Two Nephilhim sought to avenge their decapitated ally, their ASPs vomiting writhing tendrils of yellowish lightning at Grant and the robot, the blasters tearing into the earth around Grant's improvised foxhole and driving Are5 deeper behind his ever-shrinking boulder. Grant winced as a spark sizzling off the main b̶l̶a̶s̶t̶ ̶s̶e̶ared his biceps.

"This shit did not happen w̶h̶e̶n̶ ̶I̶ had fucking guns like̶ ̶

Other titles in this series:

James Axler
Outlanders®

PANTHEON OF VENGEANCE

A GOLD EAGLE BOOK FROM
WORLDWIDE®

TORONTO • NEW YORK • LONDON
AMSTERDAM • PARIS • SYDNEY • HAMBURG
STOCKHOLM • ATHENS • TOKYO • MILAN
MADRID • WARSAW • BUDAPEST • AUCKLAND

First edition August 2008

ISBN-13: 978-0-373-63859-8
ISBN-10:   0-373-63859-0

PANTHEON OF VENGEANCE

I do not love the bright sword for its sharpness, nor the arrow for its swiftness, nor the warrior for his glory. I love only that which they defend.

—J. R. R. Tolkien

The Road to Outlands—
From Secret Government Files to the Future

Almost two hundred years after the global holocaust, Kane, a former Magistrate of Cobaltville, often thought the world had been lucky to survive at all after a nuclear device detonated in the Russian embassy in Washington, D.C. The aftermath—forever known as skydark—reshaped continents and turned civilization into ashes.

Nearly depopulated, America became the Deathlands—poisoned by radiation, home to chaos and mutated life forms. Feudal rule reappeared in the form of baronies, while remote outposts clung to a brutish existence.

What eventually helped shape this wasteland were the redoubts, the secret preholocaust military installations with stores of weapons, and the home of gateways, the locational matter-transfer facilities. Some of the redoubts hid clues that had once fed wild theories of government cover-ups and alien visitations.

Rearmed from redoubt stockpiles, the barons consolidated their power and reclaimed technology for the villes. Their power, supported by some invisible authority, extended beyond their fortified walls to what was now called the Outlands. It was here that the rootstock of humanity survived, living with hellzones and chemical storms, hounded by Magistrates.

In the villes, rigid laws were enforced—to atone for the sins of the past and prepare the way for a better future. That was the barons' public credo and their right-to-rule.

Kane, along with friend and fellow Magistrate Grant, had upheld that claim until a fateful Outlands expedition. A displaced piece of technology…a question to a keeper of the archives…a vague clue about alien masters—and their world shifted radically. Suddenly, Brigid Baptiste, the archivist, faced summary execution, and Grant a quick termination. For

Kane there was forgiveness if he pledged his unquestioning allegiance to Baron Cobalt and his unknown masters and abandoned his friends.

But that allegiance would make him support a mysterious and alien power and deny loyalty and friends. Then what else was there?

Kane had been brought up solely to serve the ville. Brigid's only link with her family was her mother's red-gold hair, green eyes and supple form. Grant's clues to his lineage were his ebony skin and powerful physique. But Domi, she of the white hair, was an Outlander pressed into sexual servitude in Cobaltville. She at least knew her roots and was a reminder to the exiles that the outcasts belonged in the human family.

Parents, friends, community—the very rootedness of humanity was denied. With no continuity, there was no forward momentum to the future. And that was the crux—when Kane began to wonder if there *was* a future.

For Kane, it wouldn't do. So the only way was out—way, way out.

After their escape, they found shelter at the forgotten Cerberus redoubt headed by Lakesh, a scientist, Cobaltville's head archivist, and secret opponent of the barons.

With their past turned into a lie, their future threatened, only one thing was left to give meaning to the outcasts. The hunger for freedom, the will to resist the hostile influences. And perhaps, by opposing, end them.

Chapter 1

Artem15's flat treaded, semiclawed metal foot sank into the hillside with all the ponderous weight of her three-thousand-pound, clockwork-geared frame. The robot's pace seemed to be leisurely as she topped the small swell in the terrain, but it was just the illusion cast by her towering fifteen-foot height. Each swing of her long, mechanized legs was accompanied by the soft, melodic whistle of polished joints grinding against each other.

Artem15 was a decidedly female construct. There was no disguising her feminine breastplate, contrasting with the masculine-sculpted copper torsos of her fellow mechanically suited warriors. Her head, a camera-laden module with ruby-red optics placed where the eyes would be in a bronze-forged representation of a woman's face, was hunched between shoulder-mounted guns. A mane of glimmering golden ribbons of polished and colored steel wool hung like real hair.

Diana Pantopoulos, who piloted the one-and-a-half-ton mobile war suit, was one of the elite. Thus she had been rewarded with the identity Artem15. A mere combat drone bore a singular red ID number painted onto a coppery simulation of a pectoral muscle. The rank-and-file drone pilots strode into battle with ID stencils, not names drawn from the gods of ancient Greece. The mane of Diana Pantopoulos's

suit glimmered like fire in the sunset, two fat, braided ropes
of gold-polished cable falling forward to provide her metallic
breasts a modicum of modesty, keeping the Artem15 armor
from flashing naked breasts on the battlefield. Though the war
suit pilot called the metals that made up the armor copper and
bronze, they weren't. They were far older materials, crafted
by beings whom Hera Olympiad had identified as the gods
themselves. The specifics really didn't matter to Diana,
because inside the robot walker, she was not just another
subject of the New Olympian nation state; she was Artem15,
the Artemis of the third millennium.

She swiveled her camera head to the left, spying Are5,
with his green copper Mohawk jutting from forehead to the
back of his neck, as sharp and aggressive as a circular-saw
blade. A glance to the right showed Apo110, his burnished
yellow locks a more masculine rendition of her own red-gold
wig.

The three of them were Hera's representatives of the
pantheon known as Strike Force Olympus. The three towered
twice as tall as a man, and they bristled with cannons and
wielded massive manipulator claws that could fold into fists
easily capable of crushing a boulder. The god-themed robot
warriors had their own weapons, based on their larger-than-
life inspirations, while the robot drones that they led were
styled after helmeted Spartan warriors; one forearm was con-
cealed under a buckler five feet in diameter, while the other
arm ended in a spike-knuckled claw that could fold into a
two-foot-wide monster fist.

Artem15 looked down into the valley. The commander
units and their squadron of Spartan troopers were standing
as a copper-colored wall, overseeing a writhing mass that she

knew could be nothing but the opposition. The dark one, Thanatos, did not possess the industrial means to match the mechanized might that shielded New Olympus, but the Hydrae hordes below, the warriors of Tartarus, had been produced in clone farms. Despite their primitive technology, they still posed a deadly threat to the Greeks who had striven to rise from postapocalyptic barbarism in the shattered island nation. Thanatos's legion of black, scale-skinned Hydrae snarled, glaring up as one, creating the image of a thousand-handed, thousand-eyed organism of astonishing size. Artem15 knew that the clone horde did indeed act as if it were under the command of a hive mind. Though armed only with muskets and bayonets, the simplest weapons that Thanatos could produce, they were a fearsome force that threatened to overwhelm the town Strike Force Olympus had sworn to protect.

Artem15's pilot clicked on the loudspeaker built into her head unit. "You have only one chance. Turn back, and you all shall live."

As one, the Hydrae horde surged up the hill, their bare, claw-toed feet digging into the grassy slope. The front line opened up with their muskets, and Artem15's copper-colored breastplate shuddered under a sheet of lead balls. The smooth, polished surface sported dozens of pockmarks, creating a terrain of dimples, dents and craters on the lovingly sculpted torso plate.

Artem15 triggered her shoulder-mounted guns. The built-in weapons were belt-fed blasters that fired cartridge ammunition, faster and more powerful rounds than the musket balls, but required more craftsmanship to make.

The other mechanized units matched her actions except for

Are5, who deployed his twin thermal axes. The Mohawked war machine leaped across the gulf of fifty yards between the formation of robots and the churning throng of clones, clawed feet crashing into the writhing enemy force. Are5 would engage in conflict his way, which had carried battles to success on a hundred occasions.

Three thousand pounds of machinery easily crushed a dozen Hydrae under the huge, four taloned feet. The force of Are5's impact jarred the hillside loose. A small landslide rushed down the slope, tripping up scores more Hydrae as the wave of freed soil cascaded into shins and thighs. While the other war suits relied on their shoulder-mounted machine guns, Are5 preferred a more hands-on approach. His twin double-headed ax blades, heated to five hundred degrees Fahrenheit by internal thermal elements, carved through flesh in wide, sweeping strokes that separated torsos and severed limbs all around him. The axes had been folded and stored in customized housings, and Are5 used the axes to clear a fifteen-foot-wide swath in two body-shredding swings of the robot's long arms. The clone horde had taken the war god avatar's bait and swarmed toward him, rising to the challenge of bayonet versus red-hot ax blade.

Artem15 let her shoulder guns fall silent, drawing one of her javelins. Like the goddess of the hunt she emulated, the war armor she piloted favored the slender, accurate, explosive spears. A powerful throw launched the warhead-tipped javelin at more than a thousand feet per second, and though Artem15 could easily and accurately toss the spear two miles, at the spitting-range distance between her and the savage Hydrae, it was like shooting a bullet into an anthill. The custom-tipped spear burst through relatively fragile humanoid forms, tearing them to pieces before the internal fuse was finally armed with the right amount of kinetic energy and impacted on the mass of one reptilian. The deceleration-based fuse enabled the gore-spattered missile to explode and scythe out a deadly storm of shrapnel, clearing out a crowd of mutants who rushed to overtake Are5.

To her left, Apo110 unleashed the heat of the sun itself. Greek fire consumed a flank of irate clones who had swept around in an attempt to outmaneuver the guardian war machines. Powdered, aerosol-based orichalcum reacted on contact with sunlight and flashed brilliantly, long tongues licking through the scale-skinned Hydrae and leaving behind only blackened bones. Robot drone troopers lashed out with spike-adorned, two-foot-wide metal fists even as their shoulder guns blazed incessantly. The Spartan suits featured massive arms able to deliver nearly seventy tons of kinetic force with each punch. Even without the lethal spikes, the massive paws of the clockwork warrior robots would have turned any smaller humanoid into a pulped mass of gore. The spikes were there to keep a glancing punch from merely tossing a stunned opponent to the ground.

"Dammit! Get off!" a Spartan pilot yelled.

Artem15 turned her head and spotted a swarm of scaled flesh piled into a mound twenty feet high. She watched as a clockwork fist burst through the surface before being swallowed again by the writhing melee. She triggered the shoulder weaponry, but for every two she knocked aside, four more rose. The Hydrae were indeed like their namesake Hydra as they swarmed over the cleared body.

"Artie! There's more heading to the town!" another Spartan called. "A second formation is in motion!"

Artem15 whirled away from her beleagured ally. "Airy, Pollie! Hold the line here! You two, with me!"

Hydraulic leg pistons hurled Diana into the air with enough force to shove her deep into her pilot's couch. The twenty-yard bound took her to the top of the hill. Those same hydraulics compressed on landing, cushioning the impact. The two drone infantry she'd directed to follow her were close on her heels, and together they shoved off down the far slope of the hill, riding their front and hind toes like skis as they utilized gravity and forward momentum to rocket down the hillside. Moving at more than one hundred miles per hour, they closed the distance to intercept the maddened clones charging toward the town.

The town's militia, armed with pikes and crude muzzle loaders, were braced for the enemy assault. Artem15 admired the courage of those she was sworn to protect, but she knew that the Hydrae were bred for ruthlessness, great strength and endurance. The picket line of human defenders was outnumbered by the savage attackers whose aplomb for killing made them more than a match for simple citizens defending their homes.

Artem15 opened fire with her shoulder guns, perforating the flank of Hydrae as they bypassed the mechanized hilltop force. Three pairs of machine guns, however, were not enough to counter the Tartarus hordes. Artem15 drew another of her javelins and hurled it into the heart of the group. The detonation of the 70 mm warhead devastated the back half of the column of Hydrae mutants. Bodies stumbled and tripped over downed brethren.

The town's militia opened fire with its own primitive muskets and bolt-action rifles, joining the fight. As the Hydrae at the head of the charging remnants fell with bullets puncturing their organs, the remaining attackers renewed their charge, leaping over black-scaled corpses twisted in the dirt.

The New Olympian pilot reached for another javelin, but the horde was suddenly too close to the skirmish line defending the town. They would be caught in the spear's blast radius. Artem15 leaped, soaring over the space between herself and the Hydrae as the first bayonet sank into a citizen's chest. Anger stirred inside the metal-wrapped warrior's heart. With a feral rage that Are5 would have been proud of, she landed on the necks of a half-dozen clones, her four-toed hydraulic leg squashing them into the soil with the force that only a ton and a half of metal propelled at 150 miles per hour could produce. As she landed, Diana bellowed through her suit's loudspeakers, an inarticulate, amplified war cry that froze a score more of the deadly clones.

Her backup opened fire, slicing through the stunned and distracted Hydrae, ending their vat-born lives in a hail of bullets. Artem15's throat filled with bile, however, as she saw Greek men and women twist and fall alongside the Hydrae.

"Fall back!" Artem15 ordered. "I'll hold the line!"

The horde of attackers twisted, eyeing Artem15 as she drew her javelin from its hip quiver. They lunged forward, snarling, swinging, stabbing their bayonet-tipped muskets, determined to down an elite clockwork warrior. Pike-sharp points penetrated her armor, razor-sharp steel coming far too close to Diana's all too vulnerable human body in the pilot's compartment. She didn't dare sweep the enemy away, not if she wanted to protect the New Olympians who raced back to shelter. Diana had vowed to defend the citizens with her blood.

A clawing bayonet opened a gash on her cheek. Another needled into her thigh. The strength and fury of the Hydrae horde were more than the metal skin of her war suit could fend off.

Artem15 stabbed the earth with her javelin, and the warhead belched out a sheet of flaming death and flying metal. The concussive shock wave and heat were dampened by the cushioned tub of armor that cradled her pilot's seat, and the mobile suit's armor deflected the notched razor wire that had wrapped the explosive core of the javelin's point. Hydrae corpses were hurled off the armored battle suit's massive frame.

Dazed by the nearby detonation, Artem15 looked down to her hydraulic right arm. The metal sleeve that protected the skeleton's carpal manipulators and ulna framework had peeled back like the petals of a steel flower. The clockwork gears and pistons, composed of secondary orichalcum, had withstood the powerful detonation as if it were nothing more than a stiff breeze.

The attacking Hydrae, however, were retreating, fearing another lethal javelin strike.

"Artie!" Are5 called out. "Artie, report!"

She took a tentative step, noting that the right leg's mechanisms had been knocked out of alignment. The metal components of her legs were vulnerable to explosive displacement. She'd need realignment back at the base.

"I'm still standing, Airy. So is the town," she stated. "But it'll take some extra time to walk home."

"Thank Hera," Are5 answered.

Artem15 glared silently at the two backup units as they stood between the fleeing Hydrae and the besieged townspeople. Diana pulled aside her microphone and opened the window on her cockpit. "You two!"

The pair took a step closer and their own cockpit windows opened. They both knew what was coming.

"You fired on your fellow citizens," she hissed.

"They were overwhelmed," one offered. "We couldn't rescue them. They were dead anyway."

"That is not your call to make," Diana said. She looked at the tangle of human and mutant bodies. Six Greek men and women lay among the scores of Hydrae mutants. Bite marks and bayonet wounds marred faces and chests, but she also saw the ugly puckers of gunshot wounds on the humans. "They trusted us to die for them. Instead, they died because I was too slow and you were too hasty."

The warrior drone heads lowered.

"Remember this in the future," she snarled. She turned away from the drones. "Airy, Pollie, how goes it?"

"The Hydrae are pulling back," Apo110 answered. "They no longer have any stomach for battle."

"Airy?" Diana called.

"Broke one of my axes again," Are5 complained. "But I found something in the mix. You have to come see this."

"Bring it back to base, "Artem15 replied. "I'm too slow as it is to make the walk worth it. If it's that important, then we have to show Zoo and Her Highness, as well."

Are5 transmitted his camera image to her screen. "Just look, Artie."

It appeared to be another reptilian variant, similar to the basic Hydrae clone. However, where the scaled hordes of Thanatos were naked, bony-limbed and distorted abominations, this reptilian was tall, strong and of perfect build. He also wore a second skin that conformed to his muscular frame, glinting in the sunlight like metal.

"What the hell is that?" Artem15 asked.

"Beats me, but we're bringing the remains back," Are5 confirmed.

Artem15 turned to glare at her Spartan units. "Go back with the rest of the main force. I've got some thinking to do."

As the war robot limped back to Strike Force Olympus headquarters alone, Diana looked at the stored image of the lifeless, metal-skinned newcomer, trying to cope with the mystery.

IT TOOK AN EXTRA half hour for Artem15 to return to base. When she arrived, she backed the war suit into its storage berth. Mechanics swarmed around, looking at punctured and blood-caked steel skin.

"Lord, Artie, you fucked this suit up again," Ted "Fast" Euphastus noted. He was the head of maintenance for the magnificent clockwork machines that had been discovered by the goddess-queen of New Olympus.

"Shut up and just fix it," Diana grumbled. "Where's my chair?"

"We're bringing it," Carmine, another repairman, said. He looked at the dented, distorted chest plate. "Damn shame those mutants had to mess up a nice pair of boobs. We'll get right to work on—"

Diana crawled out of her couch, glaring at the metal-breast-obsessed mechanic. Carmine froze as angry blue eyes gleamed from the half-fused mask of a burned, ruined face. "Do whatever the hell you want. Do I really look like I give a damn about a pair of robot tits?"

Carmine shook his head as Diana unplugged the cybernetic trunk cable from its port at the base of her spine. She swung the metal capped stumps of her half thighs out and into the seat of her wheelchair. Slender, ropy arms braced themselves on the wheelchair's armrests, and she lowered herself down. Her gymnast-tight arm muscles stood out as they flexed under the weight of her torso and half legs.

"You're bleeding," Fast noted.

Diana looked down at the blood that soaked through the bandage she'd placed on a bayonet injury. "I took care of it while Artie was walking on autopilot."

She peeled off her leather flight helmet and thin, straw-like hair fell in a wet tangle over her eyes. "It's just a scratch, Fast."

Fast's lips quivered with concern, but something drew his attention from the red splotch on her thigh. A silence had fallen over the hangar, and Diana spun her chair to see what was going on.

Hera Olympiad would have been impressive just with her six-foot-tall, voluptuous body and piercing green eyes. However, clad in a shimmering silver skin that conformed to her athletic body, making her appear like a naked silver statue, she truly was unmistakable as the goddess-queen of New Olympus. Only her finely featured face was visible through a window in the otherwise seamless gleaming metal skin. She strode with focus toward Diana in her chair.

"My apologies, Queen," Diana began, dipping her head in a bow to the woman who had come to Greece in search of mythic technology.

Hera had come from a place called Cobaltville, but had chosen to remain in Greece, utilizing the wonders she'd un-earthed to become the defender of the inhabitants of the shattered islands. Before Hera's arrival, their problems with barbarian pirate raiders had grown worse with the rise of the Hydrae under the command of a madman named Thanatos. With the discovery of the Hephaestian mobile suits, Hera had single-handedly ensured peace and tranquility under the protection of the New Olympians.

"No, my child," Hera said. She gestured toward the battered frame of Artem15. "Metal can be reforged, but our villages cannot be so readily repopulated. Once more, your heroism honors me, Diana."

Smooth metallic fingertips grazed tenderly down the scar tissue that made up the left side of young Diana's face. The goddess-queen's touch was cool and soothing to her numbed skin.

"Then what, milady?" Diana asked.

"Airy has shown me what he showed you," Hera said. Her emerald eyes shimmered, as if pebbles had been tossed into green ponds. "We are facing a demon from my past. I will brief you all, but the creature you discovered was not born in the vats of Tartarus."

"From where, then, my queen?" Diana asked.

Hera looked out of the slowly closing hangar doors, her silvery skin burning bright in the reflected sunset bleeding over the distant line of hills. "The creature was sent from my old home, Cobaltville. My baron had sent me, seeking an advantage over his fellow barons. Now he no longer needs that advantage."

The hangar doors clamped shut, and Hera's chrome flesh no longer shone bright. The shadows of the hangar were reflected in black hollows and voids on her mirrored skin. It seemed as if a light had been doused.

"The New Olympians must now face a real god, my child," Hera said with a sigh.

Diana followed her queen, forcefully propelling her wheelchair to match the goddess's long strides.

Chapter 2

"Anything…for…you, dear Domi," Mohandas Lakesh Singh mocked himself in a pitched, nasal tone. He would have said it softer, smoother had he not been forced to grunt from the effort it took his 250-year-old body to crawl over the boulder-strewn hillside in the Bitterroot Mountains. Born before the nukecaust in 2001, Lakesh had maintained his lifespan initially through cryogenic stasis. The gifts of new, blue eyes and the more important vital organs were due to his involvement in the Totality Concept, a supersecret program of scientific research that enabled the revival of nine godlike beings to dominate the more manageable, surviving human populace.

Lakesh's brilliance made him irreplaceable in constructing the technology behind the matter-transfer system that linked the many redoubts spanning the apocalypse-ravaged globe. He had been so important that the old barons kept him as young and healthy as their science could allow. Those medical efforts paled in comparison, though, to Sam's nano technology. Sam's mere touch had transferred an armada of microscopic nanites to Lakesh, and the miniature rebuilders had repaired the ravages of age on a molecular level. He currently appeared to be in his mid-to-late-forties.

Lakesh was pushing his physical limits on this odd little hike led by Domi, who moved with pantherlike surefootedness ahead of him. Originally a child of the Outlands, Domi had survived the sexual servitude of Guana Teague in the hellish underworld of Cobaltville known as the Tartarus Pits. Though she was often described as an albino, with porcelain-white skin, hair the color of bone and pink eyes, she was scarcely as frail and as delicate as the albinos that Lakesh had known of in the twentieth century.

Feral, not fragile, was the term most often associated with Domi, from her lapses into simple, broken English when under stress to her fury in battle when it came to defending those she cared for. When Domi became his devoted lover, Lakesh was at first concerned that he was merely the man she had chosen because the original object of her affection, Grant, had developed a relationship with Shizuka, the leader of the Tigers of Heaven. Lakesh had feared that he was either her rebound from rejection, or just a means to make Grant jealous.

That wasn't the case. Their mutual affection was real and strong. Domi remained fiercely loyal friends with Grant, the man who had stood up for her to the cruel Guana Teague, but Lakesh could see that the love the two felt for each other was not sexual at all. Grant had become the surrogate big brother that Domi had always wanted, and the little albino had filled the same surrogate sibling role for the former Magistrate.

Domi looked back to the exhausted Lakesh. Her face broke into an impish grin. "Need a rest?"

At just a hair over five feet, Domi looked as if she had been carved out of ivory. Her muscles were tight and firm, and if she were older than twenty-five years, her smooth, unlined face and near perfect physical conditioning didn't betray it. She wore cutoff jean shorts and one of Lakesh's khaki safari shirts, which billowed down from her shoulders like a tent.

She tied off the tails under her breasts, leaving her toned stomach exposed. Aside from her scant clothing, she also had a small gun belt with her equally small Detonics Combat Master and a waist-level quiver for the lightweight crossbow slung across her slender shoulders.

"Not at all," Lakesh lied, restraining his desire to gulp down air like a landed fish. "Though, Domi dearest, it would have just been easier to tell me where you like to go hunting."

Domi raised a white-blond eyebrow. She then looked at the small sheath of quarrels bouncing against her upper thigh. "Oh. This."

"I understand the feral needs—" Lakesh began, but before he could finish, she bounded down off the boulder she stood on and planted a kiss on his lips.

"You are smart about a lot of things," she replied. "But my trips aren't just about getting fresh squirrel meat."

Lakesh felt his cheeks redden. "Then what is this about?"

"Some really neat things," Domi answered cryptically. "It's not far now."

Lakesh mopped his brow, then took a swig of water from his canteen. "Mystery soon to be solved."

"Making fun of the way I used to talk?" Domi asked, but her smile and tone belied any challenge in her words.

"No, just out of breath." Lakesh sighed.

She gave him a soft pat on the cheek, then tapped his stomach with the back of her hand. "This is the other reason. You need some exercise."

Lakesh blew out a breath that fluttered through his lips in a rude response to Domi's implication. That only made the albino girl grin even more widely, and she gave his abdomen a playful pinch.

"Come on," Domi said, taking his hand in hers. They moved a little more slowly now, letting Lakesh regain his wind as they followed a narrow trail that wound to the mouth of a cave.

"Welcome to my version of an archive," Domi announced.

Lakesh's eyes tried to adapt to the dimmer illumination inside the cavern when a growl filled the air. The Cerberus scientist whirled at the sound, wishing he'd brought a firearm for himself when a small gray bolt of fur lunged at him.

"Moe! No!" Domi shouted. She intercepted the flying little fur ball inches from Lakesh's face. "Bad Moe! That's the man you're named after. Be nice."

She held up a small creature with the familiar bandit mask of a raccoon in front of Lakesh's face. A pointed, little brown nose wrinkled. "Sniff him. He's friendly. He's our friend."

Lakesh's eyes finally adjusted and he could see the little gray-and-black creature, far less menacing in appearance than in growl. Blue eyes met blue eyes as Moe touched noses with Lakesh. A moment later, a tiny pink tongue began lapping at Lakesh's cheeks.

"Hold him for a moment," Domi said, handing the animal to Lakesh. The raccoon continued to sniff and nuzzle Lakesh as the albino girl walked to where she'd stored a small battery-operated lantern. She clicked it on, and Lakesh looked around the cave, seeing plastic storage shelves and containers, each laden with all forms of odd knickknacks and faded though once garish periodicals and paperbacks. Moe crawled up onto Lakesh's shoulders, but aside from the odd feeling of tiny hands in his graying hair and the softness of fur on his nape, the little beast hadn't so much as scratched him.

Lakesh's eyes danced across cracked old figurines, time-worn stuffed animals and bald plastic dolls sitting at eye level on several shelves. "This looks like a teenage girl's room."

Domi nodded, as if doing mental math. "Maybe. That's the first stuff I collected. I might have been a teenager back then."

"You come here all the time?" Lakesh asked. His fingertips ran over a plastic crate filled with a mix of ancient comic books and ratty old magazines.

"Sometimes," Domi said. She pulled a black cartoon mouse off one shelf, inspecting it. She pushed the stuffed animal's eye back into its face, kissed its furred forehead and put it back on the shelf.

"A lot of old toys," Lakesh noted. "The things that would be at a garage sale. Old puzzles, picture books, even old LPs and tapes."

Lakesh wiped dust off an album cover, then his eyes widened. "The Blue Oyster Cult? Oh, that takes me way back."

Domi grinned broadly.

"We have a lot of this in the computer archives. You don't need to hunt all this down. Why?" Lakesh asked.

"At first, before I met Grant, I'd always wanted a room of my own. Full of stuff that I owned," Domi explained. She picked up a doll that Lakesh had thought was bald, but it was just white skinned and white haired, dressed in what appeared to be a hand-sewn version of a shadow suit. Lakesh could see where Domi had trimmed its hair, arms and legs in proportion to foot-tall doll representations of Kane, Grant, Brigid Baptiste and even himself. "In the Outlands I didn't own nothing more than the clothes I wore."

"Own anything," Lakesh unconsciously corrected. He walked to the familiar-looking dolls set on a rocky shelf. "What...what are these?"

"My family portrait," Domi said. "The people I love."

Lakesh felt his throat tighten for a moment. Domi was a fiery young woman, quick to anger and voracious as a lover, and Lakesh realized the depth of caring she possessed was evident in the loving detail applied to each of the tiny totems standing together. Each had been carefully sculpted and repainted and painstakingly dressed to be a perfect miniature doppelgänger.

Taking a step back, he felt the corner of a container scratch his calf. Lakesh looked down at the box. In large letters on top of the crate, the word Read was scrawled in marker. More boxes were beside it, but unmarked, except one with a strip of tape marked To Brigid.

"Those are ones I know she hasn't read yet," Domi said. "She gave me a list. When the box gets full, I bring 'em down for her."

Domi put her miniature self back with the rest of its family. Lakesh saw two versions of himself, the old, withered self before Enlil-as-Sam had bestowed the gift of rejuvenation upon him, and one that more closely matched his appearance now. Lakesh admitted, though, that the hook-nosed little doll seemed to be considerably more handsome than he currently felt.

"Quite a library," Lakesh said, fighting his narcissism over the miniature doppelgänger. "But why not use the archives?"

Domi shrugged. "Those aren't *my* books. This is where I am. This is me and mine here. My people. The things I've learned. The shit I think is cute. And Moe."

Lakesh scratched the butt of the fur ball on his shoulder. "Called Moe because he's so smart?"

Domi's eyes widened, lips parting for a moment as she was caught off guard. "Uh, yeah. Smart. Right."

Lakesh mentally flashed back to all of the times that Domi had sat in his lap, his fingers giving her shoulder a squeeze, or scratching her back. He could easily imagine the situation reversed for Domi and the raccoon, the young albino sitting on the floor of the cavern, Moe curled in her lap as her fingertips absently scratched its back, mirroring her pose whenever Lakesh read to her, teaching her how to read. Domi winced as she noted the mental gears turning in her lover's eyes as he figured out the equation.

Lakesh leaned in close to Domi and kissed her tenderly. He never had felt more in love with the feral girl who had grown so much since he'd first met her. "You are truly the sweetest, best thing ever to come into my life, precious, darlingest Domi."

Her cheeks turned almost cartoonishly bright red at the statement.

With an inevitability that both Lakesh and Domi had grown used to, their Commtacts—subdermal transmitters that had been surgically embedded into their mastoid bones—buzzed to life.

Bry's familiar twang sounded in their ears. "Lakesh, Domi, where are you?"

With a resigned sigh, Lakesh answered, the vibrations of his speech carrying along his jawbone to be transformed into an outgoing signal by the cybernetic implant. "We're about a two hours' hike from the redoubt."

"Two hours at your speed? Or Domi's?" the sarcastic technical wizard asked.

Lakesh rolled his eyes, eliciting a smirk from his companion and a chittering chuckle from Moe the raccoon. "What's wrong, Bry?"

"I picked up something on satellite imagery from over the Mediterranean. The remains of Greece to be exact," Bry responded. "Atmospheric disturbance indicative of—"

"Annunaki dropships," Lakesh finished, worry tingeing his words. His mood soured instantly, and even resting his arm across Domi's suddenly taut shoulders did little to help him. He looked down at the girl who was listening on her own bionic Commtact.

"Send out a Sandcat to meet us at Road 6," Domi interjected. "Marker 12. We'll be down there in fifteen minutes."

Seemingly recognizing the urgency in his mistress's voice, Moe bounded off Lakesh's shoulder. Domi gave the raccoon a loving hug and a kiss on the end of its pointed nose. "Be good, Moe."

The raccoon chittered a response, then darted out of the cave.

Regretting the hike's abrupt end, Lakesh followed Domi out of her personal archive and down the rocky slope of the hill.

KANE STOOD, a silent sentinel at the Cerberus redoubt's entrance as the Sandcat rolled up. His cold gray-blue eyes regarded the modified armored personnel carrier as it slowed to a halt, its side door swinging open to allow Lakesh and Domi out. The six-foot-tall former Magistrate was always an imposing figure, but the dour expression darkening his features gave Lakesh a momentary pause.

"They're still alive," he pronounced grimly.

"Perhaps," Lakesh replied. "Just because Bry saw evidence of a dropship means nothing. Someone else might have come into possession of one of their craft. It could have been uncovered by the Millennial Consortium, or Erica could have traded for one before *Tiamat's* destruction."

Kane's eye flickered momentarily at the scientist's suggestions, but he didn't relax. "Thanks for trying, Lakesh."

Lakesh tilted his head in an unspoken question.

"Trying to make it seem less than it could be," Kane muttered. He escorted Lakesh and Domi along the corridor toward the ops center. "But my job is to look for the worst-case scenario. Let's simply assume that one of those snake-faced bastards survived *Tiamat,* and he's making some moves."

"It's your job to be prepared for the worst. It's my job to look at all possibilities equally," Lakesh replied, trying to keep up with Kane's long strides, spurred on by his tension. "Both are important, and let us do what we do best. This is part of the synergy that has kept us going all this time."

Kane nodded grimly, slowing to accommodate his two companions, realizing the effort Lakesh expended to maintain his pace. "The only synergy I want is the blending of a bullet and an Annunaki face. I'd thought that we were done with the fucking overlords."

"The only one who died for certain was Lilitu," Lakesh said. "With our rogue's gallery, unless you see the corpse, they truly cannot be discounted. And even then, some whose corpses we've beheld as forever stilled…Colonel Thrush, Enlil, Sindri…"

"Sindri was just beamed into a storage pattern, no corpse to 'behold,' as you put it," Kane corrected, his voice taking on a derisive tone that usually accompanied any mention of the miniature transadapt genius. While Kane reserved a murderous rage for the overlords, the wolf-lean warrior harbored a deep-down annoyance for Sindri.

The three people entered the redoubt's ops center, where Bry, Brigid Baptiste, Grant and Brewster Philboyd were waiting. Bry and Brigid were at one of the computer work-stations. Philboyd and Grant were sitting at a desk, throwing cards down in a quick game of War. With Kane's entry, Grant seemed relieved, obviously tired of the card game.

"Glad you finally showed up," Grant grumbled. While Kane was an imposing figure, Grant was truly menacing. Taller than Kane, with a thick, powerful build, Grant was also a former Magistrate. Not only was the ex-Mag one of the finest combatants Lakesh had ever observed, but also his massive strength was coupled with an uncanny skill at piloting nearly any craft, air, land and sea.

"Not again," Kane replied, looking over to Philboyd.

"Grant, the game's called War. Do you fight fair?" Philboyd asked.

"It's a card game. You're not supposed to cheat," Grant replied. "What's the fun in that?"

"Now, this is hypothetical because I am not a cheater—" Philboyd began.

"Yes, you are," Grant interjected.

"Let us know when you two are finished," Brigid spoke up, a chilly disdain for Grant and Philboyd's minor quarrel weighing on her words.

"Busted," Kane said with a grin. He leaned in conspiratorially to his friend. "Besides, who else are you going to play cards with?"

"I dunno. I was thinking my partner," Grant retorted.

"Maybe if I catch amnesia and forget how much of a hustler you are," Kane said. He looked at the monitor where Bry and Brigid were busy. "That's the contrail from the dropship."

Brigid adjusted her spectacles on her nose. Years of constant reading as an archivist had left her vulnerable to eyestrain when going over fine imagery and small print. "We can't tell who was piloting the dropship. It could be anyone who gained access to one of them. We spotted the transsonic atmospheric distortions in the island chain that used to be Greece."

Lakesh frowned. "It has to be something important for the surviving overlords to risk exposure. As far as we knew, when *Tiamat* was destroyed, they all died."

"Hard to believe that something as old and big as *Tiamat* could die," Grant grumbled. "The big bitch might be down, but I don't think it's forever."

"By the time she recovers from her injuries, we'll hopefully be long dead," Lakesh noted, referring to the living megalithic ship in which the Annunaki had ridden to Earth. "Preferably of old age."

Brigid let loose a cleansing breath, pushing away the horrifying thought of *Tiamat*, the miles-long living chariot of the gods, reawakened to spread more destruction. The starship had more than enough power to scour all life from the surface of the planet. Its crippled and comatose state had accounted for lessened stress in her life, though the thought of an active Annunaki overlord was hardly reassuring. "Right now we are looking at some footage recorded from a recent conflict in that region."

Bry's fingers danced over the keyboard, and a bird's-eye view flashed on the monitor. "The footage is about twenty minutes old, and we only caught the tail end of things."

The monitor's image sharpened until Kane and Lakesh could see the presence of massive sets of coppery metallic heads and shoulders, like living statues, leaving behind a morass of green-and-black corpses.

"I've double-checked the math, and the dead creatures are

about a shade over five feet tall, and they are identical, at this magnification at least," Bry explained. "They resemble the humanoid reptilian mutants that used to roam across the remnants of the United States."

"Scalies," Lakesh mused. "But they were exterminated."

"Here on the North American continent, but you have to remember that these mutants could be artificially created," Brigid said.

"If they're about five feet tall, then how big are those constructs walking away?" Lakesh asked.

"Approximately twelve to fifteen feet, and almost half as wide," Bry stated. "What did you call them, Brigid?"

"Mecha," the archivist said. "A generic term for robotic combat vehicles."

"Giant robots," Lakesh murmured. "Larger than the ones we encountered in China. And heavily armed by the looks of them."

"Close-ups of the shoulders correlate with late-twentieth-century machine-gun designs. Belt-fed rifle caliber," Bry noted. "Grant recognized them, and utilizing the known dimensions of the weaponry, calculating the rest of the robot's size was easy."

Grant shuffled his deck of cards absently. "Brigid wants to go meet with the group that owns the robots. They seem fairly decent, according to this footage."

"Decent?" Lakesh asked. "That's a refreshing change. How did you determine that?"

"We caught a flash of an explosion while scanning the area. On image enhancement we saw that a trio of robots was assisting a line of local villagers against the mutants," Brigid said.

Bry cued up the footage, and Lakesh watched the battle

from above. He was surprised to see one of the mecha detonate an explosion at its own feet to stanch the tide of attackers. He was even more dazzled when the chest plate of the robot swung open. He couldn't see inside the torso of the robot, but apparently there was someone inside.

"It looks like one robot is talking to the others about the friendly-fire incident at the start of the recording," Kane noted.

"So they're piloted craft," Lakesh mused. "And they have rules of engagement to protect outlying communities."

"You noticed the lack of industrial capability in the town, as well," Brigid said.

"If they have only bolt-action rifles and pitchforks to deal with a mutant horde, I doubt that those people have a garage to tighten the nuts on a battle robot," Kane interjected.

"Precisely. Indeed, there aren't even any vehicles on the premises," Lakesh added.

"I am fairly curious," Brigid answered. "But Bry and I have been running comparisons between the one prone mecha being dragged back to base. Any pilot taller than five feet would be cramped inside even the most generous of compartments for the robots. Domi is well over the limit for riding in the chest, let alone operating the device."

Domi tilted her head. "Maybe Sindri's people?"

"The transadapts," Kane agreed. "The tallest of them were just over four feet. And if you have a lab that can breed scalies, you can whip up a batch of transadapts, as well."

"Trouble is, those strange little monkey men would be in conflict from the critters from the selfsame lab. And the transadapts we've encountered are hardly friendly and generous toward humans," Grant said.

"You're also talking about an abandoned people who had

been slaves," Brigid countered. "Not being oppressed and forced into submission to humans would have a good effect on them."

"Rottenness isn't a matter of genes," Domi murmured. "Remember Quavell?"

The meeting room grew quiet as each of the Cerberus staff present remembered the Quad-Vee hybrid who had taken refuge along with them for several months while she was pregnant. The Cerberus explorers had initially believed that the infant had been sired by Kane when he had been captured and pressed into stud service to revitalize the frail, genetically stagnant hybrids. When it turned out that another had fathered the child, Kane and his allies continued to protect Quavell and her baby. Quavell died, however, due to complications of childbirth brought on by the genetic transformation from the slender, delicate hybrids to the larger, more powerful Nephilim, the servants of the Annunaki overlords who had also been awakened by *Tiamat*'s signal. Especially present in the minds of those around Domi was the albino girl's shift from hatred and loathing of the panterrestrial humanoids to love and compassion for the hybrid woman.

It was a reminder that though they all had become open-minded, the nature of humanity was to harbor prejudices, something made very apparent by their encounters with the Quad-Vees and the transadapts.

"What's powering the robots?" Domi asked. "Doesn't look like it smokes like a Sandcat."

Brigid looked back to the screen, and Bry, on cue, called up the image of the downed robot. "Kane, you remember the Atlantean outpost that Quayle had discovered?"

Kane nodded. "Yeah. You missed out on that. I'm sure you

would have loved the place. All kinds of wall carvings, and a metal called orichalcum that blew up when sunlight touched it. Took out the whole joint."

Brigid leaned past Bry and tapped a few keys, drawing up a subscreen. "Greek philosophers like Plato and Pliny discussed Atlantis at length. One of the things mentioned was the legendary gold-copper alloy that was the hallmark of Atlantean society. Seeing it as a staple of decorations and animatronic statues in city plazas seems at odds with the unstable explosive compound you described."

"Fand told me what the stuff was called," Kane responded. "Besides, the outpost was a couple thousand years old and under the ocean. Who can say that the seawater exposure didn't rust it or cause some kind of other imbalance, like dynamite left sitting too long? Maybe kept away from rust-inducing salty humidity, it's great."

Brigid shrugged. "You stated that it was stored in a vault. Under excellent storage conditions. However, it could be akin to a high-energy metal like uranium. I wish you'd brought back a sample."

"Quayle kept me kind of busy for that. Plus, that whole sunlight-making-it-go-off-like-a-grenade thing dissuaded me."

Brigid locked eyes with Kane for a moment. Though the two shared an enormous affection for each other, it was commonplace for them to push each other's buttons even in the most casual of conversations. "In its stable format, orichalcum could easily prove to be a reliable power source. Given Grecian familiarity with Atlantean mythology, it's quite possible that these robots may be artifacts from an outpost placed in Greece. Or it could be a component of a highly durable alloy."

"Given the artifacts we've found around the world, it's very possible that Atlantis itself was the beneficiary of Annunaki and Tuatha de Danaan technology," Lakesh added. "The orichalcum that Kane discovered could be a manufactured element, along the lines of plutonium. But the most important thing is that they have apparently mastered a lost form of technology. We had a glimpse of it in Wei Qiang's at the Tomb of the Three Sovereigns."

"Those suckers were strong, but still only man-size. Basically, semi-intelligent muscle. Double their size and give them a thinking person at the controls, you've got some considerable power on your side." Grant nodded, for emphasis, at the image on the monitor of lifeless, scaled mutants and their shattered muskets being shoveled into a mass grave. "I wondered how those robots did what they did, I mean programming wise. They reacted to our actions with some reasonable responses."

"Ancient forms of computers have been discovered. The most prominent of these is the Antikyteria Mechanism," Philboyd answered. "The Antikyteria was an analog gear-style computer that was capable of charting star patterns. It's a fairly simple looking design and more minute versions of that gear, working in concert, could form a non-circuit-board style computer."

"Didn't Archytas also mention that he possessed an automated, steam-powered, wooden robot pigeon?" Lakesh asked.

"Around 200 B.C.," Brigid confirmed. One of the former archivist's strongest interests was research into out-of-place artifacts, examples of modern technology originating in historical eras. Philboyd seemed slightly put out that she fielded the question regarding robotics, but was used to her need to provide an explanation. "It was capable of flight, if I recall correctly."

"So they could have airborne mecha," Kane said grimly.

"Potentially," Brigid said. "But I'd presume that it would simply be more efficient to hang one off the bottom of a Deathbird. I'd consider a Manta, but the damaged armor appears ill suited for orbital use."

Grant took a deep breath. "Fifteen feet tall. Plenty big, but not as big as some of the monstrosities in myths."

"Like Talos or the Colossus of Rhodes," Brigid mentioned.

"How big would those be?" Domi asked.

"Descriptions are inconsistent," Brigid explained. "And they could have been highly embellished as mythology advanced. Talos could reasonably have been about forty to sixty feet tall, and the Colossus about twice that."

Domi looked back to the robot laying on its back. "Well, it's nice to know that we have friendly folks in control of that technology. I can see why we'd want to hook up with them right away."

Philboyd nodded. "The Greek robot pilots can fight, and they have an advanced form of technology. It'd be like the Tigers of Heaven had our Mantas from the start."

"And if the snake-faces are back and in action," Grant began, "we can use that kind of fighting power."

"Which explains the presence of a dropship in the region," Kane grumbled. "The Greeks represent a possible enemy, and the overlords don't want to have to deal with them."

"You're right. We'd better assemble an away team to meet them," Lakesh urged. "Especially if they can be potential allies."

"With a heads-up, we could make invaluable friends," Brigid noted. "What could go wrong?"

Philboyd paled, remembering the conflict with Maccan, a Tuatha prince, that had been sparked when the Outlanders visited the Manitius Moon base for the first time. Grant and Kane looked at each other silently.

"Suit up," the two partners said in harmony.

"I'm coming, too," Domi added.

"We might need backup from CAT Beta," Kane said.

"Then I'll be on scene. If necessary, the rest of my team will pop in," Domi said. "One of the ex-Mags can substitute for me."

Brigid Baptiste sighed. In asking the rhetorical question, she'd thrown out temptation for fate. She groaned softly. "Time to break out the battle bra again."

Chapter 3

Diana was just another wheelchair jockey in the meeting hall, sitting with the rest of the pantheon of hero-suit drivers. Zoo, Airy, Pollie and the rest were arranged around a bisected corpse illuminated by a searing white cone of light. The separated torso had been seared. Cauterized wounds from Airy's thermal ax had sealed in the dead thing's juices behind walls of charred flesh. The face had been cleaned up, and it was at once handsome and intimidating. Though finely sculpted, the face's beauty was sheathed in fine-scaled, lizardlike armor. Diana tried to shake off her imaginings of this creature's angelic magnetism, even in its sleep of oblivion.

She had to remind herself that this being had been fighting alongside the Tartarus mutants, joining them in a raid on a New Olympian settlement. The mutants were mass murderers, bred for attacking and exterminating humans. The wake of death and terror that Thanatos's minions had left was something that Diana would never forget. She reminded herself of the scaled thugs' horrific actions every time she touched her fused, fire-scarred cheek or forehead. The handsome snakelike humanoids that were related to the lifeless thing under the blazing light were allied with the monsters that inspired Diana to sacrifice her remaining leg so that she could fit into the cockpit of a hero suit.

The orichalcum-framed battle suits had been designed around slighter, smaller creatures. As such, even a small woman like Diana had been before the Tartarus raids had scarred and mutilated her, was too large for the cockpit. The metal caps on her thigh stumps and the cybernetic port adjacent to her lower spine were less a reminder of her wounds than they were badges of her empowerment. Her half-destroyed face was a brand of the evil that rose from the Tartarus vats.

No matter how beautiful the stranger was, the ugliness of his allegiance was unmistakable.

Z00s, the chief of the pantheon, looked at her. His furry features made his nickname of Zoo all too appropriate. "Recognize what the creature is wearing, or are you still caught up looking into his eyes?"

Diana bit back a response as she examined the burnished metal sheathing the corpse's limbs and torso. "Secondary orichalcum. The color is a bit off, but he's clothed in it."

"It's more than just that," Zoo, the Zeus of the New Olympians, noted. "It's woven, nearly clothlike, and far more flexible than anything we've ever seen except in one instance."

Diana's mind flashed to Hera's skintight armor.

"Airy's axe carved through it, but we're talking about a blade swung by a one-and-a-half-ton war machine. You can see the discoloration there and there where our small arms struck it. Bullets penetrated its limbs on only straight hits. Anything less turned into a glancing blow."

Hera looked at the bisected stranger, her silvery fingertips touching as her mind seemed to be caught in a storm. She rapped her metal-clad knuckle on the inert body's thigh. "Someone not only knows how to mass-produce secondary orichalcum, but has enough to give it out like clothing."

"How'd he get in that?" Ari "Airy" Marschene, the pilot of Are5, asked. "It's not like that getup's got a zipper."

"In a way, there is," Hera noted. She rolled over the top of the torso, revealing a knot-shaped mechanism high between the strange visitor's shoulder blades. None of the eleven pilots of the pantheon needed to be reminded of the similarity between the device and the one that enabled their goddess-queen to enjoy the protection of impenetrable silver-and-gold skin. The same knotted base for ropes of molded smart armor was a cybernetic port that Hera had been able to reverse engineer in order to allow the pilots to control their robotic war suits. Hera fiddled with the device until ribbons of metal retracted, folding back into a capsule around the cybernetic hub. The metal had only peeled away from the torso and arms, the lower part of the corpse still clad in its glimmering armor.

Zoo wheeled over as Hera pried the mechanism from the back of the corpse. "An almost exact match."

Zoo's burly arm reached out and picked up the severed forelimb, still wearing its glove of secondary orichalcum armor. Around the wrist of the grisly trophy, three tendrils of mechanical cable ended in snakelike heads. "Though apparently it still maintains its shape without the proper command impulse."

"Careful with that," Ari said. "When I went after him, he fired a burst of energy from the device still on his wrist. It had enough power to smash one of my axes. It was like nothing I'd ever seen. It's a lot more focused than Pollie's Greek fire sprayers."

Hera plucked the blaster-equipped wrist from Zoo's grasp. She seemed to be weighing it against the cybermodule in her other hand.

"So what is all of this?" Diana asked. "What has you so nervous?"

Hera looked balefully toward Diana. "I want this technology. I want all of this. If we had this kind of weaponry,
we could drive Thanatos and his mutants into the ocean. If
these become common among the spawn of Tartarus, we'll
be swept from the Earth."

"Give me a half-dozen Spartans, and I'll run a reconnaissance," Diana answered. "A quick raid, and we'll see if this
was the only one, or if there are more."

Hera shook her head. "No."

"But—" Diana began in protest.

"Do not make me repeat myself, girl," Hera snapped.

The wheelchair-bound pilots all fell silent. They had
never seen their goddess-queen this agitated in the years
that they had known her. Most of all, they had never
imagined that Hera would have growled a threat at any of
them, let alone Diana, the girl who was Hera's surrogate
daughter. The menace hanging in the air, however, was
unmistakable.

"Zoo, come on," Hera barked, urgency speeding the words
from her lips. "I'm taking this back to my lab."

The queen and her amputee consort left the conference
room without another word.

Diana watched silently, feeling a knot of nausea forming
just under her sternum. The goddess who had raised her up
from a useless cripple had delivered her a rebuke before her
peers. After all she had done for the pantheon, earning herself
a role as named pilot of a hero suit with blood and sacrifice,
Diana stung as she was discarded, tossed aside like a petulant
child. Ari wheeled over to her.

"Di, baby…" Ari began, affection purring under his words
as his deep brown eyes studied her fused mask of a half face.

"Just leave me alone," Diana answered curtly. "I'm too old to need sitting."

Ari swallowed, regretting his choice of words. The high-tech war-avatar pilot made no secret of his love for the straw-haired girl who commanded the robotic huntress. He also was very clear and careful to always treat her with respect, even though Diana had cut herself off from interpersonal ties, feeling herself unworthy of romance. He reached out to take her delicate fingers in his grasp. "Di, something is worrying Hera. Otherwise, she wouldn't be so on edge. I mean, there's a fucking alien laying on the table, and he had a laser gun and bulletproof armor. Look at it."

"I have been," Diana answered. "It's almost human, though. An alien should be...alien, shouldn't it?"

Ari glanced at the angelic reptilian once more.

"Think about it," Diana continued. "Two eyes. Two ears, vestigial as they are. Nose. Mouth. Arms. Legs. This could be something out of those cheesy old vids about the starship, where they distinguished aliens with bumps on their forehead or just some rubbery makeup."

"This is a lot more convincing than latex," Ari said. "It looks like the big brother of the Hydrae horde. The one that got all the good genes, while the others are just crappy copies."

"That's why Hera's so scared?" Pollie interjected. He'd remained taciturn as his two friends, Ari and Diana, spoke. "Think this critter is the one who supplied the template for Thanatos's clones?"

"It's possible," Diana murmured. Her friends could tell that she was in retreat, curling back into her shell. All she could think about was Hera's bitter rebuke.

Diana wheeled her chair back to her quarters, alone.

Hauling herself into her bunk, she finally allowed herself to give way to the sting of tears.

THE INTERPHASER'S HUM FADED in Kane's ears, and mistlike energy plasma dissipated around him. His keen point man's instincts kicked in, sweeping the area where they'd emerged. The interphaser's design was a godsend after years of employing conventional mat-trans visits. The psychic and physical trauma that accompanied traditional gateway jumps was greatly minimized if they used the interphaser instead. The interphaser exploited naturally occurring vortices that were spread around the globe and even on other planets. The energy points had been mapped by the Parallax Points Program, which they had discovered on Thunder Isle and then input into the interphaser.

The sky blazed a burned orange marking the sunset, and the mountaintop ruin was silent, except for the baleful calls of terns that hovered on thermals, watching the strange appearance of Kane and his companions. Kane could smell the brine of the ocean—the Agean, he'd learned from Brigid.

He set down his war bag and jogged to the edge of the weathered and cracked stone floor. Behind him, Brigid, Grant and Domi set about stowing their own equipment bags. Grant made certain to secure his huge rifle case. The container was taller than Domi was, but there was a crack in the stone floor large enough to secure it. Brigid and Domi elected to leave behind their Copperhead submachine guns and the bandoliers of grenades in their war bags. Kane and Grant opted to keep their Copperheads with them. The four Cerberus exiles were on a first-contact mission, and the two men would be out of place without something heavier than the powerful Sin Eaters in their forearm holsters. However, if all four showed up packing enough guns to fight a war, it would send the wrong message.

Kane and the others had been around enough to balance shows of strength with diplomacy. Grenades and Grant's monster-sized Barrett rifle were stashed away for contingency in the event of betrayal and disarmament. The extra weaponry disappeared under a camouflaging tarpaulin that Grant covered with dirt.

Kane pulled a pair of compact field glasses from a pouch on his equipment belt slung over his shadow suit. The high-tech polymers of the uniform conformed to his powerful muscles, providing nearly complete environmental protection from all but the most inhospitable climates. While not able to withstand rifle rounds like his old Magistrate polycarbonate armor, the shadow suit still offered minor protection against small arms and knives. In return, the suits granted greater ease of movement and offered protection against radiation and temperature fluctuation. Kane also noticed that the shadow suits were far less intimidating than the ominous black carapaces of their Mag battle armor.

"No movement," Kane announced. He turned to see Brigid Baptiste tracing her fingers over the surface of weather-beaten column. "Any ideas what this was?"

"Considering that many of the vortices were recognized by ancient peoples as places of power, aided by the influence of the First Folk, this could have been an oracle. This isn't Delphi, but it has a similar layout," Brigid answered. "Sadly, nothing of archaeological significance remains."

"So you won't be distracted by shards of pottery," Kane returned with a wink and a smile.

Brigid shook her head. "No. The only thing that could be found here would be in the form of resonant psychic energy."

Kane raised an eyebrow. "Oh, right. Because the oracles were manned by ancient psi-muties. The nodes' energy would increase their perceptions."

"That's a very good theory," Brigid said. "You've been doing some reading?"

Kane shrugged. "Continuing education. With all the crap we've encountered, and all the telepathic trespassing that's gone on in my head, it helps to be prepared. Granted, I'm going off of digital copies of the *Fortean Times* in the redoubt's library."

Brigid smiled. "I remember when you asked for that archive disk. I thought it was just to get more information on Atlantis."

"That's where it started," Kane admitted. "A lot of the theories in those old rags sounded crazy. But after slugging it out with Quayle in the outpost, I had a feeling we'd eventually run across Atlantis itself. Along the way, other articles caught my eye, mainly from personal experience."

"We know for a fact that the Annunaki took the roles of the Sumerian and Greek gods, among other identities," Brigid noted. "With that knowledge, some of von Danniken's alien-god theories come off much more plausibly...if you're willing to ignore the obvious sloppy interpretation of an Aztec sacrifice's guts being mistaken for the tube hookups on an ancient space suit."

Kane shrugged. "Lazy speculators, or just plain gullible nuts."

He sighed, getting back to the business at hand. "We seem to be on a peninsula. There's a land bridge leading down from that cliff. So far, I don't see any movement that would indicate the locals are aware of our presence."

"Thank heaven for small favors," Brigid replied.

Kane continued to scan the countryside when suddenly a column of blue-white electrical fire speared down into the land, creating huge clouds of debris and smoke from the earth. He recoiled from the power and the violence. At first, he thought it was a lightning bolt, but the searing slash of energy was too focused, too intense and lasted far too long to be a simple work of nature. Flames licked up from charred ground and, sprawled in the scarred landscape, burned corpses steamed. The dying sunset had been blotted out, overwhelmed by the brilliance of the sky fire. Cries of fear and suffering echoed in his ears, and he could smell the sickly scent of roasting human flesh.

Despair surged through him when he realized that he had been grasped firmly by Grant. Kane blinked away the flashes, and the sights, sounds and smells faded.

"Kane?" Grant asked, as if he were repeating himself. The big ex-Magistrate's Sin Eater retracted back into its powered forearm holster, though Grant appeared confused at what had caused Kane to stagger and reel.

"No, of course you wouldn't have seen that," Kane muttered. "It wasn't real."

"See what?" Domi replied. She still hadn't put her handgun away. "You froze for a moment, then started backing away from the edge."

Kane looked around the ruins. "The oracle helped me experience a psi-mutie vision."

"What did you see?" Brigid asked.

"Lightning," Kane said. "But it wasn't natural lightning. It was a weapon, and it tore the ground apart. And it was focused. It left swathes of charred corpses in its wake."

"Zeus, the king of the Olympian gods, had a quiver of

thunderbolts forged for him by Hephaesteus. Zeus's thunder-bolts were so powerful, they could destroy even the greatest monsters in the land," Brigid said. "That myth could have its basis in an Annunaki weapon."

Domi's nose wrinkled. "This shit's getting weird."

"You asked to come along," Grant chided. He glanced back at their hidden stash of weapons. "Monsters, other gods, cities, too, right?"

Brigid nodded. "Zeus obliterated anyone and anything with his thunderbolts."

"So nothing in our bags is ever going to match that kind of firepower," Grant announced. "Let's just head down the bridge and meet the locals before Zeus drops the sky on us."

Kane nodded in agreement, finally past the harrowing realism of his momentary psychic flash. "Good plan."

The arcs of future lightning were still harshly inscribed on his mind's eye, an ominous premonition of hell peeling back the sky and incinerating the earth below. He couldn't dismiss his dread, and so he threw himself into his work. Maybe knowing the potential tragedy looming in the future gave Kane the power to prevent it.

It was as good a coping mechanism as any.

THE FARTHER THEY GOT from the oracle, across the ramp of stone and packed earth sloping down from the ancient temple's remains, Kane's senses grew clearer, returning to normal. As his senses sharpened, he realized that they were not alone. He shot a glance toward Domi, knowing that her own feral instincts were also preternaturally sharp. She was on edge.

Grant picked up on his two allies' silent, brief exchange. "Where?"

"Feels like we're surrounded, at least two flanks," Kane explained.

Grant nodded. The hilly, rolling terrain was covered with sparse scrub, making it difficult for anyone to hide any closer than the hillcrests that bracketed them. Only the tops of the ridges provided sufficient concealment, as well as a good commanding view of the rut they passed through. Even with the deepening shadow of evening, their stalkers would be behind the ridges. The massive ex-Magistrate flipped down the faceplate on his black polycarbonate helmet, and vision-enhancing optics were engaged. While the shadow suits and mandibular implants had superseded most of Grant's old armor's protection and communication functions, the image-intensifying and night-vision capabilities of the black helmets were too valuable to surrender. The Mag helmet was also one of the few pieces of equipment that Grant was able to perform repairs on without compromising the fit of the Magistrate armor piece.

A heat source flared on a ridge, a head poking over the hilltop. Grant locked on to it, but the figure disappeared quickly. Still, he had enough for cursory identification. "Humanoid. Scrawny, hairless and naked according to the signature. Mammalian core heat."

"Naked?" Kane asked. "Then it's not the robots laying out this welcome mat."

"More like the mutants we saw on satellite view," Brigid said. "Strange that they have reptilian skin, but mammalian endothermic metabolisms."

"Strongbow's old crew were scaly faced, as well," Grant said. "Though they had remnants of facial hair."

"Makes you wonder about the so-called scalies often referenced in the Wyeth Codex," Brigid said.

"Less ancient history, more current events," Kane grumbled. His own faceplate was down, his point man's instinct working together with the advanced electronics of the Magistrate helmet.

"There is some historical relevance. Zeus's greatest enemy was the monster Tiamat, mother of a million tormenting beasts," Brigid noted.

"*Tiamat* is dead," Kane said coldly.

"Our *Tiamat*," Brigid responded. "But look at places like the Archuleta Mesa, or the attempted use of Area 51 to produce Quad Vee hybrids—two locations that had the technological potential to create biological constructs. It stands to reason that if Greece is a location for Annunaki-designed robots, there might also be the technology for creating monsters. Literally the womb of Tiamat. The First Folk are a prime example of Annunaki genetic tampering."

Kane's brow furrowed under the polycarbonate visor. "So whoever played Zeus the first time, long ago, made his own rogue's gallery?"

Brigid shrugged. "The towns in these islands are heavily fortified. That bespeaks of an ever present, hostile enemy in herdlike numbers. Especially considering the corpses shoved into the mass grave and the amount of damage those poorly armed humanoids were able to inflict on a single robot, we must be dealing with some sort of cloning facility."

Kane hadn't slowed his pace, and he could hear Brigid panting as she tried to keep up while applying her intellect to the problem at hand. "So they'd be akin to the mutant herds that roamed the American wasteland after the war. Bred specifically to be alien, of animalistic intelligence and a hostility toward nonaltered humans, they would be a perfect means of keeping the surviving population in check until the Program of Unification."

"Can you think of a better way to isolate communities?" Grant asked.

The two ex-Mags scanned the hilltops with their light-amplification lenses. The ground was cast in an eerie green haze by the helmet units. Though Domi and Brigid didn't have the high-tech headgear, Domi's sensitive albino eyes were accustomed to the darkness, and Brigid was wearing a lightweight Moon base visor. Brigid's eyewear was slightly bulkier than a pair of sunglasses, but the lenses were polarized to allow protection against intense light sources as well as having a built-in LED UV illuminator and lenses that filtered the tiny lamp into the visible spectrum, as well as amplifying ambient light. Still, the tall archivist envied the telescopic targeting option on Kane's and Grant's Mag helmets.

"So far, it only looks like we have one shadow," Grant said.

"It feels like more," Kane countered. He looked to Domi. She nodded, then strode off quietly.

"Be careful, girl," Grant whispered over his Commtact. The admonition brought a smile to the albino's face, a moment of cherubic warmth before her porcelain features hardened into a grim battle mask.

"You know they're going to wonder where she went," Brigid warned.

"Good," Kane replied. "That will force them to divide their focus. I'm going up ahead to further disperse them. Stay close to Grant."

Brigid looked as if she was going to protest, but held her tongue. There were times when the four Outlanders operated as a democracy, each applying individual skills and expertise to solving their mutual dilemmas. On the other hand, when being hunted by an unknown number of enemies in the countryside of a far-flung, shattered nation, Brigid would defer to Kane's warrior knowledge and hard-contact experience. His combat abilities and finely honed instincts provided him with almost instantaneous strategies that would allow the explorers to remain safe and secure from hostile foes without dithering or debate.

Brigid was also irritated by the implication that she was a less capable combatant than the highly trained former Magistrates and the feral albino girl. Compared to most of the rest of the world, she was a formidable survivor of globe-spanning conflicts. But she realized that though she could handle herself in a dangerous situation, when surrounded by a small horde of snarling mutants, reason dictated that the lifetimes of combat endured by Kane, Grant and Domi gave them an edge. Kane's warning to stay near the towering Grant was not an insult, just common sense. A lightning-quick assessment also provided her with the insight that she and Grant would form the hinge of the two-flanked counterattack by Kane and Domi. Grant needed Brigid's backup as much as she needed him.

Grant simply nodded at his partner, and Kane advanced fifty yards ahead of the pair.

Kane wasn't certain if the mysterious stalkers had access to the same optic technology that he and his allies possessed, but he doubted it. The massive warbots would be more likely to possess advanced cameras, but their stealth would be negligible compared to the scrawny mutants that Grant had spotted. From the satellite pictures, they seemed to be more proficient at using their muskets and bayonets as spears rather than rifles, which meant the complexities of electronically enhanced vision would be beyond their limited mental scope. However, if the mutants had sharp, animalistic senses, Domi's transformation to shadowy midnight wraith would be insufficient camouflage. Even with her shadow suit already blended to the darkened terrain by fiber-optic technology and the addition of a blackened head rag covering her bone-white hair and a scarf wrapped around her nose and jaw, the acute night vision of predatory animals would allow her to be spotted easily. Kane recalled, however, that most reptilian hunters didn't rely on vision when they stalked at night.

The girl would stand a chance, and even if the hunters did come at her, she'd hold them off long enough for Kane and Grant to even up the odds.

This far from the oracle's influence, and minutes separating him from his jolting psychic flash, Kane trusted his instincts again, and he felt as if violence was about to break loose like a driving rain. He activated his Commtact. "Domi, eyes on targets?"

"Ten muties close to you," Domi replied in her clipped, tense vocal cadence. When her adrenaline kicked in, she reverted to her old, primitive way of talking, dropping articles. "Dozen back by others. Haven't seen me."

Kane seized his Copperhead from its spot on his web belt. "Definitely muties."

"Too hunched, scrawny," Domi answered. "Bald and ugly, and think they can sneak up on me."

Kane smirked in appreciation of the feral girl's guts. Though Domi could, and had survived with nothing more than a knife and clad in a few rags in the wilderness, her years at Cerberus gave her an appreciation for more complex tools in concert with her sharp senses. "It feels like they're ready to make a move."

There was a grunt over the Commtact, and Kane froze. Before he could call out, something registered on his visor, an infrared trace in his peripheral vision. "Grant, on our left."

"Just spotted that one," Grant answered. "Looks like we're being herded. So the numbers that Domi announced are probably double. This could get rough."

"What else is new?" Domi grumbled.

"What happened?" Kane asked.

"Banged knee getting behind rock," Domi responded. "Caught glimpse of muties across way."

"We're going to be boxed in, and that's going to suck. Time for us to make some noise," Kane responded. He transferred the Copperhead to his left hand and flexed his forearm tendons. The sensitive actuators in the holster for his Sin Eater launched the folding machine pistol into his grasp with a loud, intimidating snap. Back when he was a Magistrate, enforcing the law for Cobaltville, the lightning appearance of the deployed sidearm broke many a criminal's will to fight. Now, the sudden appearance was the trigger for gibbering yammers of dismay from hilltop mutants.

"That got attention," Domi announced before, off to Kane's right, the throaty bellow of the albino's Detonics .45 split the night.

Kane raced, broken-field pattern, toward the surge of infrared contacts on his left on the ridge across from her position. His charge was met by a half-dozen misshapen heads popping up in response to rapid movement. They peered over the spine of the hill, and a volley of musket balls rippled down from the group.

One of them smacked, wet and hot, against Kane's chest, stopping his forward charge as if he'd slammed into a brick wall.

Chapter 4

Diana's slumber was brief, as emotionally charged dreams tormented her. It was as if she were suffering from a sweat-drenched fever. She hadn't been swamped by such stressful mental imagery since the amputation of her remaining leg. Staph infection had nearly claimed her life even as she was "upgrading" to her current existence.

The dream started out exactly as before. Instead of the sterile, pristine surgical studio where Hera Olympiad conducted the amputation, she was in a flame-lit cavern where the walls seemed carved from pulsating reptilian flesh. Shadows danced wildly behind the silver-clad goddess whose precision instruments had transformed into jagged, gore-encrusted saws and splinter-edged cleavers. Without administering an anesthetic, Hera hacked down violently. Her medical assistants had been replaced by hunch-backed, blue-scaled mutants from the Tartarus horde. Rather than handing her the tools she needed to remove Diana's healthy leg in order to fit her inside the cockpit of the clockwork war suit, their gnarled claws raked obscenely over her silver-and-gold curves, gibbering in delight at splatters of blood and wriggling pieces of flying flesh. Blue-black tongues stretched from between scaled lips to lap the offal off Hera's armored skin.

"So tasty is our daughter," a voice whispered, harsh and raw, from the shadows. "So ugly, tasty and ours."

Diana craned her neck, trying to get a look at the speaker, but her attention was seized by the metal cap crushing her thigh stump. A bolt was drilled through the bottom, grinding through bone to anchor the cap. The vibrations tore through Diana's body, and she bit her lip to keep from crying out. A hammer whacked the steel stump cap, and the mutilated girl arched her back in agony.

"Roll over," Hera demanded. Diana saw a pulsing, gel-filled black creature with barbed and hooked beetle limbs twitching in Hera's grasp. "I need to put in your interface."

Diana nodded. It was the sacrifice she had to make, to become powerful enough to fight off Thanatos's hordes. A reptilian hand caressed her cheek, scales rubbing like sandpaper on her remaining facial skin.

"It'll only hurt a moment, child," the mutant grumbled.

Diana's eyes widened with horror as she recognized the speaker, the one who called her his daughter. It was Thanatos himself, the scale-skinned lord of Tartarus, present at her conversion from fragile flesh to armored warrior goddess. She tried to pull away, but the beetle limbs speared into her back, tearing through skin and anchoring in her muscles. A stinger of venomous fire plunged into her spine, and Diana froze in feverish agony.

Thanatos let go of her face, freezing in his own horror. A hand wrapped around the monster-king's throat, and with a savage, crackling twist, Thanatos collapsed in a jumble of useless limbs.

Diana relaxed on the table, panting, looking at the new-comer who had executed the demon lord of the Tartarus horde. It was a tall, magnificent creature, even larger in stature than the corpse in the briefing room. Incredibly, its face was even more of a mix of angelic beauty and devilish intensity. Dark eyes looked down on the amputee thrashing on the cracked stone that was the operating table, then dismissed her.

It strode regally around the abattoir table, meeting Hera as an equal, wearing even more splendid skin armor than hers. A long, elegant claw stroked the armored woman's cheek.

"It has been too long, lover," the magnificent reptilian angel whispered in a disturbing, resonant, multitonal voice.

"I didn't know if you'd ever come for me," Hera replied.

Diana looked in disgust and betrayal as goddess-queen and alien angel kissed passionately.

She was ejected from the dream with a breathless pant. Her strawlike hair was matted to her forehead in the wake of the traumatic nightmare. Almost on instinct, she crawled over to her wheelchair, cable-tight arm muscles maneuvering her truncated body into its seat with acrobatic ease. Even splashes of cool water from the simple metal basin of her sink did little to ease the psychic burns seared into her mind.

She rolled out of her quarters, making her way through the New Olympian complex. Diana needed the comfort of her cramped cockpit, the womb of steel that completed her being. Outside Artem15, Diana was only a husk, a leftover that wasn't really alive. In the massive clockwork war suit, she became something much more; she was fully alive, not an animated piece of burned and fused meat. The hydraulic limbs, hooked into her central nervous system by the cyber-port on her spine, felt as natural as if she had been born with them.

Ted Euphastus was in the hangar, gnawing on a cheroot

cigar as he brought his mug over to a coffeemaker on the table. He looked at Diana as she entered. "Can't sleep?"

"Is she ready to roll?" Diana asked curtly, ignoring Fast's question. She steered her wheelchair toward the inert robotic figure standing in its coffinlike dock.

"A jolly fucking good evening to you, too," Fast grumbled. "Yeah. You can see the chest plate's been rearmored, and I realigned the leg hydraulics."

Diana rolled up to the trapeze arm off to the side of the robot and hauled herself onto the rung, swinging around on the pivoting metal pole to deposit herself in the pilot's couch. It took only a moment for her to snap the interface plug into her spine port. As the Charged Energy Modules that powered the mobile armor thrummed to life, imparting vitality into the inert robotic limbs, Diana's body tingled from scalp to stump cap. She likened the sensation to when her arm fell asleep, cold and prickly, but as the blood rushed back into the arm, warmth dispelled the numb incompletion. She was whole as her nervous system completed the circuit that activated the ancient technology cradling her. Artem15 tapped the trapeze boom out of the way, locking it back over the wheelchair. Red camera lenses glared hatefully down at the conveyance for a cripple.

As the clockwork war suit needed no refuelling thanks to the CEM's functions, Artem15 didn't need to worry about wasting resources while on an unscheduled patrol. The other pilots felt the same, enjoying the comfort of the embracing armored tubs.

"Ari and Dion have patrols out," Fast announced. "And Zoo's on the prowl by himself."

"Any particular operation, or just walkabouts?" Artem15 asked.

"No word on what Zoo is doing. He said it was private business. Are5 and D10nysus have Spartan units with them," Fast said. "Want me to rouse a couple for you?"

"Nah. I've got the radio to bring in Ari or Dion," Artem15 said. "I just need to clear my head and get some fresh air."

Artem15 gave Fast some credit for mostly concealing the ironic smirk as he considered her remark that going for a stroll wrapped in three-thousand pounds of machinery was getting some fresh air.

"Well, Hera said that you're not supposed to go on an end run into the Tartarus holdings," Fast warned.

Diana was glad that Artem15 didn't have the ability to convey facial expressions, even with the cybernetic hookup between her and the robot. "I said I was going for a walk, not out for a suicide. Speaking of which, I didn't look. I've got replacement javelins?"

"You've got a full quiver, and nine yards of ammo per shoulder gun," Fast explained.

Diana nodded, her golden-haired head bobbing between the gear-shaped shoulder gun mounts. "Thanks, Fast. Sorry about being such a whiny bitch."

Fast glanced over to the wheelchair. "It's that thing, kid. Being stuck in it would make me grumpy, too."

Artem15 put her metal claw tips to where her lips would be if she were human, then bent them back, a robotic kiss blown. That brought a smile to the wrench monkey's bearded face.

With a graceful pivot, the robotic huntress strode out into the countryside, a skip in her step as she passed through the massive hangar doors.

The gloom induced by fever dreams evaporated as Artem15 walked into the Greek sunset.

THE IMPACT OF THE MUSKET BALL was a shock to Kane. However, thanks to the high-tech polymers of the shadow suit, his remarkable reflexes and the relatively soft primitive lead musket ball, the gunshot only managed to raise a tiny bruise on his pectoral muscle. Kane's sleek, wolflike frame darted through the peppering cloud of poorly aimed fire seeking him out. Dropping into a shoulder roll, the ex-Magistrate ducked the final volley of black-powder shots.

The ancient, simple weapons couldn't be reloaded by the creatures who barely had the presence of mind to aim them. Unfortunately for Kane, the gleaming points of a dozen bayonets glared at him under pairs of feral yellow eyes. Their sharpness and the berserk strength of their wielders would overwhelm the protective qualities of Kane's shadow suit. As each blade was eighteen inches in length, the former Magistrate knew that his organs would be speared through and through.

Kane fired the Copperhead submachine gun, the weapon snarling out small-caliber rounds into naked, scale-encrusted chests. Two of the mutants dropped their bladed muskets and tumbled into lifeless tangles of gnarled limbs. The suddenly inert hordelings formed a barrier to their brethren's ferocious charge, turning two dead bodies into five more stumbling, disarmed mutants. The dozen growling creatures dropped in number to five active combatants, but their bayonets still thirsted for Kane's blood.

Kane tracked the Copperhead, aiming at the deformed face of a reptilian attacker, then he pivoted and engaged his Sin Eater. Two thundering shots from the folding machine pistol launched a pair of 240-grain superheavy slugs that blew through mutated chests as if they were soggy slices of bread. One 9 mm round glanced off a dead mutant's spine and careened at an angle into a second reptilian form, while the other Sin Eater round punctured the creature behind the first dying mutant.

The last mutant lashed out with his bayonet, but Kane batted the blade away with a sweep of the Copperhead's barrel. With a sharp kick to the mutant's knee, Kane dropped him on the rocky hillside. A kick to the temple put the mutant out just in time for Kane to address the group of sprawled hordelings that were getting back to their feet.

Their yellow eyes flashed angrily in the starlight, muskets held like spears and clubs. Kane whipped his Sin Eater around, knowing that even a moment of hesitation would allow the bayonet-armed monstrosities time to pinion him. The sidearm roared on full-auto, scything through the group with a salvo of thunderbolt rounds. The scaled half men writhed under the rain of smashing slugs, their bodies wrecked by Kane's marksmanship.

It was ruthless, but Kane reminded himself of the Greek townsfolk, their corpses visible on satellite photos. The dead people were mute testimony to the murderous intent of the charging horde.

Right now, Kane turned his attention back toward Grant and Brigid. The pair was back to back, Brigid using Grant's Copperhead while the massive ex-Magistrate attended to the charging swarm on his flank, utilizing his Sin Eater. The two full-auto weapons hammered out vicious volleys that sliced into the savage marauders charging down the slopes.

Domi was nowhere to be seen, and he didn't hear her on his Commtact.

"Dammit," Kane growled. Out in the open and heavily outnumbered, Grant and Brigid were hard-pressed by the surging reptilians. Domi at least had the advantage of broken terrain behind the hillcrest to give her an edge over her opponents.

Charging, Kane raced to bolster the defensive line held by his two companions, sending a good-luck wish to the feral albino girl.

AFTER DOMI BURNED OFF the first seven fat rounds in her compact Combat Master, she decided it was time to engage in a strategic retreat. Musket balls crackled through the air, briefly chasing after her before the mutants ran out of ammunition themselves. The hordelings expended the loads from their cheap, simple rifles and were reverting to their primal instincts of stab and smash. Fortunately for Domi, that meant that the gibbering rabble of scrawny reptilian creatures had to catch up with her first.

With a leap, Domi launched herself down the hillside, luring the mass of nine pursuing hordelings away from Grant and Brigid. She and Kane had broken off from the main group in order to thin out the overwhelming numbers of mutants, so if that meant that she had to play wounded bird to draw the cats from her nest, then so be it. She loved Grant and Brigid like family, and no risk would be too great for her.

With a speed belying her short legs, the albino girl opened up her lead over the bayonet-armed reptilians to thirty yards, far enough to give her some breathing room, yet close enough for her to be an enticing target for the misshapen lizard men. Domi paused to eject her empty magazine and shove another stick of seven slugs into the butt of the booming little Detonics .45. A particularly energetic and nimble mutant leaped to within fifteen yards of Domi, but she dumped his corpse onto the rocky hillside with the weight of a .45-caliber bullet. A cavernous chest wound further deformed his mutant body.

"Eight to go," Domi whispered, racing along to keep the hordelings from surrounding and trapping her in a killing box. The hilly land, with its sparse brush, maze of boulders and jutting rock faces was not that much different from the inhospitable, craggy terrain of the Bitterroot Mountains. As such, the reptilians didn't have the advantage of home turf, since she could navigate the sloped, uneven ground as quickly as they could.

Domi knew there was the possibility that the enemy would catch up with her, and she'd have to reload the Detonics because there were more pursuers than she had bullets. That didn't worry her too much, as she still had her wicked, sheathed knife. The mutants might have been too ferocious for farmers and townsfolk hidden behind fortified walls, but against the wilderness-born albino, the savage lizard creatures would discover that had a match for their savagery. Though outnumbered, she had the added skill of countless sparring sessions with Kane and Grant, two highly trained fighting men. Domi wasn't a martial artist, not by any stretch of the imagination, but she didn't need to be. Her natural fighting prowess, forged in the Outlands and polished by battling alongside of some of the finest combatants on the planet, had refined her technique without tempering her instinctive brutality.

A mutant raced along a hilltop to her right, screeching unintelligibly to his brothers who were strung out behind them. Domi snapped a shot at the reptilian mutant, but being on the run and not having a stable firing stance, she missed the gnarled hordeling by yards. The half man yowled in indignation and with maniacal strength, threw the musket like a javelin. Domi realized the weight and force behind the foot-

and-a-half-long bayonet would be far more dangerous than a soft musket ball. She swerved, barely avoiding the wood-and-steel missile, but the sudden change in direction caused her to lose her footing as she stomped down hard on loose shale. Her lead over the reptilians evaporated as she took a spinning crash into the gravel. Thankfully, she still held on to her .45 and she aimed it at the hilltop mutant who was running straight at her, obviously ready to rend her with his fangs and claws. Braced and stationary, Domi was equally ready to send the clone back to the hell that vomited him onto Earth.

Shockingly, the mutant seized up and exploded, detonating seven yards from Domi. One moment, the misshapen creature was charging; the next his internal organs were externalized as a cloud of red sticky mist. Domi registered the chatter of heavy blasters cutting loose behind her. The guns didn't make the familiar sounds of her friends' weapons. It took a moment for her to realize that she had to have stumbled onto one of the giant, coppery robots.

Before she could send a call over her Commtact, two screaming clones charged out from behind a boulder. Domi swung the Detonics toward them and pounded two powerful bullets into one of the mutants, stopping him cold. The other, however, had taken a flying leap, and at the apex of his path, Domi could see the lethal bayonet spearing through the air toward her face. She rolled to one side, hearing the deadly blade sink into the hard, barren soil with tremendous force.

The mutant screeched with insane frustration, trying to pry the weapon out of the ground. Domi scrambled to her feet and whipped the steel muzzle of her pistol across the mutant's jaw, shattering it with a loud pop that signaled exploding bone. The mutant collapsed into a nerveless, unconscious puddle of bioengineered twitching flesh.

It might have been a consolation that Domi only had five more mutants to face, but the creatures lurched into view all at once, hopping atop boulders. They were spread out, so she couldn't shoot them all, even if she had five bullets left in her gun. As they grinned maliciously, fangs shimmered in the starlight.

Panting, she curled her lip in defiance. Detonics in one hand, she slid her knife from its scabbard, her ruby-red eyes staring with the same rage as the pairs of soulless, yellow orbs that sized her up. "Want eats? Come and get 'em."

A gibbering chuckle escaped five pairs of lips, and they lurched forward just before freezing, yellow slits widening with horror. Domi had heard the thunderous beat of ponderous footfalls shaking the earth behind her, but now there was only silence. She would be caught in the line of fire between the machine-gun-armed robot and the savage clones anyway, so she stood her ground, ready to make the mutants pay dearly for her life. The wind rose over her head, the breeze so strong that it flicked the head wrap off her bone-colored hair, the rag fluttering away uselessly. It was a sudden, unnatural breeze that set off her instincts. Reflexively, she rolled backward, away from the quintet of hordelings, but the golden-maned titan wouldn't have landed on her. The crash of three thousand pounds of mechanized warrior shook Domi almost off her feet.

Even more stunning was the raw power emanating from the armored war machine standing in front of her.

It had landed on one mutant, and twisted limbs poked up between the giant's metal toe claws. With a grace belying its enormous bulk, the robot lashed out with long, hydraulic-piston arms. It quickly snatched up two mutants from their perches atop boulders, eliciting screeches of horror. Powerful crushing fingers closed on their toylike little bodies, gore vomiting between gigantic metal fingers. The squeals ended moments before the creatures' lower bodies plopped greasily onto the rocky ground, everything that their bellies and legs had been attached to pulverized into liquid mush. A fourth hordeling screeched in rage, lunging to attack the mechanized warrior.

Domi snapped up her pistol and blew it out of the air, .45-caliber slugs cutting it down in midflight.

Artem15 whirled at the sound of gunshots and watched the reptilian clone flop dead on the ground. Red camera lenses tightened in focus, examining the young woman she'd come to rescue.

"Lower the weapon," she ordered the albino girl.

"Not on your life," Domi said. She clenched her pistol and knife, ruby-red eyes glaring in defiance.

"Why not?" Artem15 challenged.

"Not wrapped in metal!" Domi spit. Her anger dissipated into alarm. "One's getting away!"

Artem15 whirled in response to the warning, following the flash of movement as the last mutant fled with a speed born of pure terror. Her shoulder guns chattered to life, ripping out streams of bullets that sliced the misshapen horde clone to ribbons. "Thanks for that."

"Not your enemy," Domi returned. "Thanks for your help."

Artem15 straightened and nodded.

"You speak English?" Domi asked.

"All robot pilots do," the woman in the mobile armor

replied. "But you… Where are you from? Where'd you get that gun? And what is that uniform you're wearing?"

Domi looked down at her pistol, realizing that the flood of the pilot's questions were more than she could easily explain. "My stuff's from a lot of places. Me, I'm from America. I'm from a place called Cerberus."

Artem15 tilted her head. "Cerberus?" she said with interest. "Did you come alone?"

"Three friends," Domi answered, still nervous enough to speak in her clipped vocabulary. Her ruby-red eyes widened with shocked realization. "Back this way!"

Artem15's robot cameras whirred, looking toward the direction that Domi was starting in. "Wait! I hear the fighting. Climb on!"

"Climb on?" Domi asked.

Artem15 extended a powerful, blood-slicked metal hand toward Domi. "My way's faster. Trust me."

Domi looked at the pulped remains of the mutants that had been crushed in the enormous digits. "You got to be kidding."

"I won't hurt you, and we need to get to your friends quickly," Artem15 said.

Domi grabbed on to Artem15's "thumb" with both hands and hauled herself up into the main joint that formed the robot's palm. With ridiculous ease, Artem15 carried her up to the gigantic shoulder gear housing for the robot's left gun.

"Name's Domi," she offered.

"Um…Diana," Artem15 answered. An uncomfortable silence followed the pronunciation, as if the words had somehow caught in her throat.

"What's wrong?" Domi asked.

Diana couldn't explain—and honestly didn't want to—the

sudden identity trauma she'd caused herself. "Nothing. We have to reach your friends. I'll try to explain later."

"Okay," Domi replied uncertainly.

"Hang on tight," Artem15 warned.

Domi wrapped her arms around the steel gear-shaped shoulder armor without protest. Moments later, the albino understood why as massively powerful leg hydraulics flexed, then sprung, launching both robot and girl skyward.

Domi's voice rose in a wail of dismay and shock as they accelerated into the starlit night, but the wail gave way to a crescendo of childlike glee as she realized that she was flying on the shoulder of a robotic giant.

For a moment, she allowed herself the windswept joy of sailing in flight as she'd never traveled before.

Chapter 5

He had named himself Z00s, a numerical phonetic for Zeus, when he had been remade as the first of the robot pilots of New Olympus. It was an identity he had folded himself completely into, a stark contrast to his cold and clinical title of Thurmond, Magistrate of Cobaltville. As a Magistrate, Thurmond had no given name, only his family title, an appellation that mentally conditioned him to surrender his individuality in the service of the Program of Unification. Identity subsumed behind the faceless black carapace helmet, the Magistrate was just another selfless drone, the latest edition in a lineage of protective knights who defended the villes' status quo.

Renaming himself was one thing, but the affectionate nickname of Zoo, bestowed upon him by his subordinates, was a title he wore with loving pride. Ever since he was assigned, along with fellow Magistrate Danton, to Dr. Helena Garthwaite for the expedition to Greece, Zoo had lived a whole new lifetime he never imagined. Helena had been dispatched by Baron Cobalt, partially because the baron wanted to break in a new lover, and partially because Helena had promised him that she had discovered the clues to an amazing new technology that would grant Cobalt an advantage over his fellow barons. The expedition was a harrowing journey across the wastelands of postapocalyptic America, over the tumultuous

Atlantic Ocean and finally a trek through the wreckage of southern Europe until they finally reached the Find.

Standing over it now, even in the immense fifteen-foot mobile armor, Zoo felt tiny. The Find was at the bottom of a mile-deep fissure that had been cracked open by an Earth-shaker bomb. The Earthshaker was a buried hydrogen bomb designed to cause enormous seismic trauma to a countryside, detonating with enough force to break open massive canyons, flatten mountains or hurl flatlands into mile-high plateaus. Just another of humankind's wonders created in the service of self-destruction, as opposed to the clockwork mobile armor Helena had discovered in the Find. The skeletons were designed as multiuse animatronic frames, as capable of being common workers as they were unstoppable fighting mechanisms. Helena figured out a way for them to house a human warrior, but only if the pilot was smaller than five feet in height, due to the construction of the torso framework.

The powerful Earthshaker had opened the crack down to the mile-deep, ancient Annunaki cavern, and rendered vast stretches of Greek countryside inland seas. Inside the Find, after three days of climbing and battling past territorial scaled mutants, Helena, Thurmond and Danton had discovered the prize she had been expecting, as well as hints of a secret world history that no one could have imagined. Helena, now titled Hera, had constructed the theory based on historical records uncovered among the ruins and remembered pillow talk from her time with Baron Cobalt. While it seemed incongruous to Zoo at first, there was no denying that he was now inside a man-machine interface that was far more than the sum of its parts.

With a single bound, he began his descent down into the crack in the world, hopping like a spider from cliff to cliff, secondary orichalcum claws securing him to a rocky ledge with more than enough strength to counter the downward momentum of three thousand pounds of mechanoid. He leaped and caught walls with a facility that no one would ever assume capable in a massive, clanking monstrosity. The zigzag hopscotch down the sheer walls of the crevasse turned the mile-deep descent into a gleeful ride that took only minutes rather than an arduous, life-threatening trek. Zoo whooped with delight as freefall rendered him weightless, and the hydraulic extension of his body danced through the air in showy somersaults.

Landing in a crouch, the secondary orichalcum skeleton and its Annunaki-designed hydraulics cushioned what would have been skeleton-shattering impacts. His heart felt light, the journey a cleansing experience that washed away the poisonous dread in his spirit. Zoo looked into the gaping black entrance of the Find, the cavern that was also the back door into the Tartarus clone vats. Feral yellow eyes blinked in the darkness, but the mutants didn't dare make a move against the hated thunder god that strode through the cave. The bearded clockwork giant walked with strength and confidence that no scrawny little reptilian creature would be able to harm him even if he did summon up the courage to launch his minuscule frame against the king of the clockwork war suits. Zoo ignored them, walking into the domain of his goddess-queen's publicly sworn enemy, Thanatos.

Helena Garthwaite and her two Magistrate bodyguards, Thurmond and Danton, had been raised up, with the wonders of the Find, from seekers of mythology to the very beings of legend. The technology that would have allowed Baron Cobalt an edge to sweep aside his hybrid brothers and assume the throne of Lord of the Earth, instead became the forge in which Hera Olympiad, Zeus and Thanatos were born, the core of a new pantheon that would be their first step on a ladder of continental expansion.

Zoo had remade himself the most, going under the carving saw and the spine-violating implant of the cyberport that left him legless, half a man, but only when he was away from the magnificent orichalcum skeleton and its steel armor. His mobile suit was the finest of the cache of fifty, and undeniably he was the mightiest and greatest of the robot god warriors. As a Magistrate, he was intimidating, but merely a drone. Now he was a magnificent copper-skinned exemplar of metallic godhood.

"Thanatos?" Zoo called over his loudspeaker.

The clones seemed confused, as if there was no one to give them focus or purpose. Normally, Thanatos would have strode out, greeting his brother. Something alerted Zoo's instincts, informing him that there was danger in the air, a doubt that had started when the metal-armored reptilian was discovered among the mutant hordelings.

His light-amplification optics kicked in, minor illuminators giving the lenses something to target. They picked up a massive silvery disk, taller than the mechanized war suit and so wide that it had to have had entered the chasm sideways to land. Zoo couldn't find a single aperture, no hatches or thrust nozzles on its smooth, mirror-polished surface. Something crunched under his clawed foot, and Zoo looked at the ground, seeing the charred husks of mutants ankle deep around him. The piles of dead had been incinerated by some form of high-energy weapon, and from the numbers of corpses, they had to have surged in violent, desperate defense of their cave.

"Than! Than, are you all right?" Zoo called out.

"Danton is well," an unearthly voice boomed. Though it possessed an alien intonation, it was familiar. The address of Thanatos by his old name sent an urgent jolt of menace running up Zoo's spine, but Zoo dismissed his panic, using his reason to decipher the mystery of the familiar yet alien voice.

The fifteen-foot robot genuflected, dropping to one knee in submission. It was an old reflex, stretching back to his days as a Magistrate. "Baron Cobalt, my lord!"

"Please, Thurmond." The alien voice resonated across several frequencies. "Or shall I call you Zeus?"

Zoo looked around the darkness, unable to tell where the voice was coming from, despite the fact that it didn't produce an echo due to its multitonal reverberation.

"I, too, have a new identity, my loyal subject."

"Baron Cobalt?"

Zoo finally focused on movement in the darkness. It was a seven-foot-tall figure, a silhouette of physical perfection clad in cobalt-blue shimmering metal armor that was as finely wrought as Hera's silver skin. The Baron Cobalt he remembered was only a shade over five feet and willowy, while this newcomer was carved from slabs of lean muscle and long, straight limbs. The rippling musculature under the metal, skin-conforming armor was a far cry from the frail leader he'd remembered. Finally, the stranger's face came into view of his night optics, an angelic face sculpted in reptilian skin, beautiful and menacing in the same instant.

"Please, Zoo, call me Lord Marduk."

Inside Z00s's cockpit, Thurmond's jaw went slack in awe.

MILES AWAY, another former Cobaltville Magistrate's jaw dropped in surprise, but not at the appearance of an Annunaki

overlord. Rather, Kane gaped at the sight of a gigantic mechanoid bounding over the crest of a hill, Domi clinging to its
shoulder and hooting in excited delight.

The paltry remnants of the hordeling marauders, already
in disarray from the concentrated firepower and fighting co-
ordination of the Cerberus explorers, completely lost their
nerves at the sight of a more familiar but no less implacable
enemy. Against efficient human warriors and a towering
mecha, with their overwhelming numbers depleted, the reptilian clones were helpless. A wild panic broke through the
half-dozen remaining ambushers as they scurried toward the
nearest bolt-holes.

Artem15 landed ten yards from the Cerberus explorers,
then set her hand on the soil of the valley in order to give
Domi a means to scramble down off her shoulder.

"Look what I found!" Domi exclaimed, unable to contain
her glee, especially now that she had seen that her friends were
safe.

Kane looked over the giant robot and simply had nothing
to say. He fell back on his old standby sarcasm. "Well, if you
promise to clean up after it and walk it every day…"

Domi's nose wrinkled in mock admonition. "You know
what I mean."

Kane nodded, then looked up at the fifteen-foot titan. "Uh,
hi. We saw your kind in a satellite photo, and we decided to
drop on by."

Artem15 straightened, even though she knelt to stay more or
less level with the humans. "There are still satellites up there?"

Kane's litany of surprises continued to roll, this time at the
youth and femininity of the robot's voice. "Yeah. Where we
come from, we're lucky to have access to satellite imagery."

"Wow," the voice said through the clockwork mechanoid's loudspeaker in an awed whisper. She stared at the starry veldt above. Finally she pried her attention from the heavens and returned to the four companions. "Domi and I have already made our introductions. I am Artem15."

"Artemis," Brigid repeated. "The Greek goddess of the moon and the hunt. In Roman myth, she was also known as Diana."

"Diana's her real name, too," Domi said. She still seemed high from her bouncing trip across the hills on the shoulder of the towering robot. "She helped me out against the scalies."

Grant flipped up the visor on his helmet, amused by the giddy joy in the albino girl's voice. "You okay?"

Domi wiped her mouth and came away with flakes of dried blood. "Oh, I slipped and got into some hand-to-hand with one of the mutants."

She leaned in close to Grant. "Did you see me flying?"

Grant gave the girl a calming squeeze on her shoulder. "Looks like fun, but I'll stay at the stick of a helicopter."

"This is better," Domi said softly, a wide grin splitting her face.

Artem15 cleared her throat. "Domi is right. My pilot… My real name is Diana Pantopoulos."

"I'm Brigid Baptiste. This is Kane and that is Grant. My comrades and I are from the Cerberus redoubt, and despite our guns, we're here on a mission of peace and exploration," Brigid announced. "We come as potential friends and allies."

Artem15 scanned the hills around them. "I'd have to say bringing the arsenal was a good idea. Between the four of you, you devastated a fifty-strong raider squadron. The Tartarus vats will have to work extra hard to replenish their ranks."

The mention of Tartarus brought a glance of recognition between the four Cerberus companions.

"Did I say anything wrong?" Artem15 asked.

"No, not at all," Kane replied. "Where we initially came from, Cobaltville, the Tartarus Pits were the slums under the main city."

"However," Brigid interjected, "Greek mythological terms are quite commonly encountered, as the name of our own redoubt, Cerberus, makes apparent."

"Cobaltville…" Artem15 repeated in awe. "That is where Hera Olympiad and Z00s came from."

She shifted from knee to knee in excitement over the touchstone she had in common with the far-flung quartet. "And Hera was worried about her past catching up with her."

"Well, maybe it has," Grant responded. "This isn't exactly a social call. We only took notice of this place when our satellites picked up traces of an overlord dropship."

"Overlords?" Artem15 asked. "What are those?"

Brigid looked exasperated at Grant's interruption and resumed her explanation. "The overlords are entities who are a threat to humanity. In their previous incarnation, they ruled nine cities across America as barons before an evolutionary signal returned them to their original Annunaki forms."

"Hera and Zeus are from Cobaltville? "Kane asked. When Artem15 nodded, he turned to Grant. "I don't remember anyone who could have been named Zeus."

"Me, either, but I do know eight years ago, Cobalt picked out a pair of his best Magistrates to accompany some whitecoat on an expedition," Grant noted. "Well, maybe not best. I'm kind of fuzzy on who was sent."

Brigid clucked her tongue. "You can't remember your comrades?"

Grant rolled his eyes. "It's been eight years, and even if I did have a eidetic memory like yours, I've taken a lot of knocks to the old cabbage."

Brigid shrugged.

"So would you know Zoo when you saw him?" Artem15 asked.

"Yeah," Grant replied. "Maybe even Kane, but he was a little young and wet behind the ears when those guys went out. He barely remembered my name back then."

Kane shook his head.

Artem15 nodded at the quartet joking around with one another. "The overlord dropship, it wouldn't have crew members that wore skintight, flexible armor and have scaly faces?"

"The Nephilim," Brigid answered. "So you have seen them?"

"Ari, er, Are5 killed one of them yesterday," Artem15 explained. "There's a ship full of them?"

Kane nodded. "Which is why we rushed over here. If there's at least one overlord alive, both of us are going to have to pitch in and keep them from grabbing power. Those snake-faces are cunning devils, and they have a lot of nasty tricks up their sleeves."

"Like wrist blasters," Artem15 confirmed. "Blew the thermal ax right out of Are5's hand."

"Which is why we're here," Grant offered. "It's a bit selfish— you scratch our backs and we'll scratch yours—but it's a first step. A universal show of friendship. Speaking of which…"

Artem15 tilted her head, then nodded. "Domi wondered that, too. I speak English because it's a common trade language for the Mediterranean. As well, all the members of Strike Force Olympus speak English, thanks to Hera's and Zeus's tutelage."

"Not complaining," Kane said. "Otherwise, anything you said would just be…"

"Greek to you?" Artem15 finished for the ex-Magistrate.

"You caught it before I put the brakes on that," Kane muttered. "Awkward…"

"It's okay. At least it's not butt jokes," Artem15 replied.

"Thank heaven for small favors," Kane returned. Robot and explorer shared a chuckle.

"This is why I'm the one who should do the talking," Brigid admonished. "Don't mind Kane too much. I just bring him along to kill annoying pests."

"Fighting fire with fire," Kane translated.

Grant gave Kane a slap on the shoulder. "Smart-ass to the end."

The two Magistrates shared a grin, bolstered by some hope given to them in the robot's story. Maybe the Cerberus explorers had lucked into a situation where they discovered a relatively peaceful society. The mention of Zeus as a Magistrate also seemed promising. Although Kane and Grant had battled their fellow Magistrates while they were wanted outlaws on the run from the barons, there were also those who believed in law, order and justice rather than blindly following the tyrannical status quo of the villes. The recent recruits brought into the ranks of the Cerberus away teams were as decent as Kane and Grant. If one of Cobalt's old Magistrates was the leader of a guardian force holding off hordes of human-hating mutant monsters, it wasn't a stretch for Kane to imagine that this wouldn't be as desperate a situation as he'd expected.

Then again, there was the premonition of lightning flashing from the sky, destroying the countryside and burning helpless humans to charred hulks. Some form of terrain-scouring menace was waiting in the wings, capable of laying waste to thousands of lives in a single blast of electric-blue fire. Grant frowned as he saw Kane's good mood sober.

"I don't know if anyone in your command has psychic abilities," Kane began. "But I had a momentary flash when we were passing through what apparently was an ancient oracle."

"Not to my knowledge," Artem15 answered. She grew silent for a moment, and Kane could tell that while the hydraulics of the robot were still, gears turned in its pilot's mind. "What was it?"

"A weapon in the form of lightning or some kind of electric ray," Kane replied. "I'm not sure if your group takes premonitions seriously, but I've encountered enough strange situations—"

"Kane," Artem15 interrupted. "I'm an amputee riding in the chest of a fifteen-foot-tall combat robot dating back at least three thousand years, battling hordes of cloned mutants who now apparently have the support of ancient reptile gods who fly around in spaceships and wear impenetrable metal."

Kane smirked. "You'll take my flash seriously."

"Yep," Artem15 replied.

"So all that remains now is the 'take us to your leader' request," Brigid chimed in. "Though it might get cramped if all four of us ride on your shoulders like Domi did."

Domi grinned, enjoying the prospect of riding to Artem15's base on the robot's shoulders.

"Then let me call a ride for the rest of you," Artem15 answered. "Never let it be said that the Greeks don't know how to spoil a visitor. We'll hold off on the gifts, because we know our reputation in that regard."

Diana keyed in her communicator. "Artem15 to base. I have conducted a first contact with travelers from America. Requesting permission to bring them in under hospitable security protocols, and for escort from Are5 and his patrol."

"You said amputee," Brigid said. "You cut off your legs to be a robot pilot?"

Artem15 looked down to her. "Only one, Brigid. The other…"

The red camera eyes in their helmet slit whirred, and the head turned to look at the bullet-riddled corpses of the Tartarus marauders.

"Oh," Brigid replied.

"I take it there's no shortage of volunteers," Kane said grimly.

"No. Just a shortage of suits," Artem15 stated. "I'm sure your satellites have seen the layouts of the towns and farms around this area. High walls, and sniper towers where farmers are doled out the few bits of firearms technology that we can spare."

"Other than the robots, you don't have much high tech?" Grant asked.

"Radios, and we have a small factory that turns out cased rifle ammunition and simple bolt-action rifles to supply the civilian populace," Artem15 said. "And we have stockpiles for our robots' shoulder guns."

Kane noted the wicked, wedge-shaped knuckles on her hands. "So you conserve ammo with hand to hand."

"Yeah," Artem15 answered.

"So Zoo is an amputee, as well?" Grant asked. "Was he injured by the mutants?"

"No," Artem15 said. "He was the first volunteer. That is why he is our Zeus. He sacrificed two healthy legs to be our defender."

Grant and Kane exchanged a glance. Despite the courage of some of the Magistrates they had faced, Zoo's gesture was surprising.

"Do you remember anyone that good?" Kane asked.

"Hell, back when we were Mags, we did stuff we weren't proud of," Grant replied. "It took seeing another way of life to make us what we are."

"Point made, partner," Kane acknowledged.

The thuds of three sets of feet racing across the countryside filled the air. Kane finally spotted the leader of the trio, a massive robot with a metal razor fin bisecting his helmet.

"You rang for some noble steeds, Artie?" Are5 asked, skidding to a halt. He swiveled his hand in a salute, bowing his Mohawked helmet toward Artem15.

"That's Are5," Artem15 introduced, "And Spartans 10 and 34. Are5 is a hero pilot, like me."

"The officer corps," Are5 added. "When a Greek needs help, they call a Spartan. When a Spartan needs help, they call us."

"And when we need help," Artem15 interrupted, "we call ZOOs."

"Right," Are5 agreed. The imposing robot strode toward Brigid, making a gesture of running his metal fingertips along his domed helmet. "Milady, I would be honored if you would ride my shoulder back to New Olympus."

Brigid raised an eyebrow, then smiled. "Absolutely, Ares."

Kane rolled his eyes as Spartan 10 extended a hand for him to climb up to a robotic shoulder. "He must have gotten the shovel out to lay that crap."

Spartan 10 chuckled, shoulders vibrating under Kane's

seat. A girl's voice came from the helmet. "Artie's a little too polite to let you guys know that Ari's a horny little stump."

Kane grinned and wrapped an arm around the shoulder gear. "Wing woman?"

"Two," Spartan 34 corrected, letting Grant settle onto her unisex robot shoulder.

Grant chuckled. "Finally some competition for our own horn dog."

Kane shook his head. "Some days it's not worth leaving the redoubt."

"And deny me the pleasure of having a hunk on my shoulder?" Spartan 10 asked.

Kane smiled. Together, the clockwork warriors and their Cerberus explorer riders headed toward the New Olympian base.

DANTON HAD SUFFERED a few bruises, but he was unharmed, despite being under the protection of a six-foot Nephilim. Zoo hadn't been asked to leave his battle armor, but he was mindful of the other scaled sentinels surrounding him. Zoo saw that Danton wasn't a prisoner. Danton explained that he hadn't realized that the beings from the silver disk were, in fact, friends and allies from their days at Cobaltville. He'd directed his hordelings to throw themselves at the armored aliens, believing them to be invaders.

Marduk had ended the conflict with a backhanded slap and a stentorian bellow, allowing his booming timber to cow both Nephilim warriors and the Tartarus mutants.

At least that was the story that Danton had been allowed to tell, Zoo thought suspiciously.

"A wonderful little empire you have carved out here," Marduk proclaimed. "Helena has done me proud."

Zoo watched the pacing overlord as he surveyed the breeder vats in appreciation.

"We tried to contact you," Zoo explained. "However, the atmosphere and radiation zones made it difficult to get a signal around the world."

Marduk smiled and nodded. "I believe you, Z00s. The technology you had, even the technology you currently possess, is wholly insufficient for reliable intercontinental communications. Sending a messenger would have been difficult, as well, because, after all, it took you how long to get here? A year?"

"Fourteen months. The Atlantic was a nightmare," Zoo said.

"I have seen the rough waters from the safety of my dropship," Marduk explained. "I agree, traversing those waves would have made any journey a life's gamble. Even if you did get back, it really would not have mattered to me. My Sandcats and Deathbirds were as efficient as these old Annunaki warbots, at least with the features and add-ons Helena was able to decipher and adapt. More recently, I had hordes of Nephilim equipped with ASP blasters and airborne dropships of considerable firepower at my command."

"Had," Zoo repeated.

Marduk nodded. "Yes."

"So now you need us," Zoo surmised.

Marduk's smile returned but was now slightly sinister. "You Magistrates were always a perceptive lot. Sadly, the greed of my sister Lilitu, whom you knew as the Baroness Beausoleil, has deprived me not only of my armies of minions and fleet of dropships, but of the mightiest weapon I'd ever beheld."

Zoo glanced toward Danton. "But there are more weapons in the Find?"

Marduk's nod confirmed Zoo's question. "Helena came here at my behest. Not only was I getting bored with her, but I truly was seeking a considerable advantage over by brother barons. Now, with the losses we all have incurred, I seek my old toy chest."

Zoo looked at the illuminated vats where a new generation of reptilian humanoids was brewing. "So you'll be able to construct more of your soldiers?"

"Nephilim," Marduk corrected. "Yes, I will. But they are secondary to what treasures I had deposited here."

"And what about us? What about New Olympus?" Zoo asked.

Marduk took a deep breath, then let it out. "I seek not to demote any of you. You may still remain Zeus, Thanatos and Hera, the lords of this kingdom. As ruler of the Earth, I realize that I will have to delegate my authority. Even Zeus required subjects in Olympus, did he not?"

Zoo nodded.

"In cooperating with me, helping me to defeat my brothers, you will find me a generous benefactor," Marduk stated.

"But what if Hera—Helena—doesn't want to play second fiddle to you, Lord Marduk?" Zoo asked hesitantly.

Marduk's smile contained no warmth or joy. His needle-sharp teeth would have been frightening on their own, but the demeanor of the Annunaki overlord before him made Zoo tremble in his pilot's couch.

"In that instance, you will have to find yourself another Hera."

Zoo swallowed hard, forcing his rising bile back down.

Chapter 6

The radio report of first contact put Hera on edge. That feeling of unease was compounded by the appearance of the alien soldier among Danton's clone force. She hadn't been able to get into radio contact with Danton, hence the need to send Z00s out to the Tartarus Find. It was risky to dispatch him, but utilizing an unsecured radio or an open communication hardline was out of the question. Hera reminded herself of the old saying that a secret known to two was not a secret for long.

She, Zoo and Danton-Thanatos were the only three who were privy to the knowledge that the Tartarus hordelings were at Hera's beck and call. The clone vats were her source for an easily generated bogeyman designed to give the heroic robot champions a powerful challenge, their raison d'être. Now, everything had grown more complicated. First there was the body of the alien humanoid, a creature resembling the Annunaki from the ancient computer records in the Find. Now, there were newcomers who claimed to be exiles from Cobaltville. For the first time since she'd donned the environmentally impervious silver skin, beads of nervous sweat formed on her smooth brow and a chill ran up and down her spine.

If, after all this time, Baron Cobalt was interested in a return on his investment, then it was very likely that he might have chosen agents whose origins were more obscure, she told herself. Giving himself away with familiar old faces was not characteristic of the scheming baron. Still, the presence of a truly alien opponent distracted her suspicions, as well, another factor that made her feel that paranoia was a better tactic than assuming that coincidence was merely coincidence.

Hera took a deep breath. A lot of things were happening quickly, and she simply didn't have enough information to make a snap judgment. She just wondered if she would have the opportunity to make enough observations before assassins and saboteurs brought New Olympus crashing down.

Artem15 had the right idea. Hospitable security precautions were the order of the day. The strangers' movements would be monitored, and they would be escorted through New Olympus without actually subjecting them to imprisonment or total disarmament. There would be the implication of trust. Perhaps under the illusion of freedom, the four strangers would betray their hand as saboteurs, thieves or assassins.

Hera was glad that her robot pilots were so selflessly loyal to her. Her surgical procedures enabled her to handpick only the most trusted and dedicated to pilot her mobile armor suits. She'd specifically redesigned the cybernetic interface module to accommodate those who would otherwise be helpless cripples outside of the mighty war robots. It was ingenious, she congratulated herself, that people were willing to drastically mutilate themselves for a greater cause. Then again, the horrors of the clone master Thanatos and his Tartarus mutants were inspiration enough for a full-fledged recruitment drive. Revenge for personal injury or lost loved ones and selfless duty to protect family and country were powerful motivations for her elite robot pilots. The inhuman nature of the enemy rendered impossible any chance of peace negotiations with the monstrous Thanatos or his mindless minions.

In the meantime, Hera had her invincible, heroically noble heroes who were practically helpless when not guiding their one-and-a-half-ton war suits against the implacable foe. If they should grow suspicious and turn against her, Hera easily had the means to eliminate a legless cripple confined to a wheelchair.

A preoperative volunteer, one of the Praetorian soldiers who made up the conventional military staff of New Olympus, stood in the doorway, interrupting her worries of plots and counterplots.

"Milady," he spoke up. He was clad head to toe in copper-and-leather armor, resembling both the robot Spartan drones and the baronial Magistrates that she was familiar with from Cobaltville. However, instead of the high-tech Sin Eater, the soldier was armed with a bayonet-tipped, bolt-action rifle, a crude, easily produced weapon that helped the Greeks of New Olympus feel as if they had a say in their own livelihood.

"The travelers have arrived," Hera announced.

"Yes," the soldier said. "I will accompany you to the hangar, my queen."

"Are the preparations for the meeting hall and guest quarters complete?" Hera asked, striding out into the hall, her majestic demeanor returning as she performed the duties of her regal station.

"The meeting hall is fully stocked with a welcome meal, and off-duty personnel have been assigned to make it feel more festive," the Praetorian responded. "The observers and electronic surveillance equipment are also in place for the two guest apartments."

Hera nodded, a smile spreading across her lips. "Excellent." It was good to be in charge again.

KANE WAS IMPRESSED as the giant hangar doors swung open, a massive pair of metal lips peeling apart to reveal a huge maw in the side of the mountain. The open doors exposed two lines of fifteen-foot-tall bronze robot warriors standing at attention. The walls of mechanoid giants formed a coppery corridor that led down to a tall, seemingly naked animated statue of a goddess coated in gleaming silver with threads of gold.

Spartan 10 kneeled and allowed Kane to climb her arm to the ground. The other robots did the same for his companions.

Grant gave Domi a tap on the shoulder. "You were right. That was fun."

"Told you," Domi answered. She fell silent at the gauntlet of mobile armor suits standing at attention in the hangar. "Oh boy."

"Honor guard or death trap?" Brigid asked.

"They're watching us," Kane answered. "Same way we welcome any visitors to Cerberus."

"So both," Grant added. "They want us to know that if we misbehave, we're pulp."

Two human soldiers with metal breastplates walked up to them. "Please surrender your rifles. You may retain your sidearms, however."

Kane looked over to Grant, then shrugged. It wasn't as if the Copperhead SMGs would provide any advantage to the two ex-Magistrates in the event of a conflict with twenty-five towering robot warriors. Still, Kane was glad to keep the reassuring weight of his Sin Eater on his forearm. Grant looked relieved, as well. The guards took the rifles, then pivoted to face the silver goddess at the far end of the robotic gauntlet. "Follow us, sirs and madams."

The Cerberus explorers shared a bemused look, then followed the leather-and-metal-clad soldiers.

"They look familiar?" Grant asked in a low voice, audible only over their Commtacts.

"Budget-rate Magistrate armor," Brigid spoke up immediately. "Leather and copper instead of polymer and carbon fiber. Seems as if Hera knew a good design when she saw it."

Grant made a face, remembering how ill-fitting Magistrate armor plates had pinched and chafed on him. "Good is relative."

"Oh, my God," Brigid said, eyes narrowing.

"What?" Kane asked.

"The silver skin put me off for a moment, but that's Helena Garthwaite, from the Archivist Division," Brigid answered. "She specialized in archaeological research, but she was a polymath in regards to the sciences." She glanced toward Grant. "See, some of us remember our coworkers."

"Lah-dee-fucking-dah," Grant replied.

The four explorers looked at the silver-and-gold-armored goddess standing before them. She was a curvaceous woman, statuesque in height. With her hair hidden under a skullcap of the same liquid, polished metal that made up the rest of her skin, the only part of her visible was a regal, unlined face with cold black eyes and a wide, sensuous mouth. She stood, her head tilted back, chin raised, though it was not as if she was exposing her throat to attack, the shimmering armor skin extending all the way to the tip of her chin, forming the bottom of the metallic frame for her beautiful face. Kane could hazard a guess at Hera's hair color as her slender eyebrows were light wisps of blond hair. She stood upon a three-step dais, thus allowing her to tower over the newcomers to the hangar.

"You may bow your heads in deference to our respected queen, Hera Olympiad, savior of the Greeks, lord high scientist and supreme arbiter of New Olympus," their escorts said in unison.

The Cerberus warriors dipped their heads respectively before the silver-and-gold-clad woman. It was a far less extreme show of honor than being forced to their knees, as had been the case too many times for them to count. If Hera demanded only a respectful nod, then she couldn't have been too tyrannical a leader.

"Baptiste?" Hera asked. Brigid nodded in affirmation. "My God, woman! You're looking quite healthy. I never expected to see you again."

Brigid blushed a little. "Ever since I got kicked out of Cobaltville, I've been getting quite a bit of exercise."

Hera looked appreciatively toward Kane, a slender eyebrow arching in an unspoken question.

Brigid and Kane shook their heads in a synchronized denial. "No, ma'am," Kane spoke up. "Not that kind of exercise."

"Really?" Hera asked, throwing a couple of extra syllables into the one-word response. "So, no doubt you told your friends my real name?"

"Yes, Helena," Brigid said.

"She only had time to say that she worked with you when you were both archivists," Grant added, shaking his head at the brief flash of flirtation between Hera and Kane. "Of course, Brigid seems to have forgotten that you were sent here to Greece."

Brigid glared at Grant's smugness. "I can't remember information never made available to me."

Hera smiled, letting herself relax a little in the presence of the four newcomers. Though the men were obviously former Magistrates, easily denoted due to their helmets and the Sin Eater folding machine pistols on their forearms, their presence alongside an archivist and a short little albino wisp of a woman hardly seemed to resemble any death squad dispatched by Baron Cobalt. "I am told you came to New Olympus because you detected a threat to our nation."

"Yes," Brigid answered. "It's a complicated story, but suffice to say that we believe that an entity that used to be one of the barons is operating in the islands."

Hera's wide smile faded, her lips drawn into a tight, bloodless line. She snapped her fingers and one of her assistants held up several drawings on a sketch pad. "Annunaki. You mean that they were once the barons?"

"How did you know who those snake-faces are?" Kane asked.

"Because I spent hours going over everything in the structure where I discovered the robot suits you see," Hera answered. "Deciphering Sumerian wasn't easy, but it did allow me to uncover more than a few secrets."

"An archaeological site?" Brigid asked, perking up.

"Sadly, the region containing the site is currently in the hands of New Olympus's greatest enemy, Thanatos," Hera lamented. "It would have been a joy to show off its wonders to a fellow scientist."

"You managed to get a bunch of robots out of there," Kane noted.

"Only thanks to the courage of Z00s," Hera explained. "Though, I'm pretty sure you would have known him as Thurmond."

"I remember him now," Grant spoke up, glancing to Brigid.

"Me, too," Kane added. "Thurmond and Danton were the ones assigned to some kind of top-secret expedition."

Hera's lips curled into a sneer. "The other's name is never spoken lightly within these walls, Kane. He is now Thanatos."

The Cerberus warriors grew quiet, issuing apologetic nods.

"It is not your fault," Hera said with a sigh. She stepped down from her dais and ran her silvery fingers across Kane's shoulder. "You come as friends, and as such, you deserve a friend's welcome."

"Not the way we're usually greeted," Grant muttered as Hera led them into the feast hall. The big ex-Magistrate gave a low whistle looking at tables laden with food, stretching from one end of the hall to the other. One of the tables had no chairs or benches, but the reason for the lack of seating became obvious when the Cerberus explorers glanced back into the hangar to see two dozen amputee pilots descending on trapeze rungs down into their wheelchairs.

Hera took note of Kane's observation of the elite robot pilots. "Those men and women are good people. They love and are loved by the citizens that they protect. I learned my lesson from the social experiment that was Cobaltville. Rather than leading through force and intimidation, I appeal to duty and compassion. If you are concerned for their physical being, know that they have been selfless, and the Greeks they protect are equally selfless for their sake."

Kane nodded. "We don't usually run across people this friendly. At least not at first."

Hera slid her arm to hook under Kane's elbow. Kane was surprised at how warm and supple her silver-and-gold-laden figure was. "Kane, I'm certain you'll find an embarrassment of friendliness. Your stay with us will be as welcoming as your arrival in our land."

Kane smiled, despite feeling Grant rolling his eyes at the attention laid upon him by the queen. "I hope so."

Unfortunately, the first thing that sprung to his mind were the circumstances of his arrival, a preview of apocalyptic destruction followed by a savage swarm of barbaric mutants. Kane kept silent about the doubts that correlation brought. New Olympus might have been a relative paradise, but there were few places in the world that Kane went that remained so serene. As often as the synergy of his group brought about success against impossible odds, it also involved savage conflict with monstrous enemies.

Kane figured that he might as well enjoy the party while it lasted, and took his seat at Hera's right hand.

THE BUZZ OF HER smart-metal skin's communicator lattice annoyed Hera in the midst of her meal. She didn't say anything, though she heard ZOOs's voice loud and clear without anyone else paying any notice.

"Found out why Danton has been avoiding our calls," Zoo said. "Contact me when you have a free moment."

She rose from her seat and walked out of the meeting hall. She was barely through the doorway into an empty corridor when her pleasant smile collapsed into a dour grimace. "Zoo, what the fuck is going on?"

"Cobalt's here," Zoo answered. "And he's in charge of the armor-plated lizard men."

"Where are you?" Hera demanded.

"Climbing out of the Tartarus Crack," Zoo said. "Cobalt's down there with Danton. And he's called Lord Marduk now."

"And he undoubtedly looks like an Annunaki, right?" Hera asked. "I was told that the barons evolved into those creatures."

"He's seven feet of Greek god sculpture with snake

scales," Zoo confirmed. "He says he knows how to access the secrets to the other chambers."

Hera's brain spun inside her skull. The implication of that was stunning. "The other chambers? My god…"

"But he wants us on his side," Zoo added. "If you don't bend over for old times' sake, he said he'd find himself another Zeus and Hera."

Hera didn't feel any smugness in the confirmation that she had been correct. "What are the odds against us?"

"Marduk has a flying saucer and a small army of Annunaki soldiers that had enough firepower to roast a hundred muties. Smart odds say that he's got more soldiers hidden in reserve," Zoo answered. "With Danton on our side, we might have a chance, but Marduk's keeping him on a very short leash."

Hera's grimace tightened, but she held her tongue for a moment. "It's mine."

"Excuse me?"

"The Tartarus Crack is mine. Not his!" Hera snapped.

"Marduk says differently. The Find is his old vault," Zoo replied.

"Possession is nine-tenths of the law," Hera growled.

"Well, right now Marduk has those nine and is claiming four thousand years of ownership precedence," Zoo countered. "We're fucked, especially if he opens up a vault and pulls out some kind of superweapon."

Hera's fingertips gouged deep scratches in the metal bulkhead that she was leaning against for support. The smart metal hardened to protect her from harm, enabling her to scrape loose steel. She chewed her lower lip, then glanced back to the feast, hearing the constant rumble of conversation.

"No. No, we're not screwed yet," Hera said. "Get back

here and report the presence of Mallard or Gooey-duck or whatever his stupid fucking name is. Just leave out the conversation you had with him about joining or dying, and especially leave out any reference to Danton being my puppet."

"Why?" Zoo asked. "If we go after Marduk, he's got the upper hand!"

"No. We have the advantage here," Hera answered. "You weren't here, but we've got four visitors who have fought the Annunaki before, and they've survived. If they can do it, then they can be our ace in the hole."

"Visitors? And they've fought the Annunaki?" Zoo asked. "Helena, beautiful, even if they do manage to take down Marduk, there's a strong possibility that they're going to stumble onto our scam."

"Not if they take down Duckie and Danton," Hera snapped. "They'll either bury everything and clean up our mess or they'll die trying—and weaken him enough for us to finish him off."

Zoo whistled. "That's why you're the queen, gorgeous."

"The goddess," Hera corrected. She took a deep breath, looking at the reflection of her face provided by the mirror polish of her armored forearm. "Get here fast, but not too fast. The goddess would like to savor the chocolate torte we're having for dessert."

Chapter 7

Hera was still running her tongue over her teeth, tasting traces of chocolate. Z00s had timed his entrance just right on cue for her to enjoy dessert. He provided a breathless accounting of his near-death experience while patrolling the Tartarus Crack. Zoo spelled out a tale of mutants and menace accompanied by an energy surge that had taken out his communications system and tore the gear-shaped gun housing from his left shoulder. It was a wonderful fabrication, with evidence concocted on the spot utilizing a dram of pure orichalcum to duplicate the effects of a glancing energy bolt.

She didn't doubt that Zoo could pull off the charade. He'd faked tears for nosy, snooping pilots that he'd eliminated in the mayhem of battle, and had passed himself off as the noblest of heroes for seven years. With a wry, inward grin, she thought of how talented his crooked tongue was. She had to fight off a giggle at her inadvertent innuendo. She transformed the grin into a rictus of anger, keeping the muscles of her lips and cheeks taut with anger to disguise her delight at Zoo's skillful lies.

"Bad enough that Thanatos commands the clone vats, but now he's teaming with that limp old pansy Cobalt?" Hera snarled, letting her feelings of betrayal bubble to the surface.

"Marduk is his name now," Brigid corrected. Hera did her

best to avoid shooting a dagger-laden glance at the flame-haired archivist. "As we said before, he's no longer the frail specimen that you had known."

"If I didn't know that the snake-faced asshole didn't remember his real origins while he was still Cobalt, I'd almost swear that he sent you here to sit on his cache," Kane spoke up.

"Maybe he did," Hera admitted haltingly. "Something I said inspired him to send out our expedition."

It was so easy to weave a web of lies when the truth provided their structure. Hera hung a string of misconceptions on a solid skeleton of established facts.

Brigid agreed with a nod. "Subconsciously, he may have remembered his hidden vault. While the overlords are different, more aloof in their personalities in regards to their baronial incarnations, there are underlying similarities. Perhaps the reverse is true, that some traits or experiences were available to Cobalt, passed down to him in his genetic matrix from Marduk."

"Whichever the case, we've got a crisis," Zoo panted. He was hunched over in his wheelchair, beard and hair matted to his face and scalp with a sheen of sweat. "Marduk knows where weapons even more powerful than Greek fire and the mobile suits are."

"Normally, a journey into the Tartarus Crack would be suicide," Hera said. "Which is why Zoo alone is allowed to reconnoiter the area. However, these are desperate circumstances."

"That's what we're here for," Kane said. "Between the clockwork brigade and our team, we can pull off a lightning raid."

"That's if you're up to a return engagement," Grant said to Zoo.

"It will take a while, about an hour and a half, to fix my

suit and get it back to fighting condition," Zoo answered. He looked to Hera questioningly.

"It will help to give us some time to arrange for more formidable armaments for our guests," Hera added.

"Actually, we came in with a more substantial arsenal," Brigid admitted. "We merely cached it in order to provide a less threatening appearance. We didn't think you would take kindly to us carrying weaponry capable of destroying a dropship, as such arms could easily be construed as a threat to giant robots."

Hera nodded. "Wise and understandable. It wouldn't make sense to battle an Annunaki or his mutant hordes with only a few small rifles and handguns. I presume this was at the oracle where Kane had his vision, correct?"

"Yes," Brigid answered. "I'd hate to impose, but with the aid of your pilots, Kane and Grant could finish the round trip to the oracle in the time it takes to effect Z00s's repairs."

Hera gave Brigid a magnanimous smile. "Excellent plan. Diana and Aristotle, would you aid our visitors?"

The two wheelchair-bound pilots nodded in unison.

"What about us?" Domi asked, gesturing to herself and Brigid.

"We can handle picking up our extra gear," Grant said. "Just stay here and enjoy a moment of safe haven."

"You two can explore more of the plumbing of this civilization," Kane said to Brigid.

Brigid looked around the feast hall. "Can't deny that is a tempting proposition."

Kane gave Brigid a reassuring smile. "And even if we do run into trouble, we've got Artem15 and Are5 for backup. You and Domi are good in a fight, but you two aren't fifteen-foot mechanoids armed with machine guns."

"If you put it that way," Brigid answered. "Just be careful."

"Will do," Kane replied. He gave her a brief smile and then joined Grant, Artem15 and Are5 in the hangar.

HERA WENT BACK TO HER QUARTERS, excusing herself so that she could check on the effects of the ASP bolt on Zoo's cybernetics port. It was a good way to step away from the visitors and gain access to her com link to Danton in the Tartarus Crack. Now that she knew that Marduk was in Thanatos's base, she imagined that she'd have a better chance of getting through to Danton. Zoo pumped the wheels on his chair in an effort to keep up with the impatient Hera.

"Gorgeous, what are we doing?" Zoo asked.

"We're letting Marduk know that we're throwing in with him," Hera answered.

"But you're sending Kane and the others to fight him," Zoo replied. "I thought that you wanted them to get Marduk out of your way."

"I do," Hera answered. "But do you really want Marduk launching a first strike on our base, even if they only utilize Nephilim weaponry? Unless you would like our home torn apart by wrist laser…"

Zoo shook his head. "So you'll play them off of each other. And whoever wins—"

"I'll be the one who wins," Hera cut him off. "Nothing is going to make me a slave again."

"The visitors from Cerberus don't strike me as the enslaving kind," Zoo said. "What if they win?"

"Then you and I won't be slaves, we'll be heroes," Hera told him. "We get away with murder when they erase our past and we become the biggest damned heroes on Earth. It might not be ultimate, godlike power, but seven years of being the good guys has been pretty comfortable, hasn't it?"

Zoo smirked. "That's the one thing I always liked about this. As a Mag, I was only feared. As Z00s, I'm loved."

Hera grinned. "Either way, we can't really lose."

"Unless they find out that Danton's been working for you, providing an artificial menace all along," Zoo said.

"Which is why you personally will make sure that Danton dies," Hera explained. "Hush now. Got to talk to Marduk."

Zoo held his tongue as Hera keyed in her communicator. "This is Helena, Marduk. Do you read me, sire?"

Zoo raised his eyebrows at the term "sire," causing Hera to sneer at him. The amputee pilot restrained a chuckle.

"Ah, hello, darling," Marduk's voice came over the line. Hera had been informed of the unusual vocal qualities of the ancient alien overlord, but even across the airwaves, the words sounded as if they were issued by an omnipotent being. The multitonal reverberations were disquieting. "I presume Z00s has appraised you of my offer?"

"And your generosity embarrasses me, my master," Hera said.

"Helena, I presume that Zoo mentioned my warning that you and he were completely replaceable. However, such declarations of fealty are not required. I simply want allegiance," Marduk said.

"That transparent, am I?" Hera asked. "Regardless, I need to give you a fast heads-up. Your old friends Kane, Grant and Brigid Baptiste are here, and they're specifically looking for you and your flying saucer full of Nephilim."

There was an unearthly grumble on the other end of the radio. "Do they know anything?"

"Just the story I had Zoo concoct about him spying on you and Danton being all buddy buddy," Hera said. "So right now Kane is heading to an old oracle ruin to pick up some firepower to use against you and the hordes."

"You wouldn't happen to have the coordinates of this oracle, would you?" Marduk asked.

Hera read them off with breathless, seductive glee. "It just wouldn't be a good reunion gift to you if I couldn't hand your wayward pups back to you on a silver platter, would it?"

A joyful chuckle carried over the speaker, bringing a chill to Hera's spine. "Ah, darling, I never knew how close you were to my black heart."

"Now, if you'll excuse me, I have to keep up appearances for the mindless drones who think I actually give a fuck about them," Hera replied. She glanced over to Zoo. The amputee put up his hands as if to say, "You got me, boss."

"I'll have a welcoming committee ready for Kane," Marduk snarled. "It'll be good to kill that pain in my ass."

The radio cut off and Hera turned to Zoo. "What's wrong?"

"I just don't know where we're standing anymore," Zoo responded. He looked down at the stump caps at the end of his thighs, then sighed. "So to speak."

"Where we stand is where you and I have always stood. And that's for the best interests of us. New Olympus only prospers because what's good for us is good for them," Hera explained.

Zoo nodded. "And what if Artie and Ari get hurt?"

"They'll be missed, but Artem15 was in direct disobedience of my orders," Hera growled. "She went out looking for trouble."

"She went for a patrol," Zoo countered.

"And she encountered the visitors on her way to Tartarus holdings," Hera added. "If she hadn't come across those Cerberus people, she might have stumbled across you. And if she knew you were making regular runs to talk to Thanatos…"

"I'd have had to be the one to execute her," Zoo concluded.

Hera sighed, then gave the ex-Magistrate a loving, passionate kiss. "I do care about Diana, but you have to know that we cannot allow ourselves to grow sloppy over even the best sentiments."

Zoo gave her a weak smile. "I'll just have to grow a set."

Hera gave his manhood a gentle squeeze. "You do have a most admirable set, love. You just forget you have them sometimes."

KANE ADMITTED TO HIMSELF that Domi had a point. There was a great rush, a feeling of unfettered flight as he sat on the shoulder of fifteen feet of robot running and leaping across the countryside at full gallop. At first it seemed slower than travel via the wheeled armored personnel carriers colloquially known as Sandcats, but the long legs and agility of the towering mechanical warriors enabled far quicker passage over rough terrain than the Sandcats. The giant clockwork suits had a top speed of thirty-five miles per hour, but with their ability to clear twenty yards in a single bound, and the footing to handle steep slopes or loose earth without slowing, enabled them to select far more efficient routes.

A Sandcat would have had to wind the long way around while the mobile suits traveled as the crow flies, for want of a better term. Perhaps if he could bring over spare Sandcat armor packages, the primitive snap-on plates the robots already wore could be replaced with improved protective panels. Kane was mindful of the vulnerability of pilots to bayonet-wielding savages, and the brave amputee warriors deserved more. A little work by Philboyd and the other lunar robotics experts would allow the pilots to man the suits without needing to engage in self-mutilation, as well. Throw in artificial bionic legs for those who were amputees…

"Stop getting ahead of yourself, dammit," Kane growled.

"What's wrong?" Artem15 asked.

"Thinking of the possibilities for the future while I haven't even solved the problem at hand," Kane admitted.

"Like what Cerberus and New Olympus can do for each other?" Artem15 surmised.

"Mostly how we could help you out," Kane said. "Of course, we have that whole Thanatos and Annunaki team to worry about first."

"The weapons in Tartarus especially," Artem15 replied. "Your vision seems especially frightening and relevant now."

"A lightning cannon, straight out of Zeus's yard sale," Kane grumbled. "The original Zeus, not your guy."

"I was wondering what kind of plan you have in mind," Artem15 replied.

"For the Tartarus Crack?" Kane asked. "Well, it's a cavern under a mile of rock. Bring down the roof with a good old-fashioned explosion."

"You brought something big enough to do that?" Artem15 asked.

"Nope. But where you have doomsday weapons, you undoubtedly have a quantity of doomsday-weapon-sized ammunition," Kane mused. "If they have the kind of orichalcum that blows up with sunlight, I'd especially like to see how it reacts to a satchel charge."

"Oh, that ought to be great," Artem15 grumbled, sarcasm dripping even over the suit speaker. "After all, this is an island chain that's only the wreckage remaining above water after an Earthshaker bomb. It's okay. Most of us know how to swim."

"Oh, right," Kane grumbled. "They set off one of those bastards here."

"Yup," Artem15 replied. "You never know. It might not take that much power to bring things down."

"We'll figure it out later. There's the ruins," Kane said. "I'll keep thinking of something else. I want to leave this place above water if I can."

"I didn't mean to put extra pressure on you," the robot pilot replied. "That used to be an oracle?"

"You know the place?" Kane asked.

"It's where—" Artem15 began. She cleared her throat. "My family tried to hide there."

"Oh," Kane said, momentarily at a loss, searching for a means of consolation.

"Yeah. Not only did the mutants fuck up my face and tear off one of my legs, but they killed everyone else while I was forced to watch," Diana said.

"It doesn't stop hurting," Kane replied. "I just learned to concentrate on the good memories."

"Who'd you lose?" Artem15 asked.

"My father," Kane answered. "He bought me some time to escape…."

There was a moment of silence as Artem15 paused at the base of the earthen ramp leading up to the ruins. "It's nice to not feel so alone, Kane. Thanks."

"Guys," Grant interrupted on his helmet radio. The former

Magistrates activated them because they could be tuned to transmit and receive on New Olympian communications frequencies. "I'm picking up a lot of infrared sources up around the oracle. At least seventy."

Kane and the robots glanced up, their own advanced optics kicking in. Are5 drew his thermal axes from their forearm housings, and Kane's and Grant's Sin Eaters launched into their hands. A wave of gibbering cackles wafted down from the temple ruins as the red forms of scores of mutants appeared before them.

"This is going to get messy," Are5 announced. "But we can handle it."

An energy bolt lanced down from the oracle, and Are5's right hand was engulfed in a blaze as the thermal ax in that claw blew to splinters. The orichalcum hydraulic limb was unharmed, but the next bolt would undoubtedly tear out his cockpit.

"Shit, not again!" Are5 cursed as the robots and ex-Magistrates scattered, scrambling for cover as ASP beams and musket fire rained down from on high.

Chapter 8

Domi felt a powerful empathy for Diana once she had met the scar-faced amputee without the barrier of a massive robotic form impeding human contact. All her life, the feral albino girl had been an outcast, either because of her pasty skin and bloodred eyes or her wilderness-bred ferocity that alienated her even in the savage slums of Cobaltville. Even at Cerberus, she had only a small circle of friends. In mixed company, she still felt like the odd one out simply due to her relative lack of education and everyone's discomfort with the wilderness-born savage in their midst. With the influx of Moon base personnel, there was a wider range of people to have conversations with, even though many of them were highly educated rocket scientists and quantum physicists. Lakesh had staffed the redoubt with smart, skilled but ville-bred folk. The people from the Moon were equally alien to Domi and the Cerberus staff, but displaced from the twentieth century, they reached out to everyone they could, ignoring the distinctions between Outlander and ville citizen. She enjoyed talking to the refugees from the Moon base, hearing their stories from life in the twentieth century. Philboyd was an especially amusing storyteller.

Still, here was Diana, a woman who was her own age, and suffering her own social stigmatism, though it was self-induced over being too conscious of her injuries. Watching

Diana crawl into the belly of her personalized walking tank to leave with Kane and Grant on an urgent errand made Domi feel useless. The ex-Magistrates had to get to the oracle to recover the weaponry required to take the battle to Marduk and his newfound ally, Thanatos. Their leaving, stranding her in New Olympus, reinforced the dread feeling of uselessness nibbling at her gut, especially since she didn't have the kind of cultural knowledge that Brigid Baptiste demonstrated on an almost daily basis.

"Useless," Domi muttered.

"No, you're not," Brigid countered, hearing her friend. "After all, who is the one who made a friendly first contact?"

"I still feel like a retard," Domi said. "At least Kane and Grant will have something to do if a fight breaks out."

"You've always displayed a great deal of no-nonsense honesty, Domi, and a canny skill at smelling lies," Brigid told her. "Just because—"

"Just because I have the reading skills of a twelve-year-old and the vocabulary of a 'tard doesn't mean my savage, primitive ways aren't responsible for my valued place on the Cerberus staff," Domi said. "Sorry."

Brigid smiled. "Your vocabulary's improving, at least. Right now, we're both in the unfortunate position to have a little existential meltdown. Self-scrutiny is a terrible thing. It's not as if we're in the lion's den, though."

Domi looked around at the armed Praetorians. "They make a good imitation."

"Well, we are in a strange place, and surrounded by a load of armed people," Brigid said. "If there is any intrigue, I'll definitely need someone to even the odds. And you're one of the top three people I'd pick to back me up."

The two shared a smile. Domi's grin was a little broader. "I knew there was a reason why you're my best friend at Cerberus."

The pair's wait for the return of Hera and Z00s ended a moment later when the queen and her consort turned a corner.

"Are you all right?" Brigid asked the broad-chested, wheelchair-bound pilot.

Zoo nodded. "Mostly, I took some bangs here and there, but those ASP blasters didn't cause any harm to my command port."

Brigid tilted her head. "You managed to run back here— why would that have been an issue?"

"I was limping. I'm pretty sure it was just a hydraulic alignment glitch. It happens when we suffer a hard knock in the field," Zoo admitted.

Domi's eyes narrowed as she listened to the tale, but she held her tongue.

"What's wrong, my little friend?" Hera asked, placing her long, slender fingers on the albino's knotted shoulder.

"Well, his lips look awful raw," Domi mentioned. "And it smells like something other than a checkup."

Hera chuckled. "How delightfully perceptive, little girl. Of course, the queen's consort has a few amenable extras involved in his medical checkups."

Zoo rolled his eyes. "Hera…"

"Don't mind him. Sometimes he reverts to being a stick in the mud," Hera dismissed. "Brigid, I know this will be a truncated tour, but given the circumstances…"

Brigid watched Domi tug her shoulder out of Hera's grasp. It had taken only a few moments for Domi to prove her instincts were sharp. "It's understandable, Hera. I'd prefer to preserve New Olympus for later visits."

Domi sidled closer toward Zoo, glancing at the metal caps over his stumped thighs. The amputee met her curious gaze. "It didn't hurt. Hera managed to decipher the secrets of Annunaki medical technology, and was a very savvy student. Of course, this was done in the Find."

"You were awake for it?" Domi asked.

"Yeah. Hera put something on me... What was it again?" Zoo asked Hera.

"It was a neural interrupter," Hera said. "It was a techno-organic construct, part living, part mechanical. You attach it to the back of a patient's head, and it returns all central nervous functions to a baseline. Unfortunately, the neural interrupter was only part of the technology I was able to salvage from Tartarus. Had I time to gather more, I would most assuredly have taken the sterilizer, as well."

"It proved to be a headache, especially since we lost a couple of people to staph infections. Diana was one of the first survivors," Zoo admitted.

"Mostly, we've been on the receiving end of Annunaki weapons technology. It appears to be quite a formidable science, though," Brigid stated.

Domi nodded. "Like the four-thousand-year-old China-man you ran into a while back. Seems like the snake-faces can help a person live forever, but if they want to look healthy, they have to sit inside some armor."

"Immortality?" Hera mused, her wide mouth turning up in a smile.

"Unfortunately, we had to eliminate the artifact with an implode grenade," Brigid stated. "Of course, it was either preserve the technology, or stop a tyrant from regaining his full health."

"Shame," Hera said. "This doesn't seem surprising to you, though."

"No," Domi said. "Enlil, one of the overlords, used these itty-bitty robots to rebuild Lakesh, the founder of Cerberus, to look like he's young again."

"Lakesh…that withered old freezie," Hera said, referring to the cryogenically suspended people from the end of the twentieth century. "He's what, 250?"

"Looks lots younger," Domi said. "Pretty sure if they can do that, they might be able to help Diana. If we find those…"

"Nanobots," Brigid offered.

"What she said," Domi concluded.

"Would such technology be available at the Find?" Brigid asked.

"I've seen mentions of it in the records, but nothing in the register," Hera stated. "Generally, each of the subvaults only directly references the technology that it contains. That's probably to keep snoopers from inadvertently learning about things held in other chambers."

"Sounds like the Annunaki had a robot for every size they wanted," Zoo said. "From the fifteen footers down to microscopic."

"So they can extensively reconstruct a person?" Hera asked.

"Apparently so. Many of Lakesh's bionics appear to be gone from his body, broken down and turned into more organic material to replace the natural organs they were emulating," Brigid stated. "It's very possible that with a sufficient input of mass, the nanobots could build your pilots all new legs that looked as if they were the same ones they were born with."

"I've made certain to keep an eye on the emotional and psychological state of each of my pilots," Hera said. "Though, it is quite possible that Domi is right. There couldn't be any harm in repairing Diana's face. I have some remnants of technology, but any attempt at plastic surgery would only result in tragedy."

Domi looked down. "I'm sorry. I didn't know you'd already had plans."

Hera smiled condescendingly, brushing her gold-tipped fingers across Domi's pale cheek. The albino flinched from the touch. "Young lady, you never have to apologize for looking out for one of my beloved. Just because her scarring has never had an effect upon her consummate performance as a professional does not mean that I do not care about the suffering she silently endures."

"First things gotta come first," Domi replied. "Take back the Tartarus, then you have the time to fix her up."

"Exactly, my child," Hera said. "Come, we should watch over your allies. We have camera and radio feeds to the robots."

Hera and Zoo turned and headed toward the command center, but Domi held back for a moment, Brigid standing next to her.

"What's up?" Brigid asked.

"Had like her when I tricked in Tartarus," Domi said. From the stress in her voice and the broken English in her words, Brigid could tell that Domi was spooked. "Least got from them was black eyes."

"I thought she was being sociable," Brigid said.

"Touch all wrong," Domi said softly, her ruby eyes focused on Hera. "She's predator. Don't like being prey."

Brigid frowned, walking with Domi after the pair. "She seemed a magnanimous leader."

"Crazies like her don't go big control. Want in person," Domi muttered. "Up close."

"I'll keep my eyes open."

Domi remained quiet, slipping behind a vapid little smile. Brigid had never seen the albino when she had worked as a prostitute, but Domi's smile was artificial, alien to the feral, wild thing's face. The only logical source of such a grin was that she had slipped behind an old layer of emotional armor. Brigid watched Hera and Z00s enter the command center. The archivist knew that if something frightened Domi that much, she reverted to coping mechanisms that helped her survive in the Tartarus Pits, their initial impression of Hera as benevolent leader beneath a glimmering, beautiful shell would have to be revised.

"So much for finding paradise," Brigid whispered to herself.

GRANT RACED TO KEEP AHEAD of the hail of musket balls and energy bolts hurled down from the oracle's ruins. He raked the area with his Copperhead, but the snarling, stubby little weapon was designed for close-in work, not firing 350 yards uphill. Grant tried activating his helmet's communication system, but all he could hear was the squelch of electronic interference. Are5's shoulder guns spit out streams of automatic fire, knocking bodies off the temple's columns, but more mutants lurched out to take their place, and even the machine guns on the robot weren't providing lethal hits. Being forced to run for their lives, not so much from the primitive muskets but from the Nephilim's ASP blasters, made it impossible to get any decent aim to achieve telling results.

"Great," Grant grumbled. He tried to reach Kane on his Commtact, then immediately regretted that the jawbone-mounted radio operated by sending vibrations through his skull. A resonant wail threatened to shake his teeth out of their sockets and liquefy his eardrums. He killed the implant's signal, his head still swimming from the interior sonic attack. Needing a means of communication, he picked up a rock and bounced it off of Are5's chest plate.

"What's up, Grant?" Ari asked over his speaker. At least hard-wired communications weren't affected. "I can't hear a damn thing on my radio!"

"Electronic interference," Grant bellowed. "It could be equipment that the snake-faces brought with them. They jam us, they cut down our effectiveness!"

The mohawked robot crouched behind a boulder, letting the Nephilim's ASPs carve off sections of the massive rock. At least the pounding on the stone gave Are5 a breather.

Grant shouldered his Copperhead and used the weapon's built-in telescopic sight to good advantage. Though his initial wave of full-auto was weakened by the extreme range and altitude of the shots he made, he was able to scatter the scale-hided humanoids at the temple. Now the mutants were charging down the land bridge under the cover of energy and musket fire, which meant that they were coming into the range for Grant's Copperhead. It would take real marksmanship to deal with the horde of monstrosities and not completely exhaust the supply of ammunition he'd brought with him. With the submachine gun on semiauto, braced behind a berm of solid earth and aided by the telescopic sight, Grant rattled off four head shots against the charging mutants in the space of five seconds. The reptilians fired their muskets, but in his helmet and shadow suit, Grant only had to worry about bruises to his arms and shoulders rather than flesh-tearing slugs. He emptied the rest of the 35-round magazine, getting seven more dead mutants as the swift-footed creatures got closer. A Nephilim homed in on Grant, seeing his marksmanship depleting the ranks of his allies. Grant threw himself away from the cover of the berm, diving to the bottom of the ditch as the gout of earth vomited by the energy bolt's impact rained rocks and clumps of dirt on his back.

More Nephilim joined in the assault, and Grant curled up behind the thick lip of soil that was being blasted to pieces. An explosion erupted up at the temple ruins, ending the storm of bolts raining on Grant.

"What the shit was that?" Grant shouted, looking at a cloud of smoke curling up from the temple's edge.

"Artie—Artem15," Are5 answered. "She has explosive-tipped javelins."

"Oh, and I got stuck with the 'bot with the melee-weapon fetish," Grant grumbled.

Are5 pointed one of his claw fingers in the air, and the ex-Magistrate knew that it wasn't sign language for "one moment." The mechanized warrior reached for a rock that appeared to be about the size of Grant's torso, scarred and burned by Nephilim fire that had jarred it off of the boulder. "That's the problem with having a hammer. Every situation looks like a nail."

"Wonderful," Grant groaned. "You're going to talk about the rest of the toolshed?"

"Watch this tool," Are5 countered. Pivoting around the boulder, the fifteen-foot titan whipped the stone at the clot of surviving mutants who had almost made it to the bottom of the earthen ramp. The creatures were screeching in blind rage, bayonet points ready to tear into Grant and the robot warrior when 150 pounds of rock plowed into them with the force of a missile. The stone crashed through the assemblage, tossing bodies to the left and right. Some bounced off the cliff faces on either side of the bridge, while others flopped, twitching uncontrollably as broken spines spit out dying messages to unresponsive limbs.

One figure stood, untouched by the airborne rock, a lone Nephilim that sighted down its forearm at the exposed and vulnerable Are5. Grant's Sin Eater launched into his grasp, his finger hooking the trigger on the draw. The lightning reflex movement enabled the former Magistrate to pump a 240-grain bullet into the reptilian soldier's skull, an explosion of released pressure blossoming its head, leathery hide peeled back to resemble grisly flower petals. The dying drone's ASP blast missed Are5 by yards, destructive energy dissipating into the night sky.

"Great shot!" Are5 complimented.

"Nice improvisation," Grant returned.

Two Nephilim sought to avenge their decapitated ally, their ASPs vomiting writhing tendrils of yellowish lightning at Grant and the robot. The energy bolts tore into the earth around Grant's improvised foxhole and drove Are5 deeper behind his ever shrinking boulder. Grant winced as a spark sizzling off the main bolt singed his biceps. "This shit did not happen when the bad guys just had guns like the rest of us!"

Another blast tunneled through the earth, but cut off. Far above, another of Artem15's javelins had smashed into the ruins again, driving the Nephilim snipers back behind cover with an earthshaking blast.

"Shit," Grant groaned. "We're not going to have much to recover if she keeps throwing those things…"

A figure dived into the rut next to Grant, and the big ex-Magistrate whirled. He'd expected a foe had slipped past, but it was merely Kane. "You complain when you're being shot at. You bitch when someone saves your ass."

"Well, I don't need all of our grens blown up because she overshot," Grant replied.

"She's aiming at the edge of the temple, not in the middle of it," Kane snapped. "Seems like you're never happy unless you're plain grumpy."

"I'd read somewhere that the more you complain, the longer God lets you live," Grant answered.

"Shit. You'll never die," Kane said.

Grant nodded and grinned. "That's the plan!"

"Well, I've got a better plan, and it's being given to Ari by Artem15," Kane returned.

"When were you going to get around to telling me?" Grant asked.

"Right now. They're buying us some cover," Kane answered.

Grant frowned. "We're going for a run."

"Under cover fire and with good distractions," Kane said. "It's dark enough that just our guns and helmets are going to show."

"Don't remind me…" Grant moaned. The shadow suit wouldn't protect against a charged energy bolt, which would blow a hole in him the size of a watermelon. Grant was glad he had Kane to draw fire if they failed.

"Go!" Kane barked. The two ex-Magistrates broke from cover. In the gloom, their black helmets and guns appeared to be fluttering birds, the only visible elements to the two men as they charged up the earthen ramp. It would be a long run, made even longer if the soldier drones and their mutant cohorts detected their presence. Grant's long strides helped him to keep up with the same frenetic pace as the wolf-lean and lightning-quick Kane. The two men rushed madly up the land bridge to the mountaintop temple, sidestepping or bounding over the corpses of mutants that Grant and Are5 had cut down. Bloody bodies left the soil slick, making a fifty-yard stretch of the rocky road treacherous. Fortunately, the boots of the shadow suits had more than enough traction to allow them to keep their footing.

Since Grant already had his Sin Eater in hand, he reached behind his back and drew his serrated combat knife. Kane had done the same. Right now, they were too close for the black-phosphate-coated blades to give away their presence, and both Cerberus warriors would need all of the close-quarters fighting power they could muster. The oracle's ruins were teeming with mutants, three Nephilim still standing and shooting it out with the robot warriors who threw sheets of machine-gun fire at the sides of the temple's remaining walls.

Artem15 and Are5 cut their fire, not wanting to inadvertently shoot either of the two former Magistrates.

Kane leaped, knife swinging. The razor-sharp point caught a reptilian mutant in the throat and splashed a spray of blood across the eyes of a half-dozen other creatures. The lean warrior landed, but didn't stop. His forearm snapped out to catch another of the hordelings in the throat with enough force to snap his neck.

Grant fired his Sin Eater at another Tartarus raider, knocking a hole in his chest before the scaled freak could react to the shimmering ghost-shape of Kane. The clone tried to spear his partner in the back, but Grant's quick bullet stopped him cold. Movement crunched to Grant's right, and he whirled, plunging his knife deep into the face of another of the mutated horde. With a savage yank, Grant tore his weapon free, sending the creature's body crashing into the path of a third. The big ex-Magistrate didn't waste time, putting a bullet into the stunned hordeling's face.

Kane was a whirlwind with his fighting knife, sweeping the foot-long steel edge in an arc that lashed across the chests and throats of three mutants, their blood spraying in misty clouds. A Nephilim warrior lunged at Kane, the drone's incredible reflexes caught the ex-Magistrate's knife wrist at the end of Kane's wicked slice. The powerful armored alien twisted, pulling Kane off his feet in an effort to hurl the man to his death off the edge of the cliff. Though Kane was flying through the air, he was far from helpless, folding his legs around the soldier's neck. With his throat scissored between Kane's calves, the Nephilim was thrown off balance. It had taken every ounce of agility that Kane possessed, but the warrior drone was no longer able to dash Kane against the stone floor. With a powerful flex, Kane wrenched the alien's head in a neck-shattering crunch. Spine severed, the Nephilim let go, allowing Kane to roll away.

Grant crushed the face of another mutant with a well-placed kick, then watched as two clones disappeared off to his right, swept and hurled into the night by a gigantic, powerful robot limb. On the other side of the temple, a golden-maned mechanoid brought her massive fists down with such force that the temple floor was painted with gallons of flying blood. When she stood up, a limp sack of flexible smart metal was all that remained of the Nephilim warriors that Artem15 had struck.

Grant toed one pulp-filled metal sleeve, giving a low whistle.

"I don't know what's more impressive. That this armor's still mostly intact, or that you popped these creatures like balloons," Grant said.

"Let's discuss this later," Artem15 replied. "Grab your gear and let's get the hell out of here."

"Fine by me, lady," Grant said.

Chapter 9

Brigid and Domi looked at the static-filled screens in the control center, concern etched into their faces by the ominous threat of a sphere of radio silence around the oracle's ruins. Hera turned to them, her own worry evident.

"Is this usual for the overlords?" Hera asked. "Do they use communications blackouts?"

"We'd never really encountered such tactics before," Brigid stated. "But then, there are usually only three or four of us in the field, and most places don't have advanced communications networks such as yours."

Hera's lips pursed. "Then again, you told us that this is just one overlord, and they no longer possess unlimited resources. A more clandestine approach would be logical."

"At least until they find whatever big ass-guns are in the Crack," Domi snarled derisively.

Hera observed the albino girl as she attempted to rein in her rage. "We'll stop Marduk before he gets that far."

Domi's crimson gaze locked on to the silver-and-gold-skinned goddess's face. "We'll stop him, period. And before we let him die, we'll beat him until he pukes up who else survived. Don't want no damn surprises from them!"

Hera folded her arms, coldly regarding the diminutive

Outlands girl. "You are going to take an aeons-old god prisoner?"

Domi snorted. "Ain't god. Just some snake-faced fuck with fancy toys. Sure, he takes a lot of killing, but that makes catching him easier. We don't need to be gentle, just scoop up the biggest piece, preferably with a working mouth and brain."

"The threat posed by other overlords surviving is worth the effort to take him prisoner," Brigid noted. "It'd be in your best interests, too, considering that Marduk's brethren might also be aware of the prizes hidden in your nation."

Hera looked at the static-filled screens, contemplation evident in her eyes. After a moment, the command center began receiving signals, flickering images of Grant and Kane, viewed through the robotic eyes of the towering mechanoid warriors.

"…don't care. The stealth function on the shadow suits is useless if you get 'em dirty or covered in blood. How're you going to be invisible with a clot of mud staining your chest?" Grant's complaints came over his transceiver.

"Oh, good," Brigid said. "They're fine."

"He sounds miserable," Zoo countered.

Domi grinned. "That's when he's happiest."

"Sounds like the Commtacts and helmets are back on-line," Kane mentioned. "Are you reading me, New Olympus?"

"Five by five," the comm officer answered. "What happened?"

Kane held up an orb to the camera of Are5. "The snake-faces brought along this doohickey. It put out some kind of scrambling pulse. I figured out how to turn it off."

"Damn thing still makes the right side of my head itch," Grant groused. "Remind me to thank Lakesh for putting this fuse-brained thing in my head."

"I'll do it for you, Grant," Domi replied. "I don't want you to break him."

"Girl knows me too well," Grant responded. "It looks like there were four Nephilim up here with about, oh, a shitload of these insane little muties. Half of them got knocked into the sea, and the other half are a jigsaw puzzle."

"At least this encounter has proved that your combined forces are more than a match for whatever Marduk and Thanatos can throw at you," Hera spoke up.

"And that's without our really fun toys," Kane said with a noticeable lack of enthusiasm.

Brigid watched Hera. She knew that the queen's sentiment had struck a sour note in Kane, but apparently the silver-clad goddess remained oblivious to the dread that she had sparked. Domi was still in her street-corner face, friendly and inviting, but dead eyed. She could feel the gears working between the albino girl's ears, calculating scenarios on how to slay the metal-clad queen. Brigid cleared her throat. "How soon should you be back here?"

"We're leaving right now," Kane replied. "Give us thirty minutes."

"We'll be waiting," Hera answered. "How many Spartans would you like assigned to your raider squadron?"

"I'm not sure that it will be a good idea to do anything right now," Kane responded. "Do you have contact with the villages under your protection?"

"Yes. We have ten Spartans on sentry duty, one in each of the outlying communities," Hera said.

"Call them," Kane ordered.

Zoo and Brigid picked up Kane's implication at the same time. They whirled, but Hera was already shouting orders.

"All pilots! Battle stations! This is not a drill!" the queen commanded over the base's intercom system.

"We're on our way," Kane added. "I'm not sure how many clones Thanatos can… Oh, fuck."

"Thanatos has lost hundreds between you four and Marduk's appearance of late," Hera answered. "However, he has the ability to make up those losses in a few days, as well as having a standing swarm."

"I know about the swarm," Kane answered. He pointed off camera, and Are5 turned away from the Cerberus explorer. A teeming blob of figures, their footsteps rumbling like omnipresent thunder, charged over the ridge of a hill. It sounded like a stampede, and the wave of hurtling mutants crashed into the gully that the Outlanders had traveled along only hours before.

"Preserve us," Artem15 transmitted to the control room, her whisper as chilling as an Antarctic breeze.

Kane growled in disgust. "We're not going to make it back to New Olympus in time. There's no way we can cut through that big of a crowd."

"Engage full lockdown!" Artem15 warned. "Even if they do have Nephilim in their ranks, they still wouldn't be able to cut through the hangar doors."

"Our Spartans on town duty—" Hera began.

Artem15 interrupted her. "They'll be ignored. Any suits between that mob and New Olympus, however, will be overwhelmed and torn apart!"

Brigid saw a flare of anger in Hera's eyes as she was interrupted by the robot pilot. Though Brigid didn't really need any confirmation of Domi's suspicions, the brief instant that the queen had lost her emotional disguise had betrayed her. Hera was too used to giving the order and not being interrupted, let alone countermanded. Artem15's urgency to take charge of a crisis situation had cracked the emotional reserves of the queen. Her smooth, cool silver exterior had flaws just beneath the surface.

"Pulling in the Spartans from the villages would be a mistake, because that would leave them open for attack, as well," Kane added. "Do you have any parapets or balconies? Firing ports?"

"This is similar to your Cerberus redoubt, I'd assume," Hera replied. "We decided that cutting holes in our protective mountain would defeat its perfect defenses."

"Then don't open any doors," Kane suggested. "We'll figure something out."

"Fine," Hera muttered, clearly irritated. "Though, for a god-beater, your plans seem to draw on the painfully obvious."

"Sometimes self-proclaimed deities miss the obvious because they're too busy smelling their own bullshit," Kane snapped back.

Hera's eyes narrowed to slits, but Brigid broke into the conversation. "Kane, just get to work on pulling the mutant horde off our doorstep, and stop the pissing contest with our friends."

"Right, Baptiste," Kane answered. "Sorry, Queenie. I was talking about Marduk. Over and out."

Hera glared down toward Brigid from her raised position in the center of the control room. The archivist searched for any sign of reproach but caught only a smile.

"He turns into a smart-ass sometimes," Brigid said by way of apology. "But he is essentially correct about the arrogance of the Annunaki."

Hera answered her with a single nod. "Lock down all entrances. I want five Spartan suits just behind the hangar doors in the event of a breach. Praetorian guard units at ancillary entrances with radios and automatic rifles. Double the guard allotment for the ventilation ports, as well. Sidearms, swords and rifles are to be supplied to all nonessential personnel."

Zoo grimaced, then reached into his wheelchair's backpack pouch and withdrew his old Sin Eater holster. He strapped the motorized holster onto his forearm, then laid a pouch of spare magazines in his lap.

Hera took a deep breath, then locked eyes with Z00s's. "I'm going to retrieve the ASP from my quarters. I am a fighting queen, and will not ask my people to do what I cannot."

She whirled and left Zoo in charge of the command center. Brigid and Domi were struck silent by the sudden emergency.

HERA ENTERED HER QUARTERS, and as she stepped through the doors, her self-control broke and her face twisted into a mask of anger. She made a beeline for her comlink to Danton and Marduk.

"Marduk, are you there?" she growled.

"Darling, you sound upset," Marduk cooed over the airwaves.

"What the flying fuck are you doing?" Hera demanded. "And tell me just why I don't cram forty robots up your scaly ass just to show you how to behave toward me?"

"Oh, the little mutant siege I'm staging for the rebels' benefits?" Marduk asked.

"Staging," Hera grumbled. "One or two thousand scalie little fuckers setting off seismic tremors even under the mountain is faking it?"

"No Nephilim are with the mutants, dear," Marduk explained. "The horde has no weaponry capable of getting into your humble abode. They can pound all year on that steel and not even scratch the paint."

"But we're not going out for fresh air any time soon," Hera answered.

"The purpose of the legion on your doorstep is to eliminate Kane, who will undoubtedly stage some rescue attempt," Marduk told her. "I know the interfering little ape. He will either pull some insane stunt to lure away the thousands at your gates, or come here, into the Crack, to deal with me directly."

"And when Kane's dead?" Hera asked.

"Quite elementary, Hera. My forces withdraw from the hangar doors," Marduk said. "The great hope of New Olympus fades with the death of your cat's-paw, and you have to sue for peace before the ruler of the Earth."

"Surrender," Hera said coldly. "What if I don't?"

She could feel Marduk's smile stretching across his face, even over the miles between New Olympus and the Tartarus Crack. "It will take me only a short time to fire up the artificial intelligence modules for the gear skeletons. Once I do that, then equip them with GS-portable energy mortars and combat shell armor, you won't even be able to hide under a mile of rock."

Hera swallowed, her mouth gone dry.

"Tell me, girl," Marduk snarled. "Is your precious pride that important to you to spur me to drop my undivided, focused wrath upon your sorry, pretty head?"

Hera felt her knees buckle but held herself standing at the counter.

"Do you honestly think that you can outplot me, silly little bitch? You imagine that I couldn't discern that you would pit two hated enemies against each other for the sake of your personal profit?" Marduk pressed.

Hera swallowed again, this time to push a surge of bitter bile back down her throat.

"Now, recover your composure and continue whatever charade you are playing," Marduk ordered. "I will eliminate your newfound thug friends, and their tin-plated escorts. Once that is finished, we will discuss your return to slavery."

Hera remained silent. Marduk's chuckle resonated throughout her quarters, as if he were omnipresent. "Don't worry, Helena. It was inevitable that you would try to act against me. I don't take it personally. You have deluded yourself that you possessed true power, a fantasy that simply lasted far too long. But, child, you are an amateur playing against a master of this game."

Hera glared at the communicator.

"I know you're still there, girl. I hear you choking back bile," Marduk said.

"Chamber four," Hera croaked defiantly.

"What?" Marduk asked.

"Your toy in chamber four," Hera said, recovering her strength. "Oh, wait. I'm using my numbering system, not yours."

Suddenly Marduk's voice didn't sound so certain and powerful. "What did you take?"

"Look for yourself," Hera challenged. "If you can even figure out which chamber I'd looted. Then we'll see who has to sue whom for peace."

Hera turned off the com link, then wrapped the ASP blaster around her forearm. Smart metal melded to the unit, cables growing out of her neck port and writhing down from her shoulder to the energy weapon. The charged energy module of the ASP connected to her nervous system. Her body stretched, arcing in an aroused state of being. Power pulsed through every cell of her body, warming her flesh and releasing a rush of endorphins. She licked her lips, grinning at the tingling all over her skin beneath its silver-and-gold shell. The armor changed, rippling into a singular shade of gleaming platinum, scaled like an Annunaki.

"I have been a goddess too long to knuckle under to an overrated garter snake who dreams he's a dragon, Duckie," Hera snarled at the deactivated radio. "And when you learn that the Skybreaker is mine…"

She fought down a laugh. With another substantial inhalation, feeling as if she were walking on clouds, the goddess-queen of New Olympus left her quarters, making her way back to the command center.

KANE FLIPPED UP THE VISOR on his Magistrate helmet, frowning as the tail end of the horde of mutants disappeared around the bend in the gully. He could still hear their battle cries, and the undercurrent of their thousands of stampeding feet vibrated all the way so that he could feel it through the soles of his boots. He glanced to Artem15.

"Where is the Tartarus Crack?" he asked.

"It's about fifteen minutes that way," she answered. "We're going to have to go right to Marduk, aren't we?"

"We need to take the heat off New Olympus, and that's the only way I can think of right now," Kane stated.

Grant snapped a magazine into the well of his gigantic Barrett rifle. Despite its thirty-pound weight, the massive ex-Magistrate held it as if it were a regular weapon, the only sign of its added mass showing in the rippling biceps beneath his shadow suit. "Good. I'm gonna send Marduk back to space with three shoes. Two on his feet and one up—"

"You're going to harass the horde at the gates," Kane interrupted.

Grant tilted his head. "You're kidding me, right?"

"You and Are5 head back," Kane told him. "Artem15 and I are going to shake Marduk up."

"Give me one good reason why I'm not going after Marduk, especially after what he did to Shizuka," Grant demanded.

"Hmm. Let's see. You'll be under a mile of bedrock and facing off with a self-proclaimed god who hurt someone you cared about," Kane mused out loud. "What happened the last time something like that happened? Oh right. You started smacking the taste out of Maccan's mouth and brought the whole fucking pyramid of Mars down on our heads."

"You went to Mars?" Are5 asked.

Grant nodded.

"And collapsed a pyramid?" Are5 continued.

"Well, I basically kept Maccan from blasting us with his little god glove," Grant said. "He ended up blowing the ceiling out of the pyramid."

Are5 looked to Kane. "You guys are the coolest."

"We try," Kane said dryly.

"I don't know which is more stupid, me and ax-boy taking on thousands of mutants, or you dropping down Marduk's rabbit hole," Grant complained.

Artem15 stepped over to Are5. "Ari. Here—you can take some of my javelins."

"Thank you, Diana, but won't you need them more, honey?" Are5 asked.

The golden-maned robot looked down to Kane, then back to her fellow mechanoid. "We're going to have to do this through speed and stealth. If I need more than half of my javelins, then we're going to be so fucked that no amount of firepower is going to help us."

Are5 held out his metal claw hand. The robotic amazon looked down at it.

"Just a little bit of contact," Are5 stated. "I just have to get a feeling that we've still got a connection."

Artem15 laid her hand in his. "It's just metal."

"It's where you're alive, love," Are5 replied. "This is you, the only place where you really feel worthy of anything. You just have to understand, I don't care what you look like out of your suit."

Artem15 tugged her hand free, stepping back. "We'll talk about this later, Ari."

"Then make sure there's a later," Are5 responded. "Got it?"

"I got it," Artem15 responded.

Grant watched the display between the two mechanoids, impressed at how expressive the pair could be. Of course it made sense, thanks to the cybernetic cables in their backs, these were two people, acting without hindrance. The robot suits were their bodies as much as anything they were born with.

"Since Are5 and I have some reach with the new equipment, we should be able to raise some havoc from a sufficient distance to avoid the path of a mutant charge," Grant said, breaking his attention between the would-be lovers.

"That was my idea, too," Kane answered. "You be careful, partner."

"Sure," Grant replied. "But if you kiss me, I'll leave a dent in your forehead big enough to store a grapefruit."

Kane managed a grin and offered Grant a one-percent salute. "I'll try to keep that in mind."

"When you two old ladies are done, we've got work to do," Artem15 said, clearing her throat.

"Catch you on the flip side, partner," Kane told Grant as the men climbed up to their robotic partner's shoulders.

The two groups split up, each leaping off in its own direction.

MARDUK LOOMED OVER Danton, his reptilian gaze a chilling splash in the face for the former Magistrate turned prince of darkness for Hera Olympiad's new empire. Danton looked at the guards bracketing him, their grips as strong as iron, making any form of resistance futile. Even if he could wrench free of the Nephilim pair, what could he do? Outrun energy bolts that proved capable of incinerating 125 pounds of mutant into charred carbon? Danton sagged between the pair, knowing he had to accept his fate.

"Please, sire…" Danton began.

"Oh, no. The time for pleas is long since lost," Marduk replied, long talon-tipped fingers caressing the former Magistrate's cheek. "Your silver tart of a queen has taken something of mine, and I honestly do not have the patience to tear through my vaults to see what is gone."

Danton glanced up at Marduk. "What…what the hell are you talking about?"

"Don't play with me, you hairless monkey," Marduk growled. One razor-sharp talon point punctured Danton's cheek, then carved a two-inch furrow through his skin, eliciting a yowl. "Helena took one of my weapons. Which was it?"

"The only thing she took were the gear skeletons!" Danton screeched, clutching his bloodied face. "Everything else was either locked up or too ungainly to take!"

Marduk's lips pressed together, forming a wall of scales, sealed tight against each other. He looked into Danton's eyes, judging the human's reactions. "You're not lying."

"Because I like having my skin intact!" Danton countered. "Do you think I'd lie to you?"

"You rolled over fairly quickly on your old mistress," Marduk said by way of explanation. "Who is to say you wouldn't be dishonest with me?"

"Oh, I'm not sure, maybe because I'm not stupid?" Danton asked. "Throw in the fact that I was certain I'd never be allowed outside to see sunlight again, thanks to four dozen fifteen-foot killers wanting to take a chunk out of my ass—"

"All right," Marduk interrupted. "Spare me your sob story. You thought she had given you a cake assignment, and it turned out that you're just out of luck as a prisoner down here."

Danton nodded. He glanced side to side, looking to see if the Nephilim guards showed any form of emotion. It was fairly apparent by now that the drones had no mind or will of their own, were only able to respond with limited creativity in response to a problem or interpreting the orders of their overlord master. Being human, however, Danton couldn't imagine existence without thought or emotion, so he kept searching the soldier drone faces for some empathetic reaction.

"She mentioned chamber four," Marduk stated. "Do you know which one that is?"

Danton's brow furrowed. "She didn't share that information with me, unfortunately. All I was educated on were the procedures for operating the clone vats, and how to control the hordes created by them."

Marduk frowned. "Would Z00s know which chamber would be number four?"

Danton shrugged. "I'm not certain, but then, he's the one who was fucking her, not me."

Marduk's scaled brow quirked at the comment. "Ah, the poor little bastard left out in the cold. Now I see the real reason for the jealousy."

"I didn't think it was worth having my legs cut off for a piece of tail, know what I mean?" Danton asked. "So, I'm locked in the basement, playing with the baby lizards."

Marduk nodded. "My apologies for your discomfort. But at least you've given me something to work with."

"Oh?" Danton asked.

"Well, whatever Helena took, it had to be of relative small size. Otherwise she couldn't have snuck it out the back door without your notice," Marduk stated. He ran his clawed thumbnail along his scaled chin, his eyes slits as he concentrated upon calling up ancient memories from across the millennia. "She also said that she had the power to wipe me out if I threatened to move in on her."

Danton leaned closer, as if trying to listen in on Marduk's thoughts. It was a futile gesture, but curiosity consumed the Magistrate-turned-devil. The Nephilim to his left reached out and grabbed his shoulder roughly, pulling him back away from the Annunaki lord. Danton winced at the powerful grasp of the Nephilim but held his tongue, not wanting to appear more hostile toward them than was good for his health. All he could do was wait for the overlord to plumb the depths of memory and ancient eras long since gone.

Suddenly, Marduk's eyes snapped open, his face twitching in a semblance of emotion. "The Skybreaker."

"What's that?" Danton asked.

Marduk's eyes narrowed, studying Danton as if he were

peering through the human's skull, looking for abnormalities in his brain. "The Skybreaker is a self-evident name. I assume you know how a mirror works, correct?"

"It reflects light, doesn't it?" Danton asked.

"Consider this a form of electricity reflection," Marduk stated. "It's a two-part unit. The main piece is a ground-based electrical generation coil. The secondary part is an airborne direction module. The coil pumps the direction module full of voltage, and once its capacitors are charged, it's aimed and fired at a ground- or air-based target."

Danton swallowed. "Controlled lightning."

"It's simple, elegant and quite powerful," Marduk replied. "Each of its bolts can generate thirty thousand Kelvin."

"Could it destroy your other weapons?" Danton asked.

"The mean temperature of the surface of the sun is over six thousand degrees Centigrade," Marduk repeated. "Lightning is ten times hotter. The Skybreaker can vaporize anything on this planet with a full second's worth of contact."

"So, that's bad," Danton answered himself. "But we'd be safe in here, right?"

"If it were that simple, but the redirection module could be flown into the crack while retaining its charge. Then all it would have to do is fire, and everything down here would be incinerated," Marduk explained. "That bitch…"

"What do we do?" Danton asked.

"I'm not going to waste time," Marduk responded. "It's time to get into New Olympus. Send your command to the legion. Look for any entrance into the redoubt."

Danton nodded, smiling. He reached out and slid his head into the wire cage that transmitted his thoughts to the mindless mutant hordes surrounding New Olympus.

"Now, my children," he whispered. "We tear down the gods themselves…."

Chapter 10

With New Olympus surrounded by thousands of mutated humanoids, there was no reason to keep Brigid and Domi under close surveillance or armed only with handguns and knives. Hera handed Brigid a compact Sten machine pistol.

"Sorry we don't have anything that matches the arsenal you apparently brought," Hera apologized. "But as long as we have the ability to make pipes and springs, this is as good as it gets."

"I'm not going to complain," Brigid answered. She loaded a magazine into the side but didn't chamber a round. It went against her instincts to not have the Sten instantly ready, but given the primitive firing mechanism, if the weapon dropped to the ground, there was a good chance that 9 mm bullets would be chasing people around the halls. Spare magazines were tucked into the outer pockets of her shoulder bag.

The archivist glanced at Hera. "Have you given that thing a test fire?"

Hera beheld her ASP forearm blaster. "I don't need to. It's communicating with me through the interface in my armor."

Brigid raised a slender eyebrow. "It's communicating with you?"

"Annunaki cybernetics are amazing. The uniform, as you can tell, changed its appearance when the ASP blended with it," Hera stated. "As much as I can control it with a mental impulse, it also communicates back to me. It told me how it works, sort of. I know the reflexes necessary to fire it, and how much energy it can unleash before needing to cool down."

"Fascinating," Brigid answered. "Obviously more advanced than our Commtacts. Honestly, there isn't much of a feeling of feedback."

Brigid watched as Hera's forearm pulsed, the cables from the ASP flexing and writhing like living veins all the way up her arm. It was at once obscene and enthralling, a living example of superhuman power. She remembered the descriptions of Maccan's Silver Hand of Nuadhu in action. Where the Tuatha de Danaan technology didn't appear to be an animated symbiote on Maccan's hand, this particular unit was a living extension.

"It's more than feedback," Hera responded. Her full lips curved up in a smile. "It's like being plugged in, more alive than I've ever been before. It's frightening, actually. I might never have the will to take it off again."

"I've never seen that behavior in the ASPs before," Brigid said. "But then, no human has ever interfaced with one. It could be the emotional simplicity of an Nephilim drone soldier doesn't inspire reactions in the cybernetic systems."

"It could be," Hera said. "From what I've read of the Nephilim, they're only pale copies of the Annunaki, mentally and spiritually castrated."

"Which makes sense," Brigid said. "The overlords appear to have the ability to transfer their consciousness. Enlil, the leader of the overlords, had several incarnations that we've encountered, basically going full circle from Dragon King, to the android Colonel Thrush, to the human child Sam, to an all-new Annunaki Dragon King body."

"So they keep their drone minions around in order to have a body to pop into if things go sour for them," Hera mused.

"Apparently," Brigid explained. "When the Annunaki were reawakened, Kane pushed Enlil over a dangerous drop that would have killed anything. There was incontrovertible evidence that he was severely injured, but when he came after us at Cerberus, he was in good health. Couple that with the fact that they bragged about *Tiamat* being able to produce countless bodies to effectively make the overlords immortal…"

Hera's face was grim. "Which is what Domi meant when she said that the snake faces need a lot of killing. Granted, there is Danaan technology hidden around the globe that conveys powerful healing energies, such as another Annunaki's lair in Sinai. The clone vats of the Find will give Marduk the means to maintain his immortality."

"That's what we're afraid of," Brigid said. "Whether Marduk destroys his surviving brothers or uses his replication technology as a carrot to control them, it's not going to be anything good for humanity as a whole."

Hera nodded. "Then we have to make certain that the secrets of the Tartarus Find are erased forever."

"As much as I hate to admit it, sometimes knowledge is too dangerous to exist," Brigid replied. "If that means bringing down the roof, then so be it."

Hera's smile crawled enigmatically across her lips. "So be it."

Brigid frowned, wondering how Domi was faring as she made her rounds with Z00s.

DOMI ENJOYED THE SIDEARM she'd been assigned. The two-foot leaf-bladed sword was well balanced and razor sharp. Giving it a couple whirls to see how well it maneuvered in her hand, she gave a nod, then slid it back into her sheath. Z00s regarded her with a modicum of curiosity. "Certain you wouldn't want something with some range?"

Domi patted her Detonics. "Good enough for long distance. The sword, though, is very nice. This is my speed."

Zoo smiled. "Probably a better idea than a gun anyway. Given the numbers outside, you won't run out of ammunition for that blade."

Domi winked. "There's always a method to my madness. Plus, it might be primitive, but no blaster I ever held took off an arm or a head with one hit."

Zoo chuckled, wheeling his chair toward one of the ventilation access ports. "Cobaltville would get interesting after I left it. Shit."

"Always room for more out at Cerberus," Domi said, walking along with him. "Hang with us, you get to see the dark corners of the world."

"Yeah, like this joint," Zoo mentioned as they got closer to the maintenance area. His eyes narrowed and he looked around. "There should be a squad of Praetorians on hand."

Domi's nose twitched, and the sword was in her hand instantly. "Get more."

Zoo's eyes widened, and the Sin Eater snapped into his hand, his old Magistrate reflexes allowing him to catch the motor-launched folding machine pistol. His other beefy paw dropped to the walkie-talkie hanging around his neck.

The albino girl had broken into a run, sprinting to the end of the corridor. Domi knew that if she didn't force the hand of the mutant infiltrators, then they'd swarm the pair. And even though Zoo was well armed, there would have been no way for him to handle himself at hand-to-hand range, given his wheelchair. As she entered the maintenance area, the faint aroma of blood that had kicked her instincts into gear became an overwhelming stench. Scaled, yellow-eyed monstrosities crouched over slaughtered Greek soldiers, their chests pried open. There had been three soldiers, and the access hatch to the main vent had been battered open. The lethal mutants numbered a half dozen, at least those who were still standing. Four clone corpses were sprawled on the floor, with a fifth dangling over the bottom of the forced hatchway. Domi saw one of the reptilian mutants gnawing on a kidney, then she growled at it.

"Kreeeyah!" the man-eating clone shrieked, tossing aside the half-eaten organ and hefting a bayonet-tipped musket like a spear.

Domi didn't even bother vocalizing a response. She was a bolt of black and white, hurtling across the room and lashing the leaf-shaped point of her sword in a vicious slash across the center of the screaming mutant's head. The creature's jaw stretched farther, ripping apart savaged cheeks, the top of the head tottering back for a moment before coming loose and splashing on the floor.

Loud hoots issued forth as the other mutants lunged into action. Domi grabbed the decapitated monster's body by his scrawny upper arm and twisted, swinging the corpse into the path of the charging killers. The body jerked, pushed forward as bayonet points poked through his chest like metallic nipples. Domi grimaced and kicked the dead mutant in the stomach, driving the corpse down and levering the muskets out of their owners' hands with 150 pounds of deadweight. A third mutant leaped, fingers tipped with ragged, tough nails raking the air like claws.

The albino girl flicked the point of her sword in his direction, ducking her head. The mutant's talons flashed through her bone-white hair, missing her scalp. Domi's new sword, however, plunged into the belly of the Tartarus invader, razor-edged steel carving through viscera and bowels as if she were unzipping it from navel to sternum. Fetid breath blasted into Domi's face, the final issuance from frantic lungs. With a hard push, Domi propelled the disemboweled mutant into one of her unarmed foes. The corpse toppled into another mutant, knocking both away in a sprawl of tangled, scrawny limbs.

Domi had bought herself a breather, but she took a moment too long. Scaled knuckles cracked into her jaw as another reptilian jabbed at her. The blow was strong but imprecise. Had it caught her solidly, or been delivered with a good follow-through, the albino woman would have been tossed to the floor like a sack of wet laundry. Instead, the punch only managed to enrage her, and her ruby eyes snapped back, locking on her assailant with bloody rage. Her Detonics was already in her hand, and a big .45-caliber slug boomed in the confines of the room, taking most of the mutant's face with it in a spray of skull fragments, globules of brain matter and a wet cloud of blood.

"Fucker!" Domi grunted. She hacked her leaf-bladed sword, the serrated, sharp edge cleaving through the forearm of a mutant and producing a fountain of gore that gushed all over the floor.

"Down, Domi!" Zoo shouted, breaking through the outlander girl's blood fury. She hurled herself to the floor in a dive that plowed her through blood and entrails as Zoo's Sin Eater thundered down the hall.

Mutants screeched horribly as powerful slugs ripped through their deformed bodies, tearing the life from them on exit.

Domi got to her knees, her shadow suit and face caked with blood, an unearthly light in her glassy red eyes. She activated her Commtact. "Brigid, they got in!"

Zoo was on his own radio, calling to alert other maintenance areas. A screech of terror sounded down the vent, and Domi peered into the duct. She glanced down and saw the gravity-broken bodies at the bottom of the massive air passage. There were Praetorians down there, but it was mostly mutants who hadn't been agile enough to keep their balance in a spider climb. She glanced up toward the sky and saw more mutants, arms and legs splayed to buttress against the sides of the duct, a precarious balancing act as they spider-walked down the vent.

Domi pointed her Detonics up and fired off the remaining rounds from the gun, then pulled back as the first mutant corpse dropped past, too close to her head. Had the tumbling body even struck a glancing blow, it would have broken her neck. Screaming and dying creatures wailed ominously down the air passage, stopping as they crunched messily on the bottom.

"There were supposed to be eight men in here," Zoo stated. "Did you see any other bodies?"

Domi nodded, pointing to the bottom of the vent. Right now, she was too pumped to say anything clearly. The adrenaline rush of ferocious close combat surged through her veins. She held up four fingers, and Zoo frowned. "This is the only level they managed to penetrate."

Domi knelt beside one of the dead creatures, looking it

over in the light. As she ran her fingers across the scaled skin, her lips drew tight in observation.

"What's wrong?" Zoo asked.

"Never saw one before," Domi answered. "Not lizard skin."

"Looks like it," Zoo responded.

"You eat enough armadillos and lizards, you know the difference," Domi stated. "Scales are just hardened plates of hair."

"So these aren't imperfect copies of the Annunaki?" Zoo asked.

"Armored mammals," Domi replied. "Why they have body heat when they look like lizards?"

"To tell the truth, as long as they die from gunshot wounds, I don't give a fuck whether they're animal, vegetable or mineral," Zoo told her.

Domi shrugged. "Needed something to kick my brain into gear."

Praetorian guards showed up, armed with short swords and Sten machine pistols. They surveyed the carnage of the maintenance area.

"Secure this chamber. A repair crew is also en route to replace the hatch," Zoo stated. "Any sounds in the vent, you cut loose."

"Yes, sir," the leader of the sentry squad stated.

"Come in by air, might try water next?" Domi asked.

"We have a water treatment plant on the lower levels," Zoo answered.

"Won't hurt to look there," Domi mentioned. "Maybe more guards to the vents, too."

"Consider it done," Zoo replied. "You push, I'll delegate."

Domi grabbed the handles of Zoo's chair, grinning. "Hang on."

Albino and amputee, unusual partners, hurtled into the

hallway, Domi with one foot on the crossbar of the wheel-chair, the other pumping the floor to maintain their speed. Zoo barked orders into his walkie-talkie all the way. The odd couple raced to the nearest elevator bank to head down to the water treatment plant, weaving around guards en route to their battle stations, drawing curious stares all the way.

ARTEM15 LANDED ON ALL FOURS just a few yards from the edge of the rift in the earth known as the Tartarus Crack. She stayed quadrupedal to allow Kane to drop to the ground, then walked beside him to the drop-off. Kane had his Magistrate helmet's visor down, and he exploited its light-amplification and magnification features. Kane could hear the robot's own cameras whirring wildly, scanning the sheer cliffs.

"There isn't any easy way down there," Artem15 replied.

"I'm picking up some odd impressions here and there," Kane noted. "Looks like something bounced off the walls."

Artem15 directed her cameras to where Kane pointed. The gigantic hand- and footholds were unmistakably large enough to be the creation of a mechanoid.

"Z00s was going down there to spy on the enemy," Kane replied. "Maybe at a slow climb, he'd be noticed, but hopping from wall to wall, he moved too quick to be stopped. And it's not like those mutant freaks have radio communications."

"Still, wouldn't it make a hellacious amount of noise?" Artem15 asked.

Kane glanced up to her. "There'd only be one way to find out. Of course, if I'm going to be riding piggyback, I don't think I'll last too long."

"You've lasted well enough for the rest of my jumps," Artem15 responded. "There's a property to the hydraulics or the secondary orichalcum, or both, that negates kinetic energy. And Z00s never looks like he's been through the wringer on his espionage runs."

Kane looked down, then swallowed. "What the hell. It's only a mile down."

"Thanks for reminding me, Kane," Artem15 answered. "And you've got the nerve to say Grant bitches a lot."

Kane crawled up the giant mechanoid's arm. "That wasn't a complaint. That was just stating the obvious. Big difference."

"Well, it took the wind out of my sails," Artem15 replied. "You might want to strap in tight up there."

"Already working on it," Kane responded. He'd taken a fifteen-foot length of strong nylon rope from his pack and now swung it around the neck of the robot several times. He left one loop slack enough to slide around his waist, and then tied the ends of the rope together, spacing knots to put his hands between. The ex-Magistrate remembered something he'd heard in an old vid about the American Wild West. "Ride 'em, cowboy."

"Oh, great, now I'm a cow?" Artem15 grumbled.

"No. They rode horses," Kane said. "They just herded cows."

"I heard of cows, too," Artem15 replied.

Kane looked over her shoulder into the crack. "Dumb jokes aside, we're going to have to do something by morning."

"Yeah, yeah," Artem15 said. Inside her cockpit, she took a deep breath, trying to calm herself. "You tied in tight back there?"

Kane felt the rope creak in his grasp, and though he couldn't see his knuckles through the gloves of the shadow suit, he knew that they were white from his death grip. "As tight as I'll ever—"

Artem15 leaped off of the drop-off before Kane could complete his sentence, eliciting a howl of surprise as he rode three thousand pounds of mechanoid into the darkness of the Tartarus Crack. Sailing through the night, the robot reached the far wall and her clawed hands sank into stone, limbs folding under her weight. Hydraulics hissed, compressing to absorb the impact.

"…cking do that again when I'm not ready and…" Kane grumbled, holding on to his improvised harness for dear life.

"Good, you're alive up there," Artem15 said. "Any injuries?"

"No, but I'll have to change my underwear when we get to the bottom," Kane answered. "You were right. The hydraulic skeleton of this thing absorbs impacts pretty well."

In her pilot's couch, Diana's muscles were taut in sympathy with her piston-driven limbs. "Yeah, it's a little wet in here, too. Sorry about that."

"I understand," Kane muttered. "Might as well just make the leap before you talk yourself out of it."

"What were you going to do when I made another leap and you weren't ready?" Artem15 asked with a chuckle.

"Something along the lines of giving you one of my feet," Kane muttered. "But in reality, it would have just been making a stain on the back of your robot."

Artem15 laughed. "Much as I'd like to have feet again, I don't think one in my ass would be any replacement."

Kane chuckled. "Well. We took the first step. Ready for the next?"

The towering mechanoid didn't answer out loud, but this time when Kane let out a howl, it was one of pure adrenal rush, fear becoming excitement as man and machine hopped from cliff to cliff.

GRANT LOOKED THROUGH the scope on his Barrett, scanning the teeming ranks of scale-hided clones swarming the hangar doors. He realized that he didn't have to worry about the horde surging through them. While the doors were smeared with blood from burst knuckles hammering on un-yielding steel, they hadn't been budged. The cloned monsters had maniacal strength in comparison to a human being, but it was insufficient to dent four feet of metal, and even if they managed to get their fingers between the interlocking seals of the two doors, not even two hundred of them had the muscle to overwhelm the powerful locking mechanism of the doors.

"I've got movement on top of Olympus," Are5 replied. "Looks like about fifty or sixty are hanging around the vent intake shaft."

Grant swung up his Barrett, following the mechanoid's aimed finger. "It doesn't seem like they're trying to get in there now."

"They tried once before," Are5 responded. "Eight Praetorians were killed, but Domi and Z00s took care of the ones who got in."

Grant nodded, filled with pride at Domi's actions. "Are there any other means into the mountain? Do you have water pumped in from somewhere?"

"Underground springs," Are5 said. "However, unless Thanatos learned how to clone these muties with gills, there's no way they could get to the water pipes. Plus, the designers of that redoubt weren't stupid. There's grids of pipes, running parallel. This way, you can literally flow an entire river into the base, but unless you're the thickness of a garter snake, you're not getting through the pipes."

"How'd you know that?" Grant asked.

"Z00s told me, after Domi took a swim to the bottom of a treatment tank," Are5 replied.

"Sure. We're out here in the wild outdoors, and she's taking a dip in the pool," Grant said. "Glad someone double-checked, though. So that leaves the bunch at the intake shaft."

"Sooner or later, they might try again, this time sending down more than just a dozen," Are5 noted.

Grant flicked off the Barrett's safety. "Let's put a little scare into that bunch."

The massive .50-caliber rifle spiked violently against Grant's shoulder. The polymer fibers that made up his shadow suit absorbed the impact, and even though the massive ex-Magistrate felt the hard punch, he wouldn't suffer a bruise on the joint.

Three-quarters of a mile away, Grant's first shot struck a mutant clone in the small of the back. The powerful slug tore a horrendous hole through the belly of the creature and lost very little of its penetration power, even at that extreme range. The bullet punched into another, then another mutant, three bodies plowed into oblivion by the single shot.

Hordelings scrambled, racing away from the intake vent.

Are5 let a low whistle leak through his speaker. "Do they make that in my size? Sure, it'd only be a handgun…"

Grant grinned. "I'm sure we could whip something up for you. If you keep it in your ax sheath, it'd be like a mechanoid-sized Sin Eater."

"That's got me smiling," Are5 responded. The warbot's head pivoted, looking down the slope of the hill they were on top of. "Aw, shit."

Grant looked down, seeing a swarm of clones pooling at

the base of their perch. "Scared the ones up there, but gained some attention down there."

Are5 drew one of Artem15's javelins, then hurled it toward the clot of seething mutants as they began their climb. The warhead sailed like a rocket as it was powered by the giant's hydraulic musculature. By the time it hit the ground, it was going fast enough to vaporize a single mutant at the front of the group, scaled flesh proving as resistant as gossamer in the path of the robot-thrown javelin. The impact fuse hadn't encountered enough resistance to go off until it struck the ground, at which time the javelin detonated in a thunderous explosion. Body parts sailed from the swarm of deformed creatures, shrapnel and concussive force shearing apart limbs and torsos.

Grant pumped three shots from his Barrett downhill, taking out mutants who had climbed outside of the deadly radius of the javelin blast. Each .50-caliber bullet hurled a mutant back to the ground, staking it in place with ferocious energy.

"Now we've got their attention," Grant noted. "Unfortunately, it's only a small portion of the main horde."

Are5 swept the surviving mutants with his shoulder guns. "The main body of the force isn't even paying attention. Small groups seem to be breaking off to try alternate routes up here, which means we'll be surrounded pretty soon."

Grant pointed toward a hilltop a half mile away. "That looks like a good, defensible position. Think you can hop us over there?"

Are5 lowered his shoulder, allowing Grant to climb up the arm. The pair made its way toward Grant's suggestion, knowing that they'd have to move again.

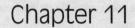

Chapter 11

Artem15 and Kane reached the bottom of the Crack, landing in a slope of relatively loose soil that absorbed their impact. Kane extricated himself from the harness and slithered to the ground, Copperhead slung down from his shoulder. He knelt for a moment, withdrawing a grenade launcher to affix to the submachine gun's short barrel, stuffing a fat gren round into it. He glanced up to the golden-maned robot huntress.

"I'll keep in radio contact," Kane told her. "I'll have a better chance sneaking among them alone and on foot."

"But if it comes to a hard contact, I'll hear the gunfire and come running," Artem15 replied.

"Depending on how far I have to go," Kane mentioned. "After the pyramid and *Tiamat* and all the other shit I've seen, why am I always surprised at how fucking big the snake-faces build their places?"

Artem15 stood her ground, watching Kane disappear into the shadows, even with the enhancements of her telescopic and infrared cameras. "Just be careful."

"Will do," Kane replied.

The ex-Magistrate walked heel-toe, his eyes and ears open, electronic enhancements heightening his own human senses. If anywhere could spawn the horde of monstrosities that stampeded through the countryside, this massive cavern had

the room for such unholy creation. Certainly, Kane was bris-
tling with weaponry and spare ammunition, especially with
the extra crowd-clearing power of a grenade launcher, but the
army of mutants that might be lurking in the darkness could
have been a reserve force capable of overwhelming Artem15
and him ten times over.

So far, after covering five hundred yards of the cavern
floor, there hadn't been a single infrared contact, though the
carbonized remains of ASP-blasted mutants littered the floor
in a knee-high layer of incinerated corpses. Kane wove
through the bodies, noting the presence of the looming
Annunaki dropship off to one side. It was powered down and
silent, but that was no guarantee that there weren't Nephilim
on board who would be watching him. For all of his conflicts
with the overlords, Kane had been inside one of the space-
craft only once, so he wasn't comfortable being near it.

Still, it was a tempting target, so he crossed over to its
underbelly, removing magnetic charges from his backpack.
The remote mines, packing twice the power of an antiaircraft
missile, undoubtedly had the power to rip open the smooth-
skinned transatmospheric craft. The only problem was that
the hull was nonferrous, which prevented the limpet mines
from adhering to the metallic-seeming skin. Kane looked
over his shoulder, making certain that nothing stalked in the
near complete darkness. Rather than waste time seeing if
duct tape would stick to the alien craft's hull, he simply
packed the mines where the body of the ship rested on the
earth.

Kane would just have to take the chance that he could
detonate the mines by remote control before the dropship
took off. He crawled out from under the edge of the smooth-

skinned saucer and scanned the surrounding area. Only the clink of a smart-metal boot on the lip of a hatchway gave the former Magistrate any warning, but it was all he needed, somersaulting forward and out of the way of the Nephilim as he leaped down, driving his fist into the dirt floor of the cavern.

The warrior's punch trapped his fist in place for a heartbeat, but that was all Kane needed to whip his leg around, kicking the Nephilim in the jaw with all the power of a crocodile tail. The blow snapped the armored warrior's head around, stunning him and dumping him to the ground. Kane pivoted and got to both feet, drawing his knife, not wishing to engage in gunplay yet. The Nephilim tried to recover his senses and lifted his forearm to aim at Kane's stomach. A sharp knee blow knocked the Nephilim's arm out of the way, and Kane grabbed his knife handle with both hands, spearing the point into his opponent's neck. The serrated blade carved through reptilian skin, bouncing into the gap between vertebrae.

Kane gave the knife a savage twist, popping neck bones apart, the dead Nephilim's head dangling limply on muscle and sinew. He stepped back, looking around, then noticed the open hatch in the side of the skimmer. Kane rushed back and retrieved two of his four limpet charges, then crawled inside the Annunaki craft. His low-light illuminator didn't show anything through his night vision, just a smooth, featureless deck with organic-metal-seeming ribs running alongside the interior of the craft. There were apertures in the floor at regular intervals, and on one side of the deck was a single seat next to the only control apparatus in the dropship.

To Kane, it felt as if he were inside the torso of a living

creature, making him imagine the space between a turtle and its shell. It felt eerie, spurring the ex-Magistrate to secret his limpet charges against the wall ribs. He glanced at the control panel and saw two membranes in the face of the craft. Given the symbiotic nature of their smart-metal uniforms and the ASPs, Kane wasn't too surprised at the idea that the pilot plugged himself into orifices in the ship. He had seen Enlil pilot another craft, but that was from a special chair in the heart of the deck. Given that Brigid had explained to him that the jewel interface had been specifically keyed to the Annunaki supreme leader's mental energy, it wouldn't have been to outré to imagine that lesser pilots would require more direct neurological interfaces. Kane didn't relish the idea of having to pilot one of these craft in an emergency.

"You've got it easy, Artie," Kane whispered.

"Why?" the robot pilot asked.

"You don't have to ram any part of you into a sphincter on your robot," Kane explained. He hurried outside of the dropship and hopped to the ground. The cooling corpse of the dead Nephilim was the only indication that anything had once lived in this section of the cavern.

"You talking about the Annunaki ship?" Artem15 asked.

"Yeah," Kane replied. "I think I'll stick with human-made ships."

"Thank the goddess for her modifications," Artem15 agreed.

Kane lurked deeper into the darkness of the cave. So far, he'd been lucky, but he remembered a saying: "The only way to never run out of luck is to die young."

I'm way too old for that, Kane thought, getting closer to the heart of the Tartarus Find.

DANTON GRIMACED, his eyes darting to the left and the right, picking up images over the metallic telepathic web he wore on his clean-shaved skull. To Marduk, it was as if the man were experiencing seizures. Danton winced in pain, feeling his mutant minions torn asunder by various weapons.

"The main ventilation shaft is a loss," Danton wheezed, reclining back and pulling the web off of his skull. He wiped some blood from his right nostril. The strain of taking control of so many creatures and receiving psychic trauma from their violent deaths obviously took a physical toll, as well as mental.

"I thought your hordelings had gotten in," Marduk said.

"They did, and while the guards killed a few of them, they managed to take up a position inside. It was a girl," Danton said. "A girl and that fucking, self-righteous cripple Thurmond."

Marduk smirked. "Thurmond is patrolling New Olympus for infiltrators?"

"And shooting them," Danton grumbled. "Then I was distracted by two attackers at the hangar gates. I sent some mutants after them, but they had shifted their position."

Danton held up a cloth to his bloodied nose. "I hate when I'm in contact and they start killing large numbers of my clones."

Marduk nodded. "Two attackers?"

"A man and a robot. Unfortunately they evacuated their position when the responding mutants got up there," Danton said. "However, they left behind an antipersonnel mine."

"That's why you took off the telepathic web," Marduk surmised.

"I'm going to have to let my little mutants work on their own for a bit," Danton explained. "Granted, I only receive a tiny fraction of the trauma that my mutants receive, but when we're talking about them dying a dozen at a time, it's like being punched in the face every few minutes."

"You are keeping the pressure on New Olympus, though," Marduk said. It wasn't a question, and Danton gave his nose another wipe.

"We've got a job to do, so yes, the mutants are looking for every chance to get in there. They aren't that bright, but they will look for a way in. As well, the ones hunting for the man and the robot won't stop until they're feasting on human flesh," Danton explained. "They're very single-minded, and it takes a lot of fear to pull them off the case."

Marduk looked at the telepathic web. He hid his grin as best he could. The device was meant to enhance natural telepathic ability, something native to all Annunaki, even when they were only the hybrid barons. He remembered the agonizing blow he'd felt when one of his brother barons had been slain by the renegades. Even through his evolutionary change to his true nature, the searing brand of that psychic blow still resonated, years later.

The telepathic web was a way for Marduk to connect with the lower, base minds of the mammals of this world, such as humans, or the deformed mutants that he and his brothers had crafted the hairless monkeys into. It was impressive to Marduk that Danton even possessed the ability to direct the ape-based hordes with the enhancement webbing, though it was obvious that a mere human didn't have the psychic strength and defenses to deal with traumatic feedback.

Something tickled the overlord's mind and he turned, looking in the direction of the dropship.

"Kane's here," Marduk said.

"Kane?" Danton asked. The former Mag drew his Sin Eater on instinct.

"One of my Nephilim is dead," Marduk explained. Cold eyes regarded the human. "Connect and let loose the hounds."

Danton glanced at the silver-cabled lattice, then placed it on his clean-shaved head again. Imagining the cavern, he sent out the silent call for his clone guards to begin scouring the darkness for Kane. A distant prickling clawed on his mind, but it wasn't the same as the group slaughter caused by high explosives. His hordelings at New Olympus were getting closer to the two interfering raiders who had been harrying the swarm.

He glanced to Marduk. "One of your Cerberus opponents may soon be dead."

Marduk ran a talon along his scaled chin, allowing himself a smile. "This will be a fine night, then."

IT WAS AN OLD TRICK, but Grant assumed that the primitive mutant horde was not well versed in basic diversion tactics. Settling in to a sniper's roost, the ex-Magistrate picked off the Tartarus raiders one at a time, utilizing the raw power of the Barrett to draw them closer.

All the while, Grant knew that he was making himself a slab of irresistible bait to the raving, raging creatures. Forty attackers were galloping along the mountain ridge between his and Are5's original position and the current one. While they were howling with such rage that at even three hundred yards Grant could hear them, they were paying far too much attention to the lone rifleman, simplistic minds never taking into account the missing fifteen-foot mechanoid who had been alongside him.

"Come closer, you scaley fucking freaks," Grant whispered. "Come to papa."

Grant transitioned to his Copperhead, using the smaller

gun's built-in scope to pop rounds into the scrawny but murderous beings. It was a piecemeal decimation of the enemy's force, as he'd only dropped four of the clones permanently, others ignoring their glancing flesh wounds to continue their suicidal charge against Grant.

"Okay, Ari," Grant called. "They're in the box."

With a bounding leap, the mohawked robot warrior sailed out of a space between two boulders, his thermal ax describing a blazing streak in the night. The mutants glanced up and wailed in surprise at Are5's sudden appearance. The three-foot edge of his superheated ax blade caught five of the monstrosities in a single sweep. Bayonet-armed hordelings charged at the towering creature, their eighteen-inch lethal spikes poised to puncture the pilot as they leaped at Ari's chest plate.

Grant swept the bounding attackers, his Copperhead raking across their scrawny forms on full-auto. It wasn't precision fire, or pretty, but the murderous attackers were swatted out of the air, some with injuries, others slapping lifelessly against the powerful bulk of the towering mechanoid. A second sweep of Are5's thermal ax hurled severed limbs and shorn torsos into the air in a grisly cloud of devastation.

It was a good start, but there were still twenty-five mutant clones to deal with, and one of them sank a bayonet into the copper carapace over Are5's cockpit. Grant ripped the monstrosity apart with another squeeze of the Copperhead's trigger, snarling all the time. "Ari? You hurt?"

"Son of a bitch!" Are5 responded, tearing the musket out of its chest plate and shattering its stock across the heads of three savage monstrosities. "Son of a bitch!"

"Ari, pull back!" Grant bellowed over the radio. "I've got 'em!"

The ex-Magistrate reloaded the compact Copperhead as fast as he could, but the fifteen-foot robot warrior punted another of the mutants a hundred feet over the side of the cliff. Grant grimaced, unable to fire his grenade launcher as long as Are5 was in the middle of the savage mutants. All he could do was fan the thickest flanks of the swarming beastlings, carving them off of his friend's legs a handful at a time. Are5 stood his ground, punching and chopping with his thermal ax, or stomping his massive clawed feet on the diminutive attackers. Another mutant was about to plunge his bayonet into Are5's cockpit, but this time Grant was able to get off a telling shot, turning the creature's skull into a sieve, brain matter jettisoning through holes blown through bone.

"Ari! Get the fuck over here!" Grant shouted. "I can take them out!"

Are5 turned, looking bewildered, then flexed, leaping away from the crowd of marauders. In three leaps, he was far enough away for Grant to trigger a high-explosive shell into the surviving clones, scattering them to the winds with its powerful shock wave. Grant scanned the hilltops and down the slopes for signs of more attackers homing in on their position, then watched Are5 sag to his knees fifty yards out.

"Shit," Grant growled, scooping his first-aid kit out of his war bag and racing over to the robot. "Ari, talk to me, man."

"Took a poke in the side. Blood's all over the place," Are5 answered.

Grant reached the kneeling robot and hammered on the chest plate. "Open up. I'll take a look at it."

The sealing clamps hissed, and the chest plate swung open. "Too many of them."

"Shut up," Grant said. He scooped up the amputee as if he were a child. "Ari, unplug yourself…."

He reached to the small of his back and unhooked the control interface from his cybernetic port. Are5's joints clanked as they froze in place, a safety feature for the robot. Grant lowered Ari to the dirt and took a look at him. Though the pilots wore protective vests, the bayonet was still able to punch a narrow hole level with his lower ribs.

It took a few moments to unbuckle the protective leather, then tug up Ari's shirt.

"Oh, that hurts." Ari winced. "I can't breathe."

Grant looked at it. "Exhale hard for me."

The amputee pilot did so, and Grant shone a flashlight into his nostrils and open mouth. "Okay, no aspirated blood. The point missed your lung."

"Hurts like shit," Ari said.

"Maybe a broken rib," Grant answered. "The blood's too dark to be arterial. You're lucky."

"Lucky? I damn near got stabbed to death in a one-and-a-half-ton war machine!" Ari snapped.

"Calm the fuck down, Ari," Grant replied. "What kind of name is Aristotle for a god of war anyway?"

"Warrior philosopher," Ari answered, taking slow, shallow breaths so as not to aggravate his wound. "Hera picked it for me."

"She's got a hell of a sense of irony," Grant replied, applying a compress to the injury after washing it out with a squirt of saline solution. Grant didn't know if the mutants coated their blades in anything, but bits of rusty bayonet flowed out of the stab wound. The compress was taped firmly in place, and he followed it up with a roll of elastic bandage around

Ari's chest to keep a possible broken rib from floating around and poking into his lung.

"Yeah, well, I do get a little bloodthirsty against these little fuckers," Ari replied. "Hence the war-god stuff."

"Hell, my woman is a samurai. She has all of this Zen philosophy stuff she keeps telling me," Grant told him. "She says that a warrior without a good ethical foundation is merely a thug."

Ari winced. "What's your philosophy?"

Grant grinned. "Fuck 'em up first."

Another wince crossed Ari's face. "Don't make me laugh, you big bastard. It hurts too much."

"If you can complain, you can fight. Get back in your suit," Grant replied.

"So you're always ready to fight?"

Grant nodded. "Would seem that way."

"Gimme a hand," Ari requested. Grant lifted the amputee back into his couch. Blood dripped from the bottom of his armored tub.

"You'd think that they could find better chest armor for you," Grant noted. "If those little creeps can get a bayonet through your cockpits…"

"We barely have enough metallurgy to make the pipes and springs for our Sten guns and rifles," Ari replied. He plugged in his cyberport, then rocked back onto his heels, standing. The carapace swung shut. "I feel pretty damn lucky to have this much armor in front of me. Besides, any more and I wouldn't be able to open and shut the door. Not like the ass end of this tub."

Grant nodded, but the explanation didn't sound too good.

"Listen, Grant. This isn't like back where you come from, where you've got storehouses full of steel and polycarbonate," Ari continued. "You go to war with the army you have, not the army you wish you had."

"Frankly, that shit sounds half-assed," Grant grumbled. "We brought what we could."

Are5 sighed. "Some of us don't have those nice big American supply stockpiles. Listen, we appreciate the concern…"

"Yeah. We've got real work to do. We can discuss improving your protection later," Grant responded.

Are5 glanced back toward the heart of the writhing multitude of mutations by the hangar doors. "Sorry, Grant. I didn't mean to snap at you."

Grant gave the mechanoid's thigh a friendly slap, since patting the robot's shoulder would have involved a standing high jump twice his own height. "It's cool, Ari. I'm just frustrated that you'd got hurt. Still pals?"

Are5 held down his massive hand, palm up. "Climb on up, friend. We've got uglies to harass."

Grant grabbed on to the giant's wrist and rode up to Are5's shoulder. "Yippie ki-yay!"

Man and robot raced toward their next position to renew their harassment of the horde.

BRIGID AND HERA CAUGHT UP with Domi and Zoo as the pair emerged from the elevator that led down to the water filtration plant.

"You look a fright," Brigid said, noting Domi's wet hair was now a sickly yellow cap hugging her skull.

"Should have seen me before my dip in the pool washed off all the blood," Domi replied with a cock-eyed grin.

Brigid wrinkled her nose. "I'll have to take your word for it."

Hera interrupted the outlanders' reunion. "We have activity

in ventilation maintenance bay three. So far, though, it looks as if your strategy is working well, Zoo."

The bearded man nodded. "The narrow, long corridors leading to each vent access looked like an ideal shooting gallery. There are no vital components that could be caught in the cross fire, so putting up a controlled barricade gives the Praetorians a fallback point to snipe at any intruders as if they were fish in a barrel."

"Don't forget about leaving level three unlocked," Domi reminded Zoo. "That was nasty bait."

Zoo's cheeks reddened above his beard. "I figure either the mutants learn their lesson from heavy losses, or we just continue to kill them off. Either way, even when they just make the attempt, one in four of them slips on the climb down."

"Splat," Domi announced, dropping one hand into the palm of the other with a loud clap. She seemed to remember something, taking the shine off of her glee. "Anyone get the Praetorians from the bottom of the shaft?"

Zoo and Hera both glanced at the albino girl. Hera spoke up first. "It will be too dangerous opening the vent access to recover their bodies right now, darling. But we will retrieve them for a proper burial."

Domi nodded. Zoo rested a beefy paw on her shoulder. "Right now, our priorities are the living. The dead have time to wait."

Domi nodded at the man. "Understood."

"With our situation secure, we should check on the progress of the others," Brigid suggested.

"Then let's head back to the control center," Hera said. "Though you say you have contact over your Commtact implants."

Brigid nodded. "It's one way that we can't be disarmed, at least in terms of communications."

"What is the word from Kane and Grant?" Hera inquired.

"Are5 was injured during an attack on the swarm. Grant applied first aid to him, however. It was a bloody but superficial wound," Brigid answered. "Kane and Artem15 are at the bottom of the Crack, but currently are split up. Kane's making a stealth reconnaissance."

Hera frowned as soon as Brigid mentioned Kane's presence in the mile-deep cavern. "They had best be on their guard. With the Nephilim and the Tartarus mutants on the same side, that will be the most dangerous spot in New Olympus."

"Well, Kane once said, in a moment of bravado, 'The deadliest place in the world to you is Tuesday for me,'" Brigid confessed with a weak chuckle. Domi bumped her shoulder against Brigid's arm, her ruby eyes cast upward to meet Brigid's emerald-green gaze, a bridge of emotional support between the two women.

Hera provided a grin for the pair. "Let's hope Tuesday is one of his better days."

She turned her attention to Zoo. "Dear, do me a favor and check in on my contingency. Should Marduk take a more direct approach, I'd like to have a knockout punch ready."

"Contingency?" Brigid inquired. "Any hints as to what it is?"

"Something from the Tartarus Find," Hera answered. "A form of remote energy projection capacitor drone. I've been trying to discern its capabilities."

"Oh!" Brigid exclaimed. "Let's hope it doesn't come to that."

"Why?" Hera inquired.

Brigid frowned. "I doubt that even Marduk is so arrogant that he would design a weapon that he doesn't have a defense for. Even if it would be a remote control."

"This is all under my control, Baptiste," Hera concluded sharply, her black eyes smoldering.

Brigid remained silent, Kane's vision of lightning bolts laying waste to Greece crackling across her mind's eye in a storm of destruction.

Chapter 12

Kane had the advantage in the darkness, his black helmet and shadow suit blending into the murk while the red, orange and yellow blobs of scaled, warm-blooded humanoids stalked the cavern floor, bright in contrast to the blues, greens and blacks of the cold pit. It was eerie, watching the world solely through infrared vision, but the light-amplification unit, with its UV illuminator and optic filter didn't allow him much range, only bringing the cave into contrast for thirty feet in front of him. Thermal imaging picked up far more distant sources of body heat.

The Tartarus guardians seemed to be avoiding him, though Kane had no idea how they could detect him. The shadow suit was a one-piece garment and lacked only an air supply to perfectly isolate him from the atmosphere. Since those factors combined to make him olfactorally neutral, Kane ticked off other senses that could have been alerting the stalkers in the murk. He eliminated sight and smell as betraying indicators of his presence, and except for his brief flurry of combat next to the skimmer, he hadn't made much of a sound. He was either doing extraordinarily well at avoiding the mutant patrols, or something else was at work.

His point man's instinct was gnawing at the base of his neck, letting him know that some malevolent power was manipulating the situation, inspiring the hordelings to circumvent him as they started toward the base of the Crack.

"Eyes open, Artie," Kane whispered over his helmet microphone. "Patrol heading down your way."

"Affirmative," the robot answered. "Do you need support?"

"No, just stay out of sight," Kane said. "Something's weird here."

"I feel it, too," Artem15 agreed. That gave the former Magistrate a moment of pause, remembering how she had barely survived the night in the temple of the oracle when the mutant horde had swarmed and slaughtered her family.

"Ever have any other strange dreams?" Kane asked.

"You think this is the time for psychoanalysis?" Artem15 countered.

Kane grimaced under his polycarbonate faceplate. "I'm not trying to head shrink you, but you've lived in the area, and you're the one receiving the same psychic heebies that I'm getting."

"Oh, sorry," Artem15 said in apology. "No. Unless you count the nightmares from my fever."

"Do they recur?" Kane wondered aloud.

"Once after surgery, and once before you came here," Artem15 replied. "But they were vivid enough to get me walking toward the temple."

"Where we ran across each other," Kane added. The mutants now had him cut off from the pilot and her robot. There was a gap in the cavern wall, and it was obvious that the creatures had bracketed him in and were herding him toward the entrance. "We'll talk about this later. Brigid might want to hear about those dreams."

"What's wrong? Kane, there aren't mutants approaching me. Are you okay?" Artem15 asked.

"I'm being steered toward an entrance," Kane said. He glanced back, seeing that there were more skimmers parked along the side. "Thought that Zoo said he saw one large ship."

"He did," Artem15 replied. "Why?"

Kane stood and walked straight toward the cave mouth. The mutants around him stayed a minimum of twenty yards from him, as if they didn't want to incur the wrath of the man in black. "All I see are little twenty-five-foot skimmers."

"So the Annunaki don't have ships in between minis and space whale?" Artem15 asked, referring to *Tiamat*.

Kane rapped his knuckles against his helmet. "Right. Dammit… I forgot about Kharo-Khoto! The scout ship. It was old and all fucked up, but *Tiamat* could have held dozens in her belly."

"Kharo-Khoto?" Artem15 inquired. "Oh, dear… I see the mutants now. But they're basically just a firebreak between you and I."

"These things are controlled by some kind of intelligence. My bet, it's Thanatos," Kane said. "Yeah. Kharo-Khoto, the Black City of Genghis Khan. Held all kinds of ancient super-technology, which, in retrospect, was Annunaki stuff."

"Kane, if you know what's good for you, you'll tell your girl-bot to come in here with us," a voice interrupted. The ex-Magistrate winced, recognizing the unmistakable dulcet tones of an Annunaki overlord.

"Hey, Duckie," Kane greeted. He flipped up his faceplate as the stone archway he walked toward began to glow. Marduk was unmistakably present, seven feet of perfectly carved physique, clad in cobalt-blue smart-metal armor. A wry grin was evident on his reptilian face as he stood next to a bald man wearing Magistrate armor. "Ah, going for the retro minions? Does this mean I have to call you Baron again?"

Marduk shook his head, his grin spreading. "I swear you'd be cracking wise on your deathbed, Kane. Oh, wait, this is sort of your deathbed, isn't it?"

"If you want to try, let's make it a big sleep-in," Kane said. "One move toward me, you and Danton will be eating a gren."

Marduk laughed, an unnerving sound spanning multiple octaves at once. "That's what I enjoy about this arrogant little monkey. Here I am, one of the beings who raised his kind from eating lice out of their mate's hair, and he thinks a mere firearm can harm me."

Kane kept the grenade launcher leveled at Marduk. "Said the arrogant gila monster."

Marduk answered the remark with another chuckle. "So, is Artemis going to grace us with her presence?"

Kane shrugged. "I'm pretty sure she wasn't born yesterday, so that's a big no."

Marduk took a step closer, but the cavernous mouth of Kane's grenade launcher rose. Even Marduk didn't have enough faith in his smart-metal armor to press the point any further. The overlord glanced to Danton. "Send your lads to get her. She's smart enough not to risk explosives with Kane here."

Kane grinned. "That's the thing with us arrogant little monkeys…"

He thumbed the firing stud on the remote control mines he'd left in and under the skimmer. Hundreds of yards back up the tunnel, the silver-skinned ship somersaulted on a blossom of fire, cartwheeling for a second before shattering in two. Against the backdrop of fire, Tartarus mutants scurried, arms waving in the air as blazing, slashing shrapnel tore at them.

"Move it, Artie!" Kane bellowed into his microphone.

"You cursed little ape!" Marduk snarled. "Danton!"

Kane was already in motion. He knew that he was going to be trapped in the cavern, as his ride was obviously going to be leaping to safety. The grenade launcher fired, its 40 mm shell glancing off Marduk's chest before its impact fuse triggered a powerful blast ten yards behind the Annunaki. The shock wave hurled Marduk and Danton, who was shielded by the overlord's massive form, to the ground. A quarter of the snarling ring of mutants were also thrown to the ground, but lacking the protection that their human and Annunaki masters wore, most of them were shredded by the violent eruption of the round.

The nearby concussion left the rest of the mutant horde off balance, allowing Kane time to rake more of their rank and file with a full magazine from his Copperhead. Unfortunately, the shock of nearby brethren blown off their feet spurred the deformed minions to action. Bodies launched at Kane, snarling unintelligible death threats.

Kane batted one, then another aside, the stock of his weapon cracking facial bones with each savage swing, but scrawny arms whipped around his waist and legs. He flexed his forearm to launch the Sin Eater into action, but a yellow-eyed clone had snarled his arm, trapping the gun even as the electric motor tried to vault the handgun into his grasp. Kane speared the barrel of his empty Copperhead into one of those yellow eyes, the hot barrel steaming as the orb ruptured under the impact. A nerve-grinding screech issued from the half-blinded mutant. The Sin Eater wasn't responding to his forearm muscle flex command, staying in its holster. Once more, improvisation came into play, and Kane launched a wicked punch into the face of a hordeling, centrifugal force snapping the machine pistol to his waiting grasp.

"Down, Kane!" Artem15's voice ordered over his helmet radio.

Kane bit off a protest, then picked up a scrawny mutant by the throat, swinging him up as a living shield. Artem15's shoulder guns crackled, sweeping much of the crowd from around Kane in a display of precision that impressed the ex-Magistrate. Kane kicked himself free from the scaled humanoids, holding out his arm to give Artem15 something to grab on to. Her palm came up with a jarring impact to his ribs, but he was lifted away from the crowd of mutants.

Marduk rose to one knee, glaring at man and robot. "Kane!"

"You…" Artem15 gasped over her loudspeaker.

"Shoot him!" Kane ordered.

The robot's right shoulder gun rattled off a long burst, but it only chewed up the dirt next to the Annunaki overlord as he got to both feet. It was a far different situation than the precision marksmanship displayed only moments before. Unfortunately, Kane had a strong feeling about why the Greek pilot had been so shaken by Marduk's appearance.

Artem15 whirled and charged through the tunnel, racing toward the conflagration. She didn't worry about mutants in her path, her four-clawed feet smashing bodies to a pulp whether they were already dead on the dirt or trying to flee from her path. Their flimsy bodies did nothing to slow her rampant progress as she charged to the base of the Crack.

Kane clambered onto her neck, sliding into the rope harness that she still had in place. The thick nylon weave remained undamaged by her journey through the flames that seared off of the wreckage of the destroyed skimmer. "Artie…"

"Got to go. Got to fucking go," Artem15 said. With a leap, she was ten yards up the side of a cliff, springing up again as soon as her claws found resistance. The acceleration upward threatened to tear Kane from his rope harness, and his arms protested as he held on for dear life.

Kane kept quiet. She needed all of her nerve and concentration to make the ascent, though it was a less perilous proposition than the descent. Her panic, however was understandable.

She had just seen a demon from her nightmare come to life.

MARDUK GLANCED DOWN to Danton, who, except for a ringing in his ears, seemed to be just fine. Fortunately, the grenade shock had torn the telepathic lattice from his head, though its smart-metal construction had kept it from coming to harm. Marduk dusted it off and handed it back to the former Magistrate.

"He shot a grenade at us," Danton said, sneering.

"Yes. I was there. It was all very exciting," Marduk deadpanned.

Danton's eyes glared up with a rage that surprised the Annunaki overlord. "That goddamn little toe rag fired a fucking grenade at me!"

"And what shall you do about it?" Marduk asked.

Danton set the lattice over his bald pate. Electric sparks crackled along the wire pathways that made up the web. Stunned and injured mutants, any with enough life to stand, did so, ignoring personal pain. They turned as one toward Marduk.

"This is supposed to impress me?" the Annunaki asked.

Danton remained silent, his eyes alive with a churning rage. The mutants turned and started toward the Crack. Relaxing his concentration, Danton glared at Marduk, the trickle of blood from his nose indicating the monumental telepathic effort he'd undertaken.

"I'm sorry," Danton grumbled. "I was just ordering the survivors to go after that slag-head and bring me his picked-clean skeleton. Were you saying something to me?"

Marduk shook his head. "Good work. Perhaps you should take it easy with the telepathic web."

Danton pulled off the latticework, stalking away toward his quarters. "Don't try to baby me, Marduk. I know what I'm doing to my body. But frankly, that's my decision. I didn't volunteer to have a gren fired at me."

"Well, then, there's no reason for me to fine-tune your command matrix if you're so willing to endure cerebral hemorrhage for the sake of revenge," Marduk spoke up.

Danton stopped, looking back at the overlord. "Tune it?"

"You're operating that device while it's been set for Annunaki brain waves. I've been amazed that your eyes haven't melted out of your skull," Marduk stated. "Perhaps you're just a little more evolved than these apes, a bit of Tuatha de Danaan in your family tree."

Danton shrugged. He held out the telepathic web for Marduk. "Then, sir, if you would, I'd be honored."

"And what do I profit from your increased power?" Marduk inquired.

Danton pressed the telepathic web into Marduk's claw. "Undying loyalty, and your enemies torn to shreds by the screaming hordes of hell."

Marduk caressed the smart metal with his fingertips, jew-ellike knobs forming at each juncture. His talons danced across the gemstones, each lighting up with a touch as he played a soft, eerie melody on the orbs. The lattice's gem-joints faded back to shimmering silver, as if a swelling had reduced.

He dangled the device before Danton. "Master of the Tartarus clones, prince of the underworld, I present you your crown."

Danton reached for it, but Marduk held it back.

"Thanatos is too limiting a name for you. You deserve a more appropriate title," Marduk mused out loud. "Hades, the brother of Zeus."

"Z00s isn't my brother," Danton snarled.

Marduk clucked his tongue. "That mere ape? Thurmond has as much in common with me as he had with you. I was Zeus when the monkeys of this land wore togas and branches in their hair. I alone have the right to name you my brother Hades."

Danton swallowed, a tear forming in the corner of his eye. The smart-metal lattice rested in his palm, and he slid it atop his clean-shaved skull. A thrum of energy pulsed through his body, and he felt connected to the world around him. A swarm of images flooded his mind, including visions of the fleeing Artem15 and Kane. He could even feel the thoughts of Kane, the man who'd fired upon him.

"Kane," Hades said out loud. The Cerberus explorer whipped his head around, hearing his name spoken. "Oh, yes. You heard me. I'm so much better now."

Hear this, Kane thought back. A flash image involving Hades engaging in intimate relations with livestock struck the web-enhanced being.

"Droll, Kane," Hades stated. "Perhaps my minions will reenact your little delusion before I allow them to kill you."

Kane fired the Copperhead over his shoulder, sweeping a crowd of mutants that had gotten closer to Artem15 and the Cerberus fighter.

"Too complicated," Marduk said. "Your link to other humans is tenuous at best, simply because you are more than they are."

Hades nodded. "I would dearly love to crush his mind."

Marduk rested his clawed hand on Hades's shoulder. "You will have to do that the old-fashioned way."

He concentrated for a moment as Nephilim warriors stepped out of the gigantic scout ship. "Clear away the wreckage of the skimmer and get the others into the air. It's time we stopped being nice and gentle."

The Annunaki nodded in unison.

"Allow me my chance," Hades pleaded. "With my new contact with the mutants, I will be able to operate more subtly."

"You have until the sun reaches its peak," Marduk allowed. "When that time comes, one of my enemies shall be dead, or I will take over."

Hades bowed before his master.

He reached out across the miles, searching for the proper tool.

HERA BROUGHT BRIGID before the device, an orb that stood on four vestigial legs. Brigid worked to keep her dinner down, recognizing the obscene, half-alive nature of the thing on the floor. To one side, a golden column, wrapped in steel rings at various points along its length and topped with an onion-shaped crown of platinum and clear gems. The column was as tall as Brigid and approximately four times that in length.

The tapered point itself was large enough to seat a human inside its gossamer-thin screens of platinum.

"The contingency," Brigid said.

"Skybreaker, the ancient records called it," Hera replied. "Given the nature of Zeus, and the Annunaki texts proclaiming Marduk and Zeus to be one in the same, this must have been the mighty thunderbolt crafted for him."

"Zeus was said to have a quiver full of thunderbolts," Brigid noted.

"There were other canisters similar to the one I'd found this in. However, even with the power of an Annunaki gear skeleton, I didn't have enough power to free the others like it," Hera noted. She glanced to Brigid. "Kane saw the countryside blown to hell by a powerful lightning weapon."

Brigid nodded.

"Did he see if they were humans or mutants who had been annihilated by my righteous vengeance?" Hera inquired. "Or could he simply not see because of the brilliant discharges set off?"

Brigid glared uncomfortably at the column, then its techno-organic counterpart. It wasn't often that the archivist had been thoroughly repulsed by any display, her curiosity usually inuring her against such emotions. Still, the warted skin and the freakish tiny feet that the orb rested upon got under her skin, unsettling her concentration.

"Baptiste?" Hera cut in.

"Sorry," Brigid replied. "He just saw bodies in silhouette."

Hera walked over to the knob of living technology, smartmetal armor flowing away from her fingertips so that she could rest her flesh against its unnatural hide. Brigid couldn't tell if it was the queen or her prized weapon that had twitched upon first contact, but she wanted to pull her weapon and fire upon them both. Given the nature of Hera's second skin, it would be a futile gesture with anything less than the far more powerful guns of Kane or Grant.

"Awaken, sweetheart," Hera whispered.

The orb flexed, cracks appearing in its alligator hide. Sticky mucus stretched between the lips of its skin, making stomach-churning slurping sounds with each movement as it attempted to awaken. Hera stepped away from the techno-organic weapon, the curved ball halves spreading apart, joined to the underbody by a veiny, gnarled joint. The circular cups flattened, starting to flap up and down in undulating waves of freakish vitality. The "skin" beneath the withdrawn wings was gray and mottled, resembling spongy growths akin to coral that she had seen photographs of in old *National Geographic* magazines. Blue marbles dotted the thing's skin, each flickering with a weak internal light.

Hera had strode over to the column, caressing a topaz the size of a dinner plate. As her fingertips ran across its smooth, dark surface, the giant gem's coloration changed, glowing with internal fire wherever she interfaced with it. The bulbous tip of the column hummed, the jewels lining the gridwork between the slender platinum screens lighting up under their own power. "I'd don some protective eyewear, Brigid."

The archivist fumbled in her belt pouch, drawing out the Moon base advanced optics, their polarizing lenses already darkening as the fierce fire within the heart of the minaret-shaped point grew in intensity. Brigid took a step back, her skin feeling dried out from the heat generated.

The flapping wings continued to flow as if they were banners animated by an autumn breeze. An arc of lightning shot between the point into the body of the drone, a writhing tendril of energy that was unbroken, no matter how its length twisted and bucked between the two parts. The wings began to move faster, and it rose off the four vestigial feet, the puny limbs slurping into its belly. The vibrating appendages whipped up a wind that picked up Brigid's red-gold hair and lashed it across her cheeks. She grimaced at the torrent that pushed on her body. Finally the throbbing umbilicus of electricity between the bejeweled column and the techno-organic abomination broke, the blue nodules embedded in its flesh throbbing with increasing brilliance and inner lightning.

Hera strode over to a second large gem, this one pyramid shaped. It had risen out of the body of the column. Brigid winced at the glow of the alien orb and the winds pouring off its strumming wings, her ears pounding with the reverberations of their vibrations. But between blinks, even behind her polarized glasses, she could see Hera making familiar gestures along the surface of the pyramidal stone.

"A Threshold?" she whispered, too soft to be heard over the brain-assaulting hum of the drone's wings. Brigid's suspicions were confirmed when tendrils of plasma energy surrounded the hovering abomination. It had to be an ancient Threshold device, the Annunaki's original means of global transportation between parallax points. In a flare, the Annunaki bioweapon had disappeared from sight.

"How…" Brigid began.

"Presumably how you had gotten here," Hera replied. "Through use of a parallax point here, I transported the drone to the oracle temple."

"How will it be recharged?" Brigid asked. She glanced toward the tip of the column, and realized that its contained glare showing through its platinum mesh darkened her polarized glasses, but only when she looked directly at it.

"Electrical energy is being broadcast to the orb. I believe that Nikola Tesla could explain the concept of broadcast electrical energy better than I could…" Hera began.

"I'm familiar with it," Brigid stated. "How much energy can that generate?"

Hera smiled. "Enough to power twenty of those orbs."

Brigid's skin twitched at the concept of the abomination having nineteen brothers out there. She gulped down a breath. "And this is capable of opening parallax points?"

"To better deliver the drones to where they are needed," Hera stated. "Marduk was a genius."

"He also wants to keep humanity in chains and on its knees," Brigid noted. "Or have you forgotten that he's sent an army of maniacs to your front door?"

"Unlike you, Baptiste, I have the ability to respect those who disgust me," Hera responded. "Especially when their weapons are so magnificent."

Brigid looked to the door, but realized that she had nowhere to go. She was trapped in New Olympus with a woman who was quickly getting drunk with unlimited power. And given that she could shrug off gunfire and unleash bolts of destructive energy from the ASP on her forearm, she wouldn't be completely mad if she felt herself unstoppably powerful.

Dread weighed on the archivist as a chuckling Hera strode past her. "Coming, girl?"

Brigid followed in silence.

Chapter 13

Domi had left Zoo in the command center, nervous energy dancing through her system. She was coming down from her adrenaline high, and she was looking for a distraction from the adrenal crash. Patrolling the ventilation maintenance bays gave her something to focus on, and allowed the feral creature inside her the potential for armed conflict.

The Praetorians had heard about the short albino stranger, and when she met with them, she was greeted warmly, with smiles, handshakes and clasps of her shoulder. She had shown concern for the disposition of their fallen brothers, not only avenging their deaths, but also wishing a kinder resting place for their bodies.

It was strange to be greeted as a hero, usually because she was more accustomed to standing at the edge of any group, observing with self-conscious silence.

"Hail Domi," one Praetorian spoke up as she arrived at their corridor. The barricade, made of sandbags and wooden frame, had one small aperture to walk through, and a long firing slit that commanded a complete view of the hallway beyond it. One of the armored Greek soldiers kept his eye on the slit at all times, even as the others took a break from their vigil to welcome the newcomer.

"Hey," Domi replied with a nervous grin. "How's everyone doing down here?"

"Well, if on edge," another Greek answered.

Domi lowered the sack she carried over her shoulder to the floor and dug in it, pulling out a box. "I brought you some biscuits and jam."

The Praetorian nodded. "You care for the living even better than the dead, Domi."

"If that were the case, I'd have brought you something to drink," she answered with a wink. "Thanks for the warm welcome."

"It is we who are honored," the first said. "You so cared for our people that you traversed the globe to fight not just the hordes of the Tartarus, but to ally alongside us in the face of a reborn god. Such courage is worthy of our greatest legends."

Domi shrugged. "It's something I would have done anyway. I ain't no hero."

"Which is precisely why you are a hero," the second said. "Many of us in New Olympus are believers in Hellenic lore. You and your companions seem to be molded from the fabric of Greek history itself. Kane being Theseus, the king and leader, as canny as he is physically powerful. Grant is Heracles, possessed of great strength and the compassion to use it for those less powerful than he. Brigid is the emulation of Athena, bringer of knowledge, as well as a goddess capable of fighting."

"And what am I? The little troll sidekick?" Domi asked.

"No," a third Praetorian told her. "You are your land's avatar of Artemis. It is just that you encountered our own Artemis. Your skin is the color of the moon, and your ease in the wilderness makes you a natural predator. Two daughters of the huntress had no choice but to find each other in the wilds of our land. It was Artemis's own hand that brought you together, and through that meeting, united Cerberus and New Olympus."

Domi thought about it for a moment. "A tidy little coincidence, tidy enough that it might have just come across the way you said it."

The first Praetorian patted her shoulder. "Thank you for your kindness and diplomacy."

Domi gave him a one-armed hug around his waist. "Naw. Thanks for being nice to me."

Something flickered in the firing slot, drawing her attention. Her ruby-red eyes locked on it, and she shoved hard against the leader of the group. "Get down!"

Domi's adrenaline kicked in midfall, and she could hear the individual thump-thump-thump of Sten machine pistol bullets firing, some smacking into the barricade, others sizzling through the air where she and the Greek had been standing a moment before. The other Praetorians followed her sharp warning with equal speed, but one of the men grimaced, a bullet creasing across his shoulder as he was a step too slow.

"Who's shooting?" the Greek Domi had driven to the floor called out.

"Muties," Domi replied.

"But…they're too stupid!" the one with the bullet wound gasped.

Domi drew her Detonics .45 and scurried along the floor to the shielded doorway. She glanced quickly around the barricade that protected the only entrance through the improvised wall and saw one of the Tartarus freaks reloading his machine pistol as another triggered his weapon. Domi whipped back behind cover, bullets hammering against the wooden slats. "Got smart. Coordinated."

"Dammit!" the first Praetorian snapped. Another man poked his Sten's muzzle through the slot and let fly with a spray of blind bullets. A mutant-aimed round slammed into the forearm of the weapon and tore it out of his grasp. Luckily, the slugs from the gun expended themselves sweeping the ceiling.

Domi activated her Commtact. "Domi to the rest. The mutants just got smart!"

"It's Danton," Kane answered. "The fucker got in contact with my mind, and he's got a howling mob hot on our heels."

"It has to be Marduk's doing," Brigid surmised. "He must have recalibrated whatever technology Danton was utilizing to command the clones from the vat."

"So they're smart enough to do what, exactly?" Grant asked. "Because the mob at the gates aren't exactly playing chess."

"Laying down suppressive fire like you and Kane do," Domi answered. "One reloads while other shoots."

"Okay, for goons that up until now only knew how to fire single-shot muskets, then use the thing as a club or a spear, that's bad fucking news," Grant replied. "But he can't do that with all of them."

"Not yet," Brigid replied. "Dammit, there's a firefight on this floor!"

"Kane, we need a miracle," Domi said.

"I'll work on it. Repel all boarders," Kane responded.

"If I can't," Domi replied, "I'll offer them biscuits and jam."

"Huh?" Kane asked as Domi turned off her Commtact. She whipped around the barrier and fired off a flurry of shots from her .45, knocking down one of the naked mutants, a pair of bullets opening up the creature's rib cage and hurling him backward. Even with the added complexity of Danton's mind guiding it, pure reflex swept the muzzle of his Sten gun across the back of a fellow clone. The wounded creature staggered out into the open, trying to deal with his injuries when a pair of Praetorians hammered it mercilessly with their rifles.

"Cover me," Domi called. She scrambled to the end of the corridor, reaching the shaft access in time to see another of the clones crawling through the hatch. Domi saved a bullet, drawing her sword and plunging it through the throat of the intruder. The creature gurgled, its lungs flooding with blood before gravity tore it free and hurled it down the intake vent. Domi poked her head in to see what was going on and saw that the dead Praetorians at the bottom of the air duct had been stripped of their weapons.

She plucked a borrowed walkie-talkie. "The muties grabbed the guns from the dead soldiers in the shaft!"

A gnarled hand lashed down, thick nails clawing at Domi's shoulder. The walkie-talkie was dislodged from her grasp. Domi tried to tear free, but the clone above her had applied a merciless grip. "Little albino bitch. Let's see how you like being thrown down a shaft!"

Domi stuffed her .45 up into the mutant's face, unable to get the sword through the hatch along with her. "Piss off, Danton!"

A pull of the trigger, and the faceless clone toppled away, snarled fingers tearing the collar by overstretching it. The creature's death grip had to have had enormous strength to have done that, and she could see her shoulder yellowing where the claws had dug into her flesh.

"Kill me once, shame on you," another mutant growled. "Kill me twice, shame on me."

Domi looked up to see a musket-wielding freak braced against the walls of the shaft, trying to level his primitive firearm at her. "Oh, fuck…"

Hands yanked her out of the path of the discharged ball, the air duct filling with black smoke. A Praetorian raked the interior of the vent with a spray of slugs from his Sten gun, and a procession of clones toppled past the open hatchway.

"They spoke," said the Praetorian who'd rescued her. "How could they do that?"

"Marduk," Domi answered. The access panel had been bent and torn, pried free from its moorings. From the cuts on its surface, Domi knew it had to have been those long, wicked bayonets. "We need something else to secure these hatches. Before, the muties didn't have the tool use and brain power to open them up. Now they do."

"Your walkie-talkie is at the bottom of the shaft," one of the Greek soldiers noted. "If you want, you can borrow—"

"No," Domi said. "What are you going to call for help with?"

She activated her Commtact again. "Brigid? Brigid, come in."

"Busy, Domi," Baptiste replied over the implant.

Domi grimaced. "Keep an eye on this hatch, and call for reinforcements."

The Praetorians saluted her as she raced back to the corridor.

A NEW STAR FLARED in the sky out over the finger of land where the oracle temple ruins remained. Kane spotted it blaze into existence, recognizing the curling clouds of plasma energy flowing off of it.

"Brigid…" Kane spoke up.

"You see it," Brigid answered. "I was going to warn you."

"The fused-out bitch is the one with the lightning gun?" Kane asked.

"That's one way I'd put it," Brigid answered, indicating she was in the presence of the aforementioned "fused-out bitch." "She looks under control, but those things are techno-organic."

"Partly alive," Kane translated.

"It also looks based on some form of life that's never been seen on this earth. It's like winged coral, and it can receive voltage from a power column here in New Olympus," Brigid stated.

"As if this day couldn't get any better. Danton gains supreme telepathic power, and now we've got some kind of alien monster ready to spit lightning," Kane muttered. "What next?"

A musket ball slammed between Kane's shoulder blades, but the microfibers of the shadow suit absorbed what could have been a backbreaking blow on his spine. Even so, it was a sufficient answer to Kane's question. "Marksmanship's gotten better, too."

Kane could hear the chatter of an automatic weapon transmitted over Brigid's Commtact, meaning that she had to be firing it, the vibrations traveling through her body. "What's going on?"

"We've had a breech in security. Danton's sent his mutants

in through the ventilation shaft," Brigid answered. "Domi's on her way down to help our floor out, so we can repel this bunch."

"Dammit!" the archivist spit loud enough to rattle Kane's teeth.

"Baptiste?" Kane returned.

"Sorry," Brigid answered. "We lost another Praetorian…."

"Reload and keep shooting," Kane ordered. "There'll be time to mourn when the enemy's dead."

"All right!" Brigid growled in return.

The firefly hovering in the sky whirled and swung through the night, blazing a trail of vibrant blue-white behind it. Kane plotted its trajectory, then turned back to see the mutant raiders closing in on the racing mechanoid's heels. Turning in his harness, he triggered the Copperhead for a long, ragged burst, but the front few hordelings collapsed, absorbing the majority of the bullets, allowing their brethren to continue on unabated, their clawed feet grinding the dead into the dirt without missing a step.

"What's going on back there? Who's a fused bitch?" Artem15 asked.

"Don't make me lie to you, lady," Kane answered, plucking an implode grenade from his pouch. He hurled it into the clot of charging mutants just as another musket ball careened off his helmet.

The implode grenade bounced twice, then went off. A vortex opened up, compacting a dozen pursuers into oblivion with its implosion. The problem was that there were scores of mutants, and the creatures filled in their lost ranks easily, howling death threats at Kane, mentioning him hatefully by name. Kane, still reeling from the bullet to his helmet, dropped another grenade into the charging creatures' path. "Thought you could move faster…"

"I could before I knocked my knee out of alignment jumping out of the Crack," Artem15 griped. "Maybe you'd like to get off and run by yourself?"

"I'm fine right here, just groggy," Kane returned. He watched as the swarming pack had another hole blown in its ranks by a second implode grenade. He figured that tossing it farther back, he would somehow disrupt them, but their telepathic taskmaster had been exacting in his orders, and nothing, not even personal injury, would slow the rampaging horde. Muskets rippled, bullets hammering against the mechanoid's back and Kane's stomach and legs. The shadow suit held under the hammering, but the volley of fire had knocked the breath out of him. The jarring impact of dozens of bullets knocked his Copperhead to the ground below.

"You stopped shooting?" Artem15 asked. Her head pivoted back, and she saw the stunned and staggered ex-Magistrate barely holding on.

"Kane!" Artem15 called, trying to awaken him.

"Just keep moving," Kane grunted. "I'll be fine."

Artem15 deployed one of her javelins from its quiver, then whipped it into the earth right in front of the swarm. Shrapnel and concussive force split the group in two, but compared to the power of the implode grenades, the javelin was even less effective. The two groups continued their mad, writhing trek across the ground, closing in on the hobbled warbot.

Kane sucked in a breath, manually pried his Sin Eater into action, and hammered off bursts into the group on the left. Artem15 spun and raked the hordelings on the right with her shoulder guns. The chattering weapons scythed through another ten, but hardly depleted the threat snapping at their heels.

"Flanking us!" Kane warned, his Sin Eater hammering away, smashing individual mutants to a pulp with heavyweight rounds, but doing little to disperse the amassed attackers.

Lightning chopped down from the heavens, a thick, fat, white-blue beam that churned through the snarling mutants, superheated ions turning their flesh to blackened char in instants. Kane looked up to see a glowing orb, odd wings hammering the air above it as it hovered above ex-Magistrate and robot. His polarized visor darkened so that he could continue to look at its blazing image, its studded body pulsing with the fires of heaven. More bolts crackled from its glimmering hide, searing through the rest of the creatures with lethal abandon.

"That what you had a nightmare about?" Artem15 asked.

"Do I have to ask the same about Marduk?" Kane countered.

"How did you know?" Diana asked.

"You froze. And you've been a fighting professional all this time. That had to be something right out of your worst dream," Kane replied as he watched the floating drone vomit electricity in writhing tendrils. Wherever the lightning stuck, bodies either disappeared in a superheated blaze, or carcasses were repelled by powerful electrical charges. By whichever means the mutant horde were dispatched, they weren't getting up.

"Hera kissed Marduk," Artem15 answered. "They were lovers."

"They actually were lovers back in Cobaltville," Kane

told her. "I was concerned that despite their changes, they were still going to be together."

"But the Tartarus clones..." Artem15 said. "They were Hera's servants."

"Don't let on that you suspect that," Kane replied. "At least until we learn for sure."

"You suspected that she was in charge of the mutants?" Artem15 asked. "Then why...?"

"We don't have any proof," Kane said. "It was just one of the possibilities that we discussed."

"So she was the one who made me into this..." Diana groaned.

"Keep it together, girl," Kane growled. "We've already been sent on one suicide run tonight."

"Two if you count the Crack," Artem15 replied.

"Just keep your head," Kane said.

The lightning drone finished its assault on the deformed mutants, bodies strewed across the countryside about them. Blackened limbs crumbled as breezes blew on them, and fires burned where incinerated corpses had lit the rough scrub on the hilltops.

"New Olympus to Artem15, are you two well?" Hera's voice called over the robots' frequency.

"I'm good," Kane replied. "Artem15's limping. Threw her leg out of alignment. Was that you?"

"The drone, yes," Hera answered. "I've been observing it in operation."

"You sure that you've got the only one?" Kane asked.

"Actually, there are more drones back in the Find," Hera stated. "I'm fairly certain that if Marduk frees them from the partial cave-in, he might be able to power them up. Why?

Concerned that I might get a little out of control with my knockout punch?"

"Just trying to figure out what the vision could have been," Kane said. "Though Baptiste did mention it might be a residual impression left by earlier tests of this weapon. Tests attributed to Marduk as Zeus fighting some horrendous monster, or you cutting loose with that thing on the thousands at the gates. The vision was vivid, but I've seen plenty of stuff that I've misinterpreted."

"It is of concern to me," Hera replied over the radio. "That kind of destruction could only have been implemented by a deranged, frustrated being. There's no guarantee that the column I retrieved is the only power unit for these drones."

"So what's the plan?" Kane asked.

"Gather with Grant and Are5 at the gates," Hera said. "I intend to demonstrate to Marduk who possesses the real power here."

"Fair enough," Kane said. "Right, Artie?"

"Yes," Artem15 answered haltingly. "We'll be there in five minutes."

"Don't tell me you're haunted, too, girl," Hera said over the radio.

"Just shaken up by the sight of Marduk," Artem15 said, folding her shock and betrayal into that. "It's not every day you run into a seven-foot alien."

"Just report, okay?" Hera asked.

"Fine," Artem15 answered.

There wasn't much conversation between man and mech-anoid on the way back to the gates of New Olympus.

Chapter 14

The throng at the hangar gates had grown agitated, and thanks to Kane's information, Grant knew it was because their master's telepathic link had given them access to more information. The scale-armored mutations were beginning to pick up on the rudiments of tool use, even without Danton at the controls, such as the small groups that had penetrated New Olympus. The buzz of wings, similar to the blades of a helicopter, roused Grant from his musings and he looked up to see a bloated distortion of a firefly hanging in the sky, a blue-white abomination that burned so bright that his helmet polarized in response to it.

"Holy shit," Are5 said. "That's what Hera's been keeping in reserve?"

"Still think Kane and I are the coolest?" Grant asked.

"Yeah. That thing looks like a cancerous testicle with wings," Are5 replied. "I'd rather hang out with the guys who've been to other planets."

Grant chuckled. "Kane and Artem15 should be here in a few minutes. She was slowed down by a knee malfunction."

"She gets emphatic when she's kicking the shit out of mutants," Are5 explained.

Grant nodded. "I'll see if I can figure out how to knock it into alignment, then."

"Cripes. First aid on me, then you're working on robots?" Are5 asked.

"All Mags know basic first aid. I have mechanic training because I'm a Deathbird pilot," Grant said. "It's not like I'm some kind of friggin' genius."

"Naw. Just saved my life, fly cool aircraft and punch out gods," Are5 returned.

"You keep this up, I'll put you in a backpack and carry you around." Grant laughed.

"Aren't you insufferable enough without a fan club?" Kane grumbled.

Grant glanced up to where Kane was perched on Artem15's shoulder, secured in place by a rope harness. "You look like you had fun."

"Loads of it," Kane answered. "Tackled by mutants. Shot up by muskets. Telepathically assaulted by Danton. Everything you'd ever want in a vacation to Greece."

"Don't forget hanging out with the local Greek chicks," Artem15 mentioned. "Even if their faces do look like the ass of a mutant."

"Diana, meeting you is the high point," Kane said, as he was lowered to the ground. He winced and limped to a boulder to sit down. Pulling off his helmet, he revealed a darkening bruise on the back of his neck, right where it had been pinched between headgear and his shoulders by a musket ball impact. Grant checked out the injury. "How's it look?"

"Nasty, but cosmetic. You can still move, so no spinal injury," Grant stated. He touched the back of Kane's head, eliciting a few winces. "Big baby…"

"Look who's talking," Kane grunted. "Gimme a couple aspirin."

"Not until I check for concussion," Grant returned, shining a penlight into Kane's eyes. They dilated normally, and Grant pocketed the light. "Okay. Take two pills and call someone who gives a damn in the morning."

Kane swallowed the aspirin dry. "Your bedside manner is incredible."

"We can't all be DeFore," Grant said. He walked over to Are5, who unhooked a war bag from a hanger on his hip joint. Grant put away the Barrett and took out an M-60 machine gun from the redoubt's arsenal. "Hera laid out the plan. We mop up what the drone doesn't hit."

Kane stretched out, knowing he'd be a mass of bruises by the end of the day. He retrieved the recoilless rifle from Grant's bag. "You brought everything for this."

Grant shrugged. "Since we were caching it, I figured we wouldn't have to worry about hauling around all the weight."

Are5 handed Artem15 back the javelins he hadn't used. "All I got are some rocks."

Artem15 glanced at the pile of medicine-ball-sized boulders stacked in a twelve-foot-tall pyramid. "Poor you."

"Yeah," Are5 replied. "Okay, this is Are5. All units are in position. Call down the lightning when you're ready, my queen."

Hera's voice cut over their radio network. "We've got aerial radar contacts heading to us from the Crack."

"Aerial contacts?" Grant asked.

"They had an Annunaki scout ship down there," Kane explained. "It had five skimmers. Four, once I blew one up."

"I'm getting fairly low on ammunition for my guns," Are5 said. "Skimmers…"

"Four contacts, heading for the drone," Hera said. "Scatter!"

Are5 scooped up two boulders as the firefly darted skyward. Two silvery disks flashed into view, swooping in light-
ning-fast arcs to chase their aerial target. "Oh, great. The
flying testicle versus the UFOs of doom."

"Flying what?" Hera asked. There was a gasp of exasperation. "Scatter!"

Energy bolts sizzled from the smooth-skinned Annunaki
skimmers, bolts chasing after the firefly drone in the night
above. Just as soon as they had discovered an advantage,
Marduk had countered it.

Grant grimaced, seeing the swarm of deadly mutants whirl
as one, staring up at the quartet of warriors. "We've got
company, too."

Kane pulled his helmet back on and shouldered the
ungainly weight of the recoilless rifle. "At least we won't feel
left out."

The teeming mass gave a unified, aggressive bark, then
charged, clawing up the cliff toward them.

MARDUK STOOD ON THE BRIDGE of his scout ship, his eyes
locked on the view screen that made up half of one wall.
Multiple displays were scrawled across the large monitor, one
an aerial display of the positions of the five craft currently in
the air, Hera's confiscated drone and Marduk's surviving
skimmers, as well as the forward cameras of his fighting
craft. His needle-sharp teeth ground against one another as
he watched the Skybreaker drone weave with uncanny agility
while his Nephilim pilots struggled to contain it.

"Just how the hell did she get so talented with that drone?"
Marduk growled.

"She's been practicing with it for seven years," Hades

stated. "There's some kind of teleportation module on the Skybreaker power column."

"Ah, yes," Marduk said. "The parallax generator. Another thing that I'd wanted back!"

The scout ship, psychically linked to the Annunaki overlord, shuddered in response to its master's fury. Hades staggered, trying to maintain his balance. He glared at Marduk. "It's hard enough to concentrate without you throwing an earthquake into the mix."

Marduk glared at the master of the clone hordes, then let out a soft sigh. "Remember whom you reproach, my friend."

"No offense meant, sire," Hades replied. "Sending thousands after four has proved challenge enough… Dammit!"

"What?" Marduk asked.

"Climb, damn you. Climb!" Hades commanded. The smart-metal webbing over his skull pulsed and flexed, intersections of its tendrils swelling into distorted, glowing jewels.

Marduk narrowed his eyes, paying close attention, but the human had not developed a nose bleed. Still, the concentration and information flowing between master and slaves was straining the power of the telepathic enhancement lattice.

Marduk looked back at his wall screen, just in time to see one of his skimmers disappear, sliced in two by a lightning bolt, its molten halves tumbling through the sky.

"Destroy that drone!" Marduk commanded. "You accursed simpletons! Kill it!"

The deadly dance continued in the night sky over New Olympus.

GRANT AND ARTEM15 THREW three streams of machine-gun fire down the slope of the mountain, but the gigantic horde clawed and scrambled up the mountainside. It was like trying to put out a fire by spitting on it. Sure, bodies tumbled, skidding down the incline, but the mutant monstrosities were so numerous that the only thing hampering their progress was the steepness of the ridge and the need for handholds.

Are5 and Kane had better luck, their boulders and 84 mm explosive shells snapping off layers of stone and creating miniature avalanches that carved through the surging horde. Even so, while the landslides pushed back dozens at a time, they didn't score large numbers of kills. Those dislodged from their climbs recovered and renewed their scrambling journey up toward the four defenders who continued their rain of destruction.

"We need to cause a bigger avalanche," Kane shouted. "Otherwise they're going to be on our necks in the next ten minutes."

Are5 pulled his thermal ax from its forearm housing. "Back off of the edge."

The fifteen-foot mechanoid dug his fingers into the ledge they stood on, then lowered himself down. With a long windup, he hacked the superheated blade into the slope. Stone split, starting to loosen. Artem15 pulled one of her javelins and launched it over the edge, arcing it down into the front rank of the snarling, climbing horde.

The detonation disrupted the swarm's climb, but only momentarily. The shrapnel and concussion were cushioned by mutant bodies too much to break off another avalanche. Are5 chopped again, splitting more rock, then called up to his robotic partner. "Diana, give me a swing forward."

Artem15 grabbed Are5's wrist, then lifted, moving him

another fifteen feet to the right on the slope. She didn't let go, anchoring Are5 to the ledge while he hacked at the cliff. Grant and Kane continued to apply their firepower to the livid slope full of mutations, slashing at the ever advancing horde.

"They're still coming," Kane said as Artem15 moved Are5 again. Kane and Grant had to scurry to get out of the female warbot's way, but quickly returned to their edge, harassing the climbing mutants. Grant had to back off and hooked another belt bag on to the side of his machine gun.

"I thought eight hundred rounds was going to be too much ammo," Grant said. "I'm on my last belt."

Kane emptied his Copperhead, then tossed it over the edge. The flying rifle caught a hordeling in the face, knocking him in a wild tumble over the heads of his brothers. "Guys, better pull your miracle…."

Are5 grabbed one of Artem15's javelins and spiked it into the crack with all the strength of his arm. The impact fuse detonated, concussive force sheering a slab of rock sixty feet wide and thirty feet tall from the face of the cliff. Are5 twisted as the avalanche tore the ground from beneath his feet, but Artem15 held on. Had it not been for the enormous strength of the gear skeleton, plus three tons of mechanoid anchoring her inches deep into the rocky ledge, the two robots would have hurtled down the slope along with the sheet of stone. Like a massive guillotine blade, it knocked outcroppings loose with ridiculous ease before it struck the first of the mutants.

"How much do you think that weighs?" Grant asked, watching the leading edge of the slab burst mutants apart, blood darkening the hurtling stone along its front.

"Think it really matters to them?" Kane asked.

Screeches of dying monstrosities rose in a crescendo as

tons of earth tore through the heart of the mob, and though the flat edge of ax-hewn rock left seething mobs on either side of its gory path of destruction, loosened rocks and boulders hammered into them. No progress was being made in the wake of the landslide that Are5 had engineered. Mutant corpses were smeared down the mountainside where the multiton missile had pulverized the naked clone creatures.

Are5 finally managed enough strength to scramble up on the diminished ledge. "Sorry I didn't get them all."

"It bought us a few minutes," Kane answered. "Artem15, our best bet is helping Hera out. We have to get those skimmers closer to us."

Artem15 looked at Kane for a long silent moment. Kane knew that the moment of indecision was born from the implication that her queen and savior was potentially a traitor and the reason for her slaughtered family. The robot pulled one of her javelins, and transmitted.

"Queen, bring the drone closer. We'll shake your enemies off!" Artem15 called.

Three hurtling silver disks tried to keep on the darting firefly's erratic path, its glowing body sizzling off sparks as it raced to keep out of the gunsights of the enemy fliers.

"How close?" Hera asked.

"Danger close," Artem15 answered. Kane and Grant didn't need to be told that "danger close" meant that there was a good chance that they could just as easily be hit by the drone as the enemy.

"Thank you, child," Hera responded. Kane didn't know what was going on in either woman's mind, but the Skybreaker drone plunged, dropping like a fiery rock.

A skimmer jolted violently, pouring off smoke. It had

been damaged when the firefly zipped out of the way, another Nephilim pilot firing at a target no longer there and instead damaging his wingman. The smooth mirror surface of the skimmer was marred, vomiting a flare of orange flame that trailed off into a cottony tail of smoke. The one craft had been slowed, crippled by Hera's superior maneuverability, but the other two Annunaki craft charged hard on the drone's heels.

"Come on," Kane said, shouldering the big pipe-shaped recoilless rifle again. He wouldn't have time to reload the single shot, so he'd need every reflexive edge that he could. The drone rocketed out of its power dive, making a perfect ninety-degree turn that would have shaken any other form of aircraft.

Unfortunately, the Annunaki skimmers' maneuverability was up to the task, one making the course correction perfectly to remain on the Hera drone's tail. The other skimmer skipped on the rock, denting and crumpling its lower level. The alien craft, despite its horrendous battering, continued to fly, slowed but still limping along. Kane focused on the one still in full-speed pursuit.

"Right down our throats, Queen!" Kane said. "I need a straight-on shot!"

"It's coming," Hera replied.

The blazing lightning drone rocketed past the quartet of defenders, followed by a hurricane torrent of wind. Kane fired the recoilless rifle, its 84 mm rocket-propelled charge leaping into the path of the speeding skimmer. Artem15 hurled her javelin at the same time, and the two explosive warheads hammered into the smooth disk.

The simultaneous concussion crumpled the front of the skimmer, denting it severely. At the speed it was moving, the sudden change in aerodynamics turned the once sleek and agile Nephilim flier into a tumbling mass of mangled metal, somersaulting over Kane and Artem15, missing them by yards after taking a bounce into the earth before them.

Are5 whirled and hurled one of his boulders with every ounce of force his hydraulic limbs could muster. Stone punched through the out-of-control chassis of the skimmer, tearing a hole through its superstructure. The final injury to the Annunaki craft was too much, a flare of smoke vomiting from the shredded wound. Another three skips on the hilltops, mirror skin peeling away like tinfoil, and the skimmer detonated in an ugly thunderclap.

Kane looked back, seeing Grant feed another 84 mm rocket into the breech of the recoilless rifle. He turned to focus on the battered skimmer that hadn't pulled out of its power dive in time. Moving at only half its normal speed, this was an easier target, and Kane punched the round into the dented, split belly of the racing flier. His shell reached the damaged ship at the same time that the Skybreaker drone belched a writhing tentacle of electrical fury at it. Bomb and bolt tore the hapless Nephilim craft asunder, fragments of the devastated craft fluttering to the earth in a glimmering snowfall of its polished skin.

An energy bolt slammed into the earth at Artem15's feet, cracking off a slab of the ridge they stood on. The warbot started toppling over the edge, but Are5 reached out, his metal claw fingers grabbing her gear-shaped shoulder gun mounting. Metal bent and twisted, deforming under its weight, but the decorative housing held in place.

"Climb!" Are5 ordered. "Climb!"

Artem15 dug in her toe claws, finding purchase in the crumbling stone beneath her, and she pushed away from a precarious, potentially deadly plummet. Down the slope, mutants screeched in complaint as rocks toppled onto them.

"Hera, we'll keep the last one off you. We need help!" Grant shouted. He fed the recoilless rifle another round, then scooped up his machine gun.

"I've got them," Hera answered. "Thank you…"

"Just burn those fuckers!" Grant pleaded over the radio. He shouldered his machine gun, leading the shot-up skimmer far enough so that the bullets would intersect the path of the hurtling Annunaki ship. The M-60 was at its extreme range to do much damage to the Nephilim transport, but it was enough to harry it, thanks to the gaping, burning hole in the side.

Kane fired the last round from his drain-pipe-sized weapon, watching the spiraling shell sear through the darkness. It flashed violently, but the blossom of detonation had struck solid bulkhead, not the damaged area. The blast ripped another smoky hole, but did nothing to hamper the flier's path.

The mountainside beneath them suddenly blazed, burning as bright as day as the Skybreaker scoured the rock with its stream of lightning force. Ionized air stank of burning mutant flesh, bodies detonating from the effects of superheating while sparks that split from the main trunk of skyfire stopped hearts wherever they struck. The Tartarus horde shuddered, devastated by the thirty-foot-wide spotlight of disintegrating power focused upon them. Sweeps of the beam hurled charred carcasses into the air to explode into clouds of ash and soot as they struck the ground below.

Kane looked at the nightmarish display of destruction raining upon the swarm that, only moments before, had been threatening to rend all of them limb from limb in an orgy of bloodthirsty violence. Seeing them reduced to screaming and dying pathetic freaks stunned him. Until now, the teeming multitude of flesh-rending monstrosities seemed unsympathetic. It took the firepower wrested from the vaults of Marduk for Kane to feel a pang of pity for the creatures as they were massacred wholesale.

The drone belched again, wiping more of the attackers off the slope, but the mutants had learned their lesson, or Hades hadn't wanted his multitude of marauders to be exterminated in one fell swoop. Scrawny forms scurried, scrambling for the cover of rocks, racing away from the battle scene.

"Is that it?" Artem15 asked weakly.

"The last skimmer is retreating from our airspace," Zoo announced over the radio.

The firefly bolted into the sky, arcing down toward the gates that had once been clotted with thousands of clones. The doors opened, a dozen Spartan units and scores of Praetorians racing to defensive positions in case any mutants had been hiding in reserve.

But the attack had been broken. All that they found were those bodies that remained intact, and the ankle-deep ashes of countless incinerated mutants.

"Hera?" Kane asked.

"She's resting," Brigid answered. "The strain of controlling the drone was too much for her."

Kane looked at his friends on the mountaintop. "We've got Marduk on the run."

Something glowed behind them and Kane turned, slowly, battered. He fisted his Sin Eater, expecting to see the blazing engines of the scout ship hovering behind him, or the detonation of an enormous explosion.

Instead, it was the sunrise, the dawn burning with the promise of a new day.

The enemy had been routed.

Grant slipped his arm under Kane's. "Come on. Let's get down to New Olympus."

Kane nodded. The past few hours had taken its toll on him. Sleep in a soft bed would be just what he needed.

DOMI WAITED IN THE HANGAR as Artem15 and Kane limped through the gates only a little more slowly than Are5 and Grant. All four of the warriors who had journeyed to the oracle walked down a gauntlet of saluting Spartan units and Praetorian soldiers. Each strode in under his or her own power, despite the hammering of the desperate battle they had waged.

Grant gave the albino girl a fatherly hug, smiling at her. "I heard you saved the day in here."

"Not as well as I could have," Domi admitted. Grant could tell that she was going over whatever mistakes she had made against the intruders. Her shoulder was wrapped in an elastic bandage.

"What happened?" Grant asked.

"I thought the mutie had only ripped my collar, but I tore a muscle pulling out of its grip," Domi answered. "You all right?"

"I didn't take half the pounding that the others did," Grant admitted. "Lucked out for once."

"Marduk's still alive," Domi returned.

Grant sneered at the prospect. "Not for long, if I get my way."

"You will," Z00s said. "If you're up to it."

While Grant had caught a glimpse of the golden-bearded titan who led the Pantheon of hero warriors for New

Olympus, it was in the form of an empty suit, not the powerful incarnation of mechanical godhood that stood before them.

"Right now, I've been busting my ass to the oracle and back. I'm not as beat up as the rest of my team, but I sure as hell don't have the stuff to go out for round two," Grant apologized.

Z00s nodded. His robot seemed larger than the Spartan units, and even the hero suits seemed slender and weak in comparison. His golden chest sparkled and gleamed despite the scuffs and scratches that had never seen the need for spot welding to repair a punctured breastplate. Grant's eyes narrowed at the sight of the worn but otherwise perfect armor.

"Is that steel?" Grant asked.

Z00s nodded. "It was scrap that we had available in the Find. I wish that I could have evacuated more of it to New Olympus during the takeover. It would have made for so many fewer funerals of my friends here."

Grant took a deep breath. "Sorry. I didn't mean anything."

Z00s glanced to his fellow robot warriors. "That's why I lead from the front, and why I undertake espionage missions alone. Mine is the most durable of all the gear skeleton armors. I'd be remiss if I didn't take the most risks."

"It would be an honor to fight alongside you someday," Grant offered by way of apology.

"As I would be to fight alongside you," Z00s replied. "All right, team! Make a hole and make it wide for these heroes!"

Z00s stood aside. He led the other New Olympian defenders in a standing salute as the battered Cerberus warriors and their mechanoid allies passed by.

Kane, leaning against Brigid, rested his head against hers. His helmet hung from his fingers, and he could smell her fiery hair, an intoxicating scent he'd never believed that he would experience again.

"If you keep that up, people might get ideas about us," Brigid said.

Kane smiled. "Baptiste, maybe just let me have a few happy, quiet moments for once?"

Brigid nodded. "Sure. You earned it."

"What happened here?" Kane asked softly.

"Hera bonded with the Skybreaker drone. She wasn't in the command center with us," Brigid replied. "Though her smart-metal armor kept us in communication with her at all times."

Kane frowned as they walked along. "She's got a communications network in that thing?"

"Among other technology. Frankly, she keeps it a jumble, so it's hard to discern which is which, but I wouldn't be surprised if she had other technology that she's keeping from the rest of her people," Brigid responded. "I also noted that an Annunaki Threshold device was in the structure of Marduk's power core. It transported the drone to the oracle ruins."

"I guessed that when I saw the light show at the temple," Kane mentioned. "Remember when we were talking about whoever played Zeus in ancient times building his own bad guys?"

"I never forget anything," Brigid answered. "You had a conversation with Artem15 about the possibility that Hera might be manipulating events to keep her in power?"

Kane nodded. "The thing is, she had nightmares alluding to Helena Garthwaite's relationship with Baron Cobalt."

"Which was no surprise. It was a rumor around Cobalt-ville for a long time," Baptiste responded.

"She also saw the Tartarus mutants as Hera's minions," Kane said.

"So what accounts for Danton's change of heart, throwing everything he had against New Olympus?" Brigid inquired.

Kane shrugged with his free shoulder. A Praetorian wheeled a chair up to the pair.

"Kane, favored of Theseus, please, rest," the Greek soldier said.

"Favored of who?" Kane asked.

Brigid managed a chuckle, maneuvering the exhausted and bruised Kane into the wheelchair. "Some of the soldiers here, believers in classical Hellenic lore, have taken to calling us the avatars of the gods. Brothers of the warriors who fight here at New Olympus."

"So who's Theseus?" Kane asked. "Was he good-looking?"

"According to the myths I recall, his ass is as narrow as yours," Brigid said with mock admonition. "Mainly because half of his butt was left behind in Hades, the Greek hell, when his best friend Heracles pried him from an ensorcelled bench. But he was the thinking man's Greek hero, as smart as he was strong."

Kane looked to the Praetorian. "Is what she's saying true?"

"In layman's terms, yes. But Theseus is much more beloved for his truly selfless acts of courage and cleverness," the Praetorian said. The soldier gestured toward Brigid. "She is Athena, the battling goddess of wisdom, born from Zeus's brow in full battle armor."

Kane remembered one of the first instances he had seen Brigid Baptiste, clad only in a damp towel. "Well, she was ready for battle."

Brigid's cheeks reddened. "You say another word, and I'll take the other half of your ass, Kane."

Kane made a pantomime of locking his lips with an invisible key, then tossing it aside. "Home, James. Or wherever you're putting us up for the night."

"As you wish," the Praetorian answered, glancing at Brigid again.

The archivist shook her head in embarrassment.

Chapter 15

Diana rolled toward her lonely, simple quarters in her wheel-chair, dread enveloping her like a choking cloud of smoke. She didn't want an iota of human contact, but something tugged the handle on the back of her chair, impeding her process.

"Wait," Domi spoke up. "I wanted to talk to you."

Diana winced, pulling down a curtain of strawlike hair to shield her scars from view. "I'm sorry. I'm very tired and really do not want to talk."

"Is that really it?" Domi asked, walking alongside her chair, letting go as a courtesy to the amputee pilot.

A lone green eye glared out from under her bangs. "Do I really need to tell you, if you're so damn insightful?"

"No, you don't need to say a thing to me," Domi responded. "At least in terms of explanation. But I did want to talk to you."

Diana slowed the chair. "About what?"

"Whatever you wanted to," Domi said. "It's not like I have a lot of people to identify with."

Diana's shoulders sagged. "You identify with me."

Domi nodded. "Okay, we couldn't be twin sisters. I look like a lab rat and always have, and you look normal."

Diana chuckled. "You're shitting me. This is normal?"

She tugged aside her hair, and Domi got a close look at the fused half mask of skin that covered the right side of her face and her forehead like a dried puddle of wax. Domi shrugged with the display. "To be honest, I used to make a living sleeping with guys more messed up than you. Gelatinous tentacles are the worst I've had to endure."

Diana let her hair fall over her face. "So we're both freaks."

"No. We both have trouble fitting in," Domi corrected. "We're strangers in the places we call home. You avoid your coworkers, unless you're inside your armor. I tend to take long hikes in the wilderness when things get to me."

Diana remained silent for a moment. When she spoke, her voice sounded choked. "It's kind of hard to feel like my coworkers are family. Especially now."

"What family do you have?" Domi asked.

Diana's green eyes met hers. "My parents and brother were murdered by the mutants. And for the past seven years, Hera has been like my mother. That'd kind of make ZOOs my father…but before you came…"

Domi took a seat on the floor. Diana paused, then realized that the albino girl was just getting a little more level with her in the chair. It was easier for Diana to look down from her chair. The amputee grinned.

"What?" Domi asked.

"No one has ever done that for me," Diana replied. "Usually it's just eye to eye with the other wheelchair jockeys, or they stand over me."

Domi scratched her nose. "I know what it's like being the shortest in the room. Sometimes it gets to be a headache."

"Thanks," Diana said. "It's not like they treat us bad, and I do have some privileges since I'm a hero pilot…."

"But you're still the sore thumb," Domi said. "Like me. Bad enough I'm some sawed-off albino, but I'm from the Outlands. I was raised there, at least for a few years. Don't remember what happened to my family after a while. I just ate what I could catch and wandered, avoiding the radiation zones until I found myself in the Tartarus Pits under Cobaltville."

"Eating what you could catch?" Diana asked. "Like what?"

"Scorpions. Snakes. Rabbits," Domi answered. "Running for my life from bigger predators."

"A regular Artemis yourself," Diana mused.

"That's what the Praetorians are calling me," Domi said. "They called us sisters. You and me."

"We're not related. I never had a sister," Diana told her.

"I don't remember if I had one, but not that way. Not sister by blood. Sister by spirit. Kind of inspired by the same goddess," Domi explained.

Diana tilted her head, her hair hanging away from the scarring on her cheek. "Avatars of Artemis."

"Brigid's been telling me stories about her, and except for that deal with the one guy who saw her naked, we do kind of have a bit in common," Domi explained. "Just like you and me. We're both uncomfortable with crowds. We keep to ourselves. We like being alone and in the middle of nowhere."

"Yeah," Diana said.

Domi shrugged. "As far as I know, I never had a sister, and you never had a sister. But the soldiers here, they all seem to think we're family."

Diana rubbed one eye. She was getting tired, but now she was no longer in a hurry to drag herself into her cot and doze off in silence and solitude.

"Want to get some coffee?" Diana asked the albino.

"You paying?" Domi countered.

Diana grinned. "It's free for the hero pilots."

Domi got to her feet. "Sounds good, but there's got to be something I can mooch off you now. Got a stereo?"

"Nope," Diana returned.

"I'll have to look for one for you when I get back to Cerberus," Domi replied, taking the handles of her chair. "Oh, and which way to the coffee?"

"I'll steer, you push," Diana said.

"Sounds good to me," the albino said, guiding the wheelchair through the halls.

ZOOS LED THE WAY, showing D10nysus and Apo110 how to make the descent into the crack. They chose to leave Her47les and P05eidon with the rest of the Spartan units on the ledge of the Crack, simply because ZOOs wasn't certain if the cliff walls would have the strength to handle a dozen robots bounding from stone face to stone face. If they all made the journey at once, there was a possibility that they'd all meet in a mangled pile of metal a mile down, buried in shattered rock.

Landing at the bottom, Zoo, Dion and Pollie scanned around for signs of mutants. All they could see in the distance was the scattered debris of the skimmer sabotaged by Kane on his previous journey. "Pollie, wait here. Herk, you read me?"

"Loud and clear," Her47les answered.

"Lead two of the Spartans down here. Pollie and I are going in, and we might need the backup," ZOOs stated. "Once Herk's down, Donnie, it's your turn."

"Roger that," P05eidon confirmed.

"Remaining Spartans, weapons free. Any hostiles, you hose them down until there's nothing left," Z00s ordered.

Apo110 took a tentative few steps into the cavern. "Still nothing on infrared."

"They lost too many mutants to pose much of a threat," Z00s rationalized. He took the lead, keeping one of his "thunderbolts," cosmetically jazzier versions of Artem15's javelins, in claw. If there was any sign of a threat, he'd turn it to paste with a well-thrown warhead.

He also knew full well that the real purpose of this trip was to assassinate the traitorous Danton before he spilled any information about the real nature of the conflict between New Olympus and the Tartarus clones. He was split, not wanting to endanger his fellow pilots, but Hera had been insistent.

"Leave nothing alive," Hera whispered, recovering in her bed. Naked, her silver armor retracted into the nodule between her shoulder blades, she was a magnificent sight atop her covers. Zoo had to fight his base desires, listening to her orders rather than concentrating on her smooth, soft curves.

"We're pretty quiet for a scorched-earth mission," Apo110 said.

"You want to make more noise?" Z00s inquired. "Wake up a swarm of cranky Nephilim who have at least one spaceship with working guns?"

He heard Pollie's sigh over the radio. They weren't using their speakers, maintaining at least some form of operational silence as they stalked in the darkness. "Point taken, fearless leader."

Zoo snorted in derision. "Fearless? I don't know about you, but I'm about ready to lay cable in my cockpit."

"One word," Apo110 replied. "Gross."

"It's not there," Z00s noted.

"What's not?" the warbot of the Sun asked.

"There was a much larger craft, back along that wall," Z00s explained. "It had been surrounded by mutant corpses."

"No bodies on the ground," Apo110 added.

"They're there," Z00s corrected. "They're just blown ash. Dammit."

"You mean the big spaceship took off? Why didn't we see it?" Apo110 asked.

"Probably because once it was out of the crack, it stayed close to the mountaintops," Z00s mused. "Strike Force to New Olympus command. Crack has been emptied. Repeat, Crack emptied. I need confirmation of radar contacts in the air."

"There was a weather anomaly before," central control responded. "We assumed it was a cloud due to its size."

"Say, about 250 feet in length, but only 50 feet tall?" Zoo asked.

"Radar contact was not that large. And it bore no resemblance to the skimmer," command replied.

Zoo grimaced. "Some form of low radar profile."

"Well, the Cerberus people did say they only detected the ship because of the atmospheric disturbance it left behind," Apo110 mentioned. "We should ask Brigid Baptiste about that disturbance, see if she can correlate it with the radar records."

"I'm here," Brigid's voice came over the radio. "They're replaying the footage now."

"So Marduk's run away with his tail between his legs?" Apo110 asked.

"It's unlikely he's gone far," Brigid noted. "Look around to see if the vaults remain secure, or if the reason he held his Nephilim in reserve was that he was loading cargo aboard his ship."

"He made off with all the secrets of the Find," Zoo said. He felt his stomach turn at the possibility.

"Which is far worse than we could have imagined," Brigid told them. "No, the atmospheric disturbance is not the same. What we picked up was a transonic deceleration accompanied by the heat of reentry. The appearance on radar simply had to do with a reduced-profile aerospace craft taking flight, then dropping under detection."

"Well, Marduk's still in town," Apo110 said. "Whether that's good news or bad news is anyone's call."

"Herk. Donnie. Get your teams over here now. I want full spotlight illumination," Z00s ordered. "Scour the cave for any signs of technology. You see anything resembling a live mutant, you kill it. See anything that looks like a booby trap, you back the fuck off and call me."

"You're going to defuse the bomb?" Apo110 asked.

"No, but if I set it off, I've got the armor to survive the blast," Z00s explained. "You trigger a bomb, we'll need a hose to get you out of your cockpit."

"Yuck," Apo110 groaned.

"Yeah. You think I wanna see that? Imagining it's bad enough," Z00s noted. "Turn it upside down, troops! Time's wasting!"

The squadron of mechanoids, spotlights flaring, searched Marduk's private vaults. Aside from locked chambers, they found little of the overlord or his clone master. Z00s in particular, familiar with the cavern, knew that the clone production vats were long gone. With them, he had the ability to create armies of creatures for which Marduk had the DNA map. All of that power was now in the hands of a foiled, vengeful god.

"ZOOs to base," he called over his radio. "We've got a bad, bad problem."

KANE'S EYES OPENED from his brief nap. A heating pack tucked beneath his long brown hair spread its healing warmth through the massive bruise on his neck. It appeared that he'd stripped down naked to sleep, despite being fairly certain that Baptiste had been present for part of his preparations for bed. Or perhaps that thought was simply a delusion formed by the painkillers flooding his system. Throwing his legs over the side of the bed, he began to rise, then suddenly froze in place, surprised to see Hera standing in the doorway.

"Uh, hi," Kane said awkwardly.

"Hello, Kane," she answered. It was a moment before he noticed that the queen of New Olympus was wearing a strapless, shimmering silver gown, strikingly different from her usual body-hugging liquid armor. The smart metal spilled down her body and pooled at her feet with elegant ease. Her short black hair lay wet against her forehead, and she smelled as if she'd just come from the shower.

"I think you're in the wrong room," Kane suggested.

"Zoo is busy. You're not," Hera said simply taking a few leisurely steps toward the bed. "Besides, he's my consort, not my king."

"Does Zoo know that?" Kane asked, pulling the sheet over his lap. A flirtatious smile lifted one corner of Hera's mouth as her gown shone faintly with its own soft light, caressing her creamy skin, melting away to reveal even more of her long, smooth legs.

"Yes. Our relationship is open. Zoo may be with any woman who takes his fancy, and I any man who takes mine," Hera explained gliding across the room to stand beside the bed. The smart-metal fabric had shifted again, and now she stood before him clad in narrow strips of silver that only just covered her crotch and slid enticingly up her body to enhance more than conceal the pert thrust of her nipples.

"Do I look good to you?" she asked, her voice a husky whisper.

Kane rubbed his forehead. "If I weren't covered with a sheet, you wouldn't be asking that."

"Why are you so shy?" Hera asked, reaching out to lightly trail the fingers of one hand along his shoulder. "We're adults, Kane. It isn't as if you have any special relationship with Baptiste, is it?"

Kane glanced up at her. The mention of Brigid had caused the muscles in his back to tense momentarily. "Your Honor…"

"Majesty, if you must be formal," Hera teased.

"Hera," Kane said. "I'm not in top condition right now."

"I've always been a strong believer in the healing potential of vigorous lovemaking," Hera countered, and in one graceful motion she slipped onto the bed and eased onto his lap, straddling him. The sheet pinned between their thighs did little to disguise the heat of her arousal. Sleek, deceptively delicate looking arms rested on his shoulders, her smoldering gaze meeting his. "And as not only the queen, but the head doctor here at New Olympus, you really should listen to your doctor's orders."

Kane cleared his throat. The image of Hera, her physical assets more than evident, and the warmth of her skin against his fought their hardest to distract him from his suspicion of

Hera's involvement in directing the Tartarus mutants against New Olympus. No matter how magnificent her body, no matter how much pleasure the heat of her sensual flesh promised, there was still the potential that she was a mass murderer, complicit in unleashing the Tartarus clones against the very people she'd claimed to be protecting.

Still, mass murderer or not, the gentle touch of her fingertips, trailing down his chest and gliding along the tight muscles of his stomach before stopping to tug gently at the edge of the sheet that covered him, quickened his breath and brought a light sheen of moisture to his skin.

Kane wished desperately for a means out of this particular moral dilemma, even as Hera's full, silky lips brushed across his, her tongue tracing his stubbled jawline back to his earlobe.

There was a rap at the door, and Kane clenched his eyes shut.

"Kane, do you know where—" Baptiste's voice cut into the room. Sarcasm dripped from the next words out of her mouth, and he could feel her eyebrow arching on her smooth, fair forehead. "Oh. I was just looking for you, Hera. I didn't expect…to see so much of you, though."

"She's naked, isn't she?" Kane asked. He could feel his cheeks reddening with embarrassment.

"Depends upon your definition," Brigid offered. Kane kept his eyes shut.

There was a moment of silence as Hera crawled out of his lap. "What's the problem, Brigid?"

"Marduk has taken several chambers worth of technology from the Find," Brigid told her. "He's loaded it aboard his scout ship and moved. We don't think he's left the island, but he is no longer in the Tartarus Crack."

"This has been confirmed?" Hera asked. Kane finally opened his eyes, and the goddess-queen of New Olympus was in her standard silver-skinned form, every inch of her body, apart from her face, coated in a millimeter-thin layer of shimmering liquid metal. From the experience of a few moments ago, he knew full well that her voluptuous figure had not been enhanced by the smart metal one iota.

"ZOOs and his team have scoured the entire cavern," Brigid answered. She looked at Kane, who tucked more of his sheet around his waist.

"Ladies, could you discuss this somewhere else, at least until I get a pair of pants on?" Kane asked. He scanned the room, but unfortunately, couldn't find even a discarded pair of sweatpants available to tug on under his sheet.

"Well, I didn't intend to interrupt anything," Brigid said in a tone that dropped the temperature in the room by thirty degrees. "However, if you're up and about, we would like to have the both of you in central command."

"We'll be there shortly," Hera promised.

Kane dragged his sheet along with him, hunting for his shadow suit. "Very shortly."

Hera tilted her head, mischief flickering in her dark eyes as she looked at his groin. "Aww. Would you like me to help with that?"

Kane grimaced. "Some days it doesn't pay to get out of bed."

Brigid spun on her heel, exiting Kane's quarters, leaving him alone again with the queen. He could hear Brigid's snort of disdain even as the door snapped shut. He released a sigh of exasperation. Hera smirked at him, her fingertips drawing down the centerline of her metal-clad body. In their passage, the smart metal molded and folded apart, breasts easing free.

"Where did they put my clothes?" Kane asked.

"I put them in the dresser drawer beside your bed," Hera answered, her voice deep and husky. "I didn't think that you'd have to cover up all that magnificence so quickly."

"Thanks," Kane said, turning and crawling over the mattress. There was a rush of air behind him, then delicate fingertips tracing down between his buttocks, one nail gently describing a line down all the way...

Kane whirled and took Hera's wrist firmly but gently. "Your *Majesty,* if you please."

"I thought I was pleasing," Hera replied. "I know I was pleased."

Kane sighed. "Trust me. If we had the time..."

"So, the little redheaded bookworm does have some hold on you," Hera said with an amused chuckle. "That what's keeping you from sealing the deal here?"

"Mainly an emergency involving Marduk running around with a 250-foot-long spaceship and Annunaki technology," Kane answered.

Hera leaned in closer, her red, full lips inviting. "Is that the only reason? Unfulfilled relationships and seven-foot gods?"

"That's not enough for you?" Kane asked, releasing her wrist. He scooped up his shadow suit and headed for the bathroom, avoiding eye contact with Hera every step of the way. Through the door, he could hear her chuckle.

"Seems as if you recovered magnificently from your prior problem," Hera noted. "See you in central command."

When Kane finally pulled the high-tech bodysuit into place and exited the washroom, Hera was gone, as well, though Grant was standing in the doorway.

"What now?" Kane asked.

"Just wondering what's keeping you." Grant asked.

"Getting dressed, if that's okay," Kane muttered, pushing past his partner into the hall.

"Oh. Because from the sound of things, I thought it was something else." Grant chuckled, then broke into an imitation of Brigid's voice. "Kindly tell your partner that new information has come to our attention."

Kane winced. "It's not enough that you're miserable. You have to have everyone else be like you."

"Misery loves company." Grant laughed. He gave Kane a soft punch in the shoulder. "Besides, I want details."

Kane grimaced, making a beeline to central command. "Just does *not* pay to get out of bed some mornings!"

Grant chortled behind him all the way to the control center.

HADES LOOKED OUT A PORTAL, watching small lemon sharks dart and coast past in the crystal-clear waters that had rushed in when Greece broke apart under seismic trauma. A smile crossed the clone lord's lips, staring out into the beautiful inlet.

"You seem pleased," Marduk said.

"Why shouldn't I be, master?" Hades replied, still marveling at the display of aquatic life. Before he could complete his statement, a school of small, gem-bright fish darted past. "We're alive. You have the clone vats, and thus the means to propagate your life, and the rebirth of lost brothers, sure to be in your debt. Hera has command of only one Skybreaker drone. And…for the first time in years, I'm seeing beauty."

Marduk glanced at the oceanic vista, nodding in agreement. "One Skybreaker drone is still sufficient to cause grievous harm to this craft."

"I'll work upon that, sire," Hades responded. He turned to the overlord. "I managed to secure some DNA that might be useful to our cause. It was part of the artifacts that I'd specifically requested be placed aboard the ship."

"Oh?" Marduk raised an eyebrow quizzically. "What do you have in mind?"

"This lattice enables me to telepathically communicate with the clones, thanks to a special matrix that the replicator implants in their nervous system," Hades said. "What if I were able to utilize cloned genetic material from a specific enemy to form a bridge between my mind and theirs? And what if, thanks to this specific psychic bridge, I were capable of wresting back control of Skybreaker?"

Marduk's eyes widened, his lips turning up in a smile. "You have Helena's genetic material? What made you think to save it?"

"We're working in mass production of clones," Hades answered. "I'd made a few…imperfect copies and had eventually given up on the process. However, the telepathic web has increased my ability to work with the replication vats. I am quite certain I am able to finesse the process to the point that I can make a usable entity."

"If you could do that," Marduk said. "Skybreaker would be useless without the broadcast core."

"You have the computer records necessary to rebuild it," Hades noted. "And how much better would it be to have New Olympus hoisted on its own petard?"

Marduk laughed. "To think, before the fall of man, the most feared wrath was that of a woman scorned. And today, you show the wrath of a man scorned by a woman."

Hades bowed his head to his overlord. "Your will be done."

The clone master stepped away with one longing glance out the window. Soon he'd be able to gaze upon beauty across the globe, so long as his plan was a success.

Chapter 16

The New Olympian briefing room was packed, wall to wall. Even Spartan pilots not assigned to guard duty were on hand, as well as Praetorian unit commanders. The mechanized sentry jockeys who weren't present were hooked in thanks to a communication simulcast that transmitted to their armors.

It was the largest audience that Brigid ever had to address, especially since the broadcast would be relayed to Greek townsfolk over the loudspeakers on the Spartan war suits. She glanced to Hera. "I'm not certain if it's such a good idea to make this an open meeting."

"Baptiste," Hera addressed her. "Right now, my nation is being threatened by powerful forces. I would be remiss if I didn't alert my citizens to the danger that is looming over them. Would you keep secrets from the population of Cerberus?"

"I'd try to keep my concerns secret from my enemies," Brigid answered.

Kane sneered at the thought. "Marduk's a conniving bastard, but even if he was listening in, we're not discussing response tactics. We're talking about the threat that he represents. Besides, I'm sure that the snake-faced bastard is busy with his own preparations for the next phase of this fight."

Brigid regarded Kane's words, then looked back to Hera, who sat on the other side of him. For a moment when Kane rested his hand on the podium, his fingertips brushing Brigid's. It was the barest of contacts, but it was enough to form a bridge between the two. Brigid nodded, a tight-lipped smile stretching her mouth. Kane returned the smile. The archivist glanced at Hera. The queen might have thrown herself naked at Kane, but the former Magistrate would never let Brigid down. When it came to what mattered, Kane's loyalty to her was unshakable, as was her loyalty to him. Bolstered with his strength, she started her address.

"This morning, Z00s and his detachment made their descent into the Tartarus Crack," she said. From there, she had the rapt attention of the New Olympians, and she wove a tapestry of relevant data into the image of an apocalyptic battle that threatened shattered leftovers of Greece. "When they searched the old facility they discovered that it had been scoured of several pieces of technology, including the clone vats responsible for siring the Tartarus mutants, as well as the ancient Annunaki analog computers from which Hera had gained her knowledge. Given that it is highly possible that Marduk has improved Danton's interface with the computer system via a telepathic neural lattice, akin to a Tuatha de Danaan teaching system we discovered, Danton has grown far more dangerous, unlocking genetic formulae for alternate life-forms, not limited to Nephilim."

Brigid paused. She directed their attention to the screen, which currently showed digital imagery that she'd had transmitted over from Cerberus's computer files. "Marduk currently possesses the power to reinstate the overlords, creating new bodies for their ancient genetic memories to download into. With a revived Supreme Council, and the capacity to generate hordes of the Nephilim soldier drones, not just Greece, but the whole world would be vulnerable to conquest."

Dion, the pilot of D10nysus, raised his hand. "You mentioned when you first arrived that the Annunaki Supreme Council was not as homogeneous a force as you had originally thought. They seemed to distrust each other to the point that they made attempts on one another's lives."

"Correct," Brigid answered. "Lilitu had attempted a coup, but the effort resulted in severe losses among the Annunaki. They also lost the living ship *Tiamat,* as well as the significant resources held within her enormous frame."

Brigid pointed to the screen. "If he were to seek the advantage of the clone vats to himself, Marduk could retain the technology to insure his own immortality. This way, he'd be the undisputed superpower among the Annunaki, unwilling to share with the other surviving overlords, if there had been any. However, considering Hera's demonstration of Skybreaker, the genetic production capacity that Marduk possessed wouldn't be limited merely to the Nephilim or replacement bodies, but also to techno-organic monstrosities like the flying drones, capable of absorbing intense charges into their bodies like capacitors and utilizing them as devastating offensive weapons."

"They are very powerful," Donnie, the commander of P05seidon, mentioned. "The preliminary casualty counts showed a death toll in the hundreds just from the lightning blasts of the biotechnology drone. However, since many of the bodies were completely reduced to carbon ash, we only have a vague estimate of 850 dead for a minute of bombardment."

Z00s nodded. "I had double-checked the chamber where

Hera had discovered Marduk's weapon, and the other nineteen constructs had been removed. I was hoping that we'd be able to increase our firepower, but we're out of luck on that front."

Brigid changed the screen image to camera footage of the vaults taken by ZOOs's team. "Given the partial roof collapse that buried and rendered their containers immobile, it was also likely that Marduk could have discovered a damaged broadcast unit hidden under the rubble of the vault. Either way, Hera's sole advantage over the lone overlord is a fleeting one, so discovery of his scout ship is of paramount importance. Currently, Praetorian teams are engaging in low-profile shore patrols. Given the fact that Marduk's scout ship is spaceworthy, and the lack of sufficient hiding places aboveground, it's our assumption that Marduk and Danton have gone underwater."

Brigid pointed out on a scale map the size of Marduk's craft, essentially a baby version of *Tiamat,* only 250 feet in length, and capable of storing six skimmers within her bowels. "Artem15, Are5, Kane and Grant accounted for four of the skimmers last night, with a fifth damaged. The potential for a sixth craft, held in reserve as a surprise weapon, is also present, meaning that all mechanoid units needed to improvise new weaponry to deal with its aerial assault."

ZOOs, who was in contact with command central, put his finger to the earbud that connected him. He raised his hand to interrupt Brigid's briefing.

"Queen, Cerberus Away Team Beta has arrived at the oracle," ZOOs explained. "They come bearing gifts."

Hera nodded in approval. "As long as there are no horses present, we should be fine."

That brought a chuckle throughout the room.

Domi excused herself from the head table to communicate with her team.

"As I was saying, your suits will need to be supplied with upgrades. CAT Beta has brought both shoulder-mounted, heat-seeking missiles and vehicle armor packages to improve your chances against more vigorous opposition," Brigid stated. "The armored couches you pilot your suits from provide satisfactory protection from behind, but for the sake of operation, your chest plates are not perfect. They certainly do the job against the primitive small arms of the old Tartarus raiders, but when it came to sheer numbers, their homicidal rage has proved sufficient to drive their reinforced bayonets through the chest armor. Z00s has been the lone exception to this due to armor materials that had been found at the Tartarus vaults," Brigid explained.

Ted Euphastus, the lead mechanic for the New Olympian suits, raised his hand. Brigid addressed him to speak. "You have enough armor for the other forty-eight suits? We only sent three Spartans to the oracle to receive the members of your team, and while they are physically strong, it would take multiple trips."

"Unfortunately, we only had enough armor packets for the eight main hero suits. However, we managed to bring along improved protection for the forty Spartan unit pilots," Brigid answered. "We have body armor with ceramic trauma plates and protective flight helmets. The trauma plates are perfectly suited to increasing the survivability of your pilots against penetrative trauma, but the Sandcat armor packs will go to the hero suits specifically to enhance their survivability in direct conflict with Nephilim opposition."

"So it's up to us to carry the fight," Herk mentioned. The

commander of Her47les brooded, looking at the other lead pilots at the table.

"Not so," Brigid countered. "Given the success of the 84 mm recoilless rifle last night, we've gone through our stockpiles. We have twenty, and right now, Fast's team is assembling ammunition pouches for the Spartan suits, based on Z00s's and Artem15's scabbards for their explosive warheads. The recoilless rifles should work perfectly as handguns for your gear skeletons."

"And the rest?" Herk inquired.

Grant took over. "Our familiarity with the COG facilities pointed out where your arsenal should have been. Unfortunately, when the Earthshaker went off, the corridors leading to that section of New Olympus collapsed. There is a team of demolitions-trained Praetorians utilizing explosives we'd already brought with us making their own corridor to your arsenal."

"If there's an arsenal, what about our own vehicles?" Donnie asked.

"They should have been in our hangar," Hera explained. "Unfortunately, across the centuries between skydark and my coming to New Olympus, raiders penetrated and scavenged what they could from the vehicles. What couldn't be driven or fueled were cut down for scrap and spare parts. You've seen farmers in our area utilizing jeep and Sandcat tires and wheels for their carts and improvised field plows."

"The upside to this is that if your arsenal is as stocked as we believe, the Spartans will be able to upgrade to polycarbonate Magistrate armor and helmets, improving their survivability even further," Grant added.

Z00s interrupted the briefing once more. "Cerberus satellites have detected an anomaly in the waters off of Island 3. We're dispatching a Praetorian spotter team to the region."

"That's got to be the scout ship," Kane spoke up. "Once CAT Beta gets here, I'm going to make an attempt on Marduk's ride."

Domi came back. "CAT Beta's just about here."

"All right," Kane replied. "Baptiste, I want you to stay here with Beta."

Brigid looked as if she were about to protest, but she knew arguing with Kane was futile. Besides, the smaller the assault team involved in the penetration of the scout ship, the better the chances of success. She knew that Kane and Grant moved swiftest on stealth assaults like this.

"We'll be in contact through Commtact, so there shouldn't be any problem," Kane added. "If we need help, then we'll coordinate with CAT Beta and the Olympian force."

Herk raised his hand again. "Wait a second. You're going after Marduk alone? We haven't had a chance to implement the improvements to our war suits. What happens if you've bitten off more than you could chew?"

"The purpose of this mission is reconnaissance, and if possible, sabotage," Grant explained. "Which is why it will only be the two of us making this run. We don't expect to be that long, but thanks to Fast and Brewster Philboyd, your suits should be up and ready to rock in the space of an hour."

Hera looked over the Magistrate pair. "New Olympus owes you a debt of gratit…"

Her words trailed off, her eyes glassy.

Brigid, standing next to the armor-clad queen, recognized the symptoms of a psychic assault. "Kane, Grant, restrain her!"

The two Cerberus men reached for her arms, but Hera's

shimmering metallic flesh thickened, growing ridged scales, fat straps of strength-enhancing smart metal running along the lines of her normal musculature. Grant managed to maintain his grasp on Hera's forearm simply because his hands were so large and powerful, but Kane's grip was popped loose as her right arm swelled, the golden tentacles of her ASP blaster slithering under his palms. Immediately they began to glow, but Hera was coimpelled to backhand Kane rather than fire the devastating energy weapon.

The blow, striking Kane in his chest, would have broken ribs if it hadn't been for the protective nature of the synthetic shadow suit fibers. Even so, Hera's armor had boosted her strength sufficiently to hurl Kane the length of the conference table, bowling over Brigid and other members of the New Olympus staff.

Brigid pushed Kane off her. Kane considered drawing his Sin Eater, but knew that opening fire on Hera would not only alienate their new allies, but would also be unfair to the queen. Currently, she wasn't in control of herself, and as long as he didn't have sufficient proof, he had to assume she was innocent of wrongdoing. Kane opted for scooping up a chair as a shield.

Hera gestured, and her blaster discharged, reducing the chair to a handful of shattered wood, two blunt clubs remaining in Kane's hands. She glared at him.

"Oh, hello, Kane. Still want me to go fuck a sheep?" an eerie masculine voice asked, venomous rage dripping from Hera's lips.

"Danton. I was wondering what you'd hide behind next," Kane growled.

Hera shrugged, hurling Grant to the floor with a surge of

smart-metal-enhanced strength. "Actually, using Hera to kill you was only an afterthought, Kane. And the name's now Hades."

"Hades, Thanatos, Danton, sheep fucker, it all sounds the same to me," Kane taunted.

Hera took three long strides, swinging a spike-laden fist at the Cerberus warrior. Kane dodged the blow, thankful that Danton's fighting skills had atrophied in the seven years he spent at the bottom of the chasm. Had his training been kept honed by practice, Kane was certain that the smart-metal spikes would have penetrated his chest and speared his heart and lungs. He was able to trap Hera's arm under his own, and he aimed a knockout stroke at the juncture of her jaw and her neck.

Hitting that spot on an unarmored person would have resulted in instant unconsciousness. Unfortunately for Kane, punching the smart metal was like punching a steel bulkhead.

Hera grinned. "I might have slowed down in my old age, Kane, but I still remember where I'm vulnerable to a knockout shot."

The possessed queen pumped her knee into Kane's groin. Liquid fire erupted in Kane's crotch, a wave of nausea boiling up into his belly. He was taken momentarily off balance and his leverage against Hera weakened, allowing the goddess-queen to lift him like a rag doll. Glancing at the crowd of New Olympians, Kane realized that wherever he was thrown, bones would break—not only his, but also those of the people he'd come to help.

Hera didn't get the chance to throw him, as Grant wrapped his thick arms around her waist and yanked her out from under Kane. He hit the floor on his hands and knees, and he looked up to see Grant flip Hera back in a suplex. The smart metal cushioned her head and shoulders, cracking floor tiles easily. She whipped her heel up and into Grant's stomach, knocking the wind out of him.

"Brigid, got a plan?" Kane asked.

"Other than stay the hell out of her way? No," Brigid replied.

Kane looked back to Grant, who wrestled to keep Hera's talon-tipped hands away from his throat. He was thinking about Sin Eater again when a pistol boomed in the conference room. The knot of Hera's armor seed jerked violently as a .45-caliber round hammered it. The smart metal stretched in violent reaction to the assault on its interface with Hera's nervous system, losing its rigid spike growths and muscular thickening. Even the ASP tendrils lost the fire in their emitters.

Kane whipped around and saw Domi lowering her pistol. Brigid had told him that the wild albino was thinking of ways to kill Hera, and Kane hoped that she hadn't succeeded in killing the beloved queen of their new allies.

"She's stunned!" Domi shouted.

Hera shook her head, her smart metal beginning to flow off of her, revealing her skin in places, black hair matted to her head with sweat. "Get. Out. Of. My. Head!"

She was on her knees, but the grimace on her face showed Kane that Hera was engaged in full-fledged psychic combat. The jolt to the cybernetic interface with her armor had given her the break she needed to wrest back control of her body. Hera punched the floor. Normally this wouldn't have worried anyone, but her hand was naked, the metal retracted from her skin, and her knuckles split with the violence of her blow against the tiles. She lifted her fist and punched again and again, blood spraying with each subsequent impact.

Kane was about to aid her, but Brigid stopped him.

"Hera's using the pain as a psychic anchor," Brigid explained. "You break her concentration, and Hades will regain what ground he's lost."

Kane could only watch helplessly, though Hera had lost the strength to pound the floor beneath her. Instead, she ground her bloody knuckles into the shards of floor tile she'd shattered. Tears flowed down Hera's cheeks as she engaged in self-torture, struggling to exorcise the telepathic intruder.

"I am Hera Olympiad! Goddess and queen of New Olympus!" she shouted with such vehemence that spittle flew from her stretched, snarling lips. "I will never be a slave again!"

Kane glanced around the room. It was apparent to everyone present that their leader was in a fight for her life, and there was nothing they could do. More than one pair of angered eyes glanced over to Domi, who had dared to threaten their queen's life with a bullet to the back of her neck. If Hera didn't win her battle with Hades, Kane knew that he'd have to fend off an enraged throng of Hera's loyalists, all hungry for Domi's blood.

Hera finally straightened, kneeling. Tears still wet her cheeks, but her face was an expressionless mask, her eyes rolled up into her head.

"This is it," Brigid noted. "If she wins, we're safe. If Hades wins, everyone in this room is dead."

"Not if I kill her first," Kane grumbled.

Brigid grabbed his arm. "Then we're dead."

"Just me," Kane snarled. "Grant will get you and Domi out of here."

Brigid understood the implication of Kane's statement, and he could feel her grasp tighten on his biceps.

The smart metal stopped draining away from Hera's skin and started reconstituting around her flesh. Her irises pivoted back into view, and she stood, looking to Kane.

"He is gone," she whispered. "He will not be back in my mind."

"What about your hand?" Kane asked, rushing to her side.

Hera chewed her lower lip, then locked her black, smoldering eyes on his. "Hurts like a son of a bitch, frankly. But the armor's setting the bones and has sealed off the bleeding."

Kane rested his hand on her shoulder. "You sure?"

Hera nodded. At this distance, Kane could hear the crackle and crunch of her broken hand bones being repositioned and splinted by the smart metal. Occasional tics flashed across her face, betraying the agony she had to have been undergoing, but she shrugged out of his grasp and walked toward Domi. The feral girl put the pistol back into her holster, regarding the New Olympians around her. She realized that she'd put Hera's life in danger, and with that action, she may have doomed herself.

Domi remained quiet, preferring to save her final words to take any blame for harm that came to the queen, drawing threat away from her companions.

Hera rested both hands on Domi's slender shoulders and smiled. "Domi, thank you. You saved my people from what could have been an unstoppable rampage. By stunning my armor, you also interrupted Hades's concentration enough for me to drive him out."

Domi nodded, her ruby eyes locked on Hera's face, searching for any sign of menace in her voice. All that she found was a gaze of warm gratitude. "I was worried that it could have hurt you. The bullet."

Hera turned Domi's palm up, then deposited a deformed slug in it. "The armor is made of far sterner stuff than either of our flesh. But not stronger than your spirit, aiding mine against Hades."

Hera turned to the crowd, one arm across the girl's shoulders. "New Olympians, the enemy has tried once more to bring war to our doorstep. What say you to this insult?"

As one, the Greeks shouted. "Death to Marduk! Death to Hades!"

Hera nodded. "Kane, I believe you have an appointment with a submerged scout ship."

Kane nodded, looking at the display of fierce loyalty that Hera had just commanded. Though it was in Hera's best interests to preserve the unity between New Olympus and Cerberus for now, should they have to act against each other, Kane knew that the Greeks would not bat an eyelash if she commanded the outlanders' deaths.

"Baptiste, I hope you're wrong for once," he whispered to Brigid. "Because if you're not, and Hera is as murderous as we think she is, we won't stand a chance."

Brigid intertwined her fingers with his, giving a reassuring squeeze. Kane didn't have to look at her to know the worry on her face.

Chapter 17

Hades convulsed violently as Hera finally broke contact with him. In the clone matrix, the half-formed, wisp-limbed abortion that bore only genetic resemblance to Helena Garthwaite was wreathed in clouds of blood that gushed from the slits that formed its mouth and nose. Its eye stalks waved in the glowing lime-green suspension fluid as they collapsed in on themselves. Had it the musculature to reach for its disintegrating face, it would have, but the unborn thing didn't even possess the strength to yawn its mouth wide open for a final death scream.

By the time Hades finished vomiting on the floor beneath him, mucus draining from his nostrils and tear ducts, the clone was dead.

"I can make another," Hades croaked.

"No," Marduk answered. "I think you've put on enough of a regurgitation escapade for the rest of the year, Hades."

"I mean—" Hades broke down coughing, his face contorting in pain with each spasm "—I mean, I can make another Hera."

Marduk looked at the floating atrocity in the tank, the pink slush of brains oozing out of a vestigial ear hole as the soft, rotten-fruit skull began to collapse upon itself. He opened his fang-toothed mouth to make a point, then closed his lips, waving off Hades dismissively. Even the Annunaki overlord didn't have enough stomach to deal with another loathsomely fragile sack of protohumanoid birthed within the replication vat.

"Sire," Hades called out as Marduk made his way toward the door. "Sire!"

"Clean yourself up, Hades," Marduk said. "You have accomplished the one mission that I directed you to."

"But the others…" Hades groaned.

"The others will be dealt with all in good time," Marduk cut him off. "Clean the vomit off yourself. The slave drones will mop this chamber up. Set the vats to continue production of Nephilim."

Hades had to have gotten the point that Marduk no longer wished to gaze upon the dead thing, floating like a fetus in formaldehyde. "I am sorry, sire."

"You are successful," Marduk told him. "Once the enemy realizes what we have wrought upon them, it will be too late for New Olympus. When Hera falls, so will her robot army. When her robot army falls, so shall the rest of her false empire. And with that, we only have one enemy, and I am ready for war against them."

Hades winced, holding his convulsion-ravaged abdominal muscles. He nodded weakly. "When I was in her mind, I learned that Kane and Grant were on their way. They have figured out where the ship is."

Marduk half glanced over his shoulder, his reptilian lips curling up in a smile. "Excellent. Then dress up, my brother. We must present our best face when we have such important company on their way."

Hades nodded. "As you command."

"And Hades?" Marduk asked.

"Sire?"

"The next time you clone Hera, wait for her to finish baking first. As it is, that thing is utterly useless, even if it had survived," Marduk said. "If you comprehend what I mean."

"I do, sir," Hades answered.

"I won't need her now, but keep that in mind," Marduk stated, leaving the cabin, isolating Hades once more.

The clone master struggled to his feet and limped toward the door to get cleaned up as silent soldier drones entered to tend to the messes left behind.

Guilt dragged on Hades as he observed Marduk's lonely walk to the bridge of the scout ship. Yes, he had connected the lone, active Skybreaker drone to the nineteen duplicates within the hold of the scout ship, but in the psychic struggle with Hera, he no longer knew who was in charge of the horrible weaponry.

He could feel the drones, loaded into launchers by Nephilim laborers, stirring at the back of his mind, but they didn't feel as if they were part of his mind. Not quite.

Hades feared that he had not waged his last telepathic conflict. He had one lone consolation. If he failed, then the furious goddess-queen would make death swift and certain.

SELA SINCLAIR WALKED into the hangar with the rest of CAT Beta, flanked by the fifteen-foot robotic gladiators who tugged along the trolley pallets laden with Sandcat armor packages. The lean, wiry black woman gave a low whistle, looking around the preparation berths that lined the walls, technicians hard at work on repairs and upgrades. Kane and Grant, clad in their shadow suits, augmented with sealed environmental hoods, were inspecting weaponry that had been recovered by the Praetorians from the recently opened arsenal.

"Now, this is what I'm talking about," Sinclair spoke up.

Grant shot a look at her. "What?"

"This," she noted, slinging her weapon over her shoulder. "Robots. This is what I'd been expecting the future to look like. High-tech shit."

Grant smirked. "Crazy freezie."

"If they were high-tech, Sinclair," Kane interrupted, "they wouldn't need replacement chest seals."

Towed by a Spartan unit, Brewster Philboyd rode in on top of a stack of six cartons, his legs crossed as if he were riding a magic carpet, surveying the land. "Nice place you got here. I like the ass-side of the moon landscaping. Very chic."

Grant shook his head in disgust. "The worst card cheat in Cerberus has to be the only jamoke smart enough to adapt these armor packs."

"Jamoke?" Kane asked.

"Picked it up from him," Grant mentioned offhand.

"Gentlemen, gentlemen, please," Philboyd said, sliding off the pallets. "Please, there's a time for business, which is now. And then there's a time for taking these poor schlubs for every single penny they have, which is after we kick Marduk's ass."

Grant grimaced.

"I'll need a partner, even if he is only the second-worst hustler in Cerberus," Philboyd mentioned.

Grant's foul mood softened, a bushy eyebrow rising at the thought.

Kane winced. "Great. I let the serpents into Eden."

"Well, it's not as if we'd be doing any harm to their economy..." Grant started.

Kane elbowed his partner in the ribs.

"So, why do you two look like you're going scuba diving?" Sinclair asked.

"Because we are," Kane responded. "Which is why we want CAT Beta here in force. Domi already had good relations with the Praetorians, as does Baptiste, so the integration of forces will go much more easily."

Sinclair nodded. "It'll be good passing the buck back to her. These knuckleheads might be good partners, but playing den mother to them requires someone with more patience than me."

"Domi? Patience?" Grant asked. He snickered.

"Oh. I brought this for you." Sinclair handed Kane a Sin Eater holster attachment. The former Magistrate hooked his blaster to it, then strapped the entire unit to his forearm. A flex of his muscles, and the folding machine pistol deployed with a loud clack. Another flex, and the weapon folded back against his arm, an unobtrusive part of his limb.

"Now I feel right again," Kane noted.

Sinclair smirked. "One of these days, you're going to have to train me on those things. Those are cool."

"Takes six months of practice and carry before you're even allowed to load it," Kane said. "Probably would take even longer if you're an old dog needing to learn new tricks."

She snorted in derision. "Kane, I've been there for the interviews of the Mags you wanted to recruit. Rocket scientists were not a high priority in that crowd, no offense to present company."

"None taken," the other members of CAT Beta called out from where they were standing. Sinclair winced, then looked at a grinning Grant.

She looked to Philboyd for sympathy, since he was a fellow inhabitant of the twentieth century. She got none.

"Welcome to the twenty-third century, Colonel," Philboyd

quipped. "All right, which one of you's named Fast? I got thirty deep-dish armor with extra anchovies!"

Sela Sinclair sighed and followed Kane's directions to Domi. The sooner she was one of the boys again, the better.

HERA STOOD AT THE SKYBREAKER core, looking at it, and if it hadn't been for her breathing, one would have thought someone had installed a beautiful statue next to it, sculpted from the purest platinum in the world. Her stillness, however, belied the turbulence churning behind her black eyes, calmness chipped away.

Diana, in her wheelchair, remained quiet, uncertain whether she should interrupt her queen's concentration, not even aware of what she wanted to accomplish here. Finally, Hera glanced over her shoulder, spotting the amputee pilot.

"Diana," she greeted, holding out her hand. "Diana, my child."

Diana rolled forward, then reached up to interlace her callused fingers with the delicate, gold-gloved digits. "My queen, you had summoned me."

Diana didn't dare to look Hera in the eye, preferring instead to remain behind her curtain of straw-colored hair. Smooth metal fingertips brushed the locks aside, cupping the girl's cheek.

"Diana, it has only been less than two days, but I feel as if we've had a gulf of years since I reproached you," Hera said, her voice soft, hurt.

Diana risked a glance up at her face. The queen had always been smooth-skinned and young, most likely due to the effects of the amazing armor she wore. However, Hera's eyes looked out over bags of exhaustion, wrinkles puckering at their corners. The stresses of the preceding desperate hours had taken their toll on her.

"Diana, I was far too harsh with you."

Diana didn't know what to do, and when she realized that she was nodding in agreement of Hera's assessment, she stopped. "No, my queen. I had spoken out of turn."

There was a weak, sad smile on Hera's face, delicate fingers gliding down to Diana's shoulder and giving it a squeeze. The silver-clad goddess took a deep breath, letting it out. "That would be the situation if this were a tyranny, my child. New Olympus is not ruled by me. I came here, I endured the title of queen and goddess, but really, you've all been a part of the important decisions. This is not a government without representation by the people."

"But—" Diana began.

Hera shook her head, cutting Diana off. "I tried to make New Olympus a better place than what I had found, and much better than the environ of hell that I walked out of nearly a decade ago. It wasn't easy. Zoo wanted me to have true authority, rather than share my power with you."

Diana narrowed her eyes, confusion flashing in her mind.

"It would have been easy to live up to the role of goddess-queen, crushing any who questioned my wisdom, but I am not that kind of person," Hera told her. "Any evidence to the contrary, it's where I buckled under Zoo's council."

"Zoo told you to be so uptight about going into the Tartarus Crack?" Diana asked. "Why?"

"I don't know," Hera answered. "All I know is that he said that his missions to the Crack were for the greater good of New Olympus."

Worry flashed across Hera's features. "Those ambushes, on Z00s's patrols. Where the others had been lost…"

Hera locked her eyes on Diana's. "Diana, do you think those losses could have been because their pilots suspected something? Did they ever say anything to you?"

Diana shook her head. "Nothing was said to me. Though I had heard…rumors," Diana added, feeling as if she were deciding death warrants.

Hera's frown deepened. "Rumors. Rumors aren't enough to prosecute on. Neither is the fact that Z00s was able to observe this supposed union between Marduk and Danton."

"What are you talking about?" Diana asked.

"Well, as has been said, Marduk used to be Baron Cobalt. And before I was exiled on this fool's errand, I had been Cobalt's lover," Hera confessed. "But like most relationships, he became bored with me. And as the ruler of one-ninth of North America, he had some considerable capacity to dismiss a boring old, worn-out piece of tail."

Hera gave Diana's hand a squeeze. "I supposed I'm lucky I wasn't just thrown to the cannibals in the wilderness."

Diana tried to resist the urge to glance back at the doorway, where Domi hovered like a blood-eyed ghost. She failed, catching a glimpse of the pale albino standing just behind the doorjamb. "Then why send Z00s and Thanatos with you?"

"Thurmond and Danton were my handlers. If I found anything, they would report back, utilizing their communication equipment," Hera explained. "This way Baron Cobalt would profit from the risks I took."

"Handlers," Diana repeated.

Hera nodded, a tear crawling down her cheek. "In more ways than one."

Diana's throat tightened. It may have been the stresses of the past few days, but the roller-coaster ride of loyalty and betrayal in the face of the queen had come full circle. Here was a woman who had been smashed viciously by circumstance and conspiracy. Diana wanted to wrap her arms around Hera, to hold her, to apologize for ever doubting that she was anything but the benevolent savior who'd returned Greece to its greatness.

"Please, Diana, be careful," Hera whispered. "Thurmond is dangerous. He would think nothing of murdering you and attributing your death to Danton."

Diana clamped her hand over her own mouth, looking back toward Domi in the doorway. "Hera…"

"It's okay," Hera said. "The people of Cerberus…they might be our only hope to completely sever our ties to the past and rid a cancer from New Olympus."

Domi stepped across the threshold. "The others have been listening in."

The girl tapped her Commtact implant for emphasis. "They know."

Hera nodded. "Keep it quiet from the others. Zoo has deluded everyone, gotten them to love him. He's been hedging his bets, and after today's show of vulnerability, he might be poised to take control. I'll be discredited by one means or another."

"We'll be on our guard," Domi promised, walking over to Diana's chair. "Watch yourself, and if you need help, then CAT Beta and I will fight by your side."

Hera's face tightened, as if to hold back a flood of tears. She held her free hand out to Domi, who took it.

"Thank you, Domi. Thank all of you," Hera sobbed. She snaked her fingers free from their grasps. "I need to clean up.

If I'm to spend my last hours as queen this day, then I don't want to be remembered looking as if I cried all night."

Diana and Domi nodded, leaving the goddess-queen's chamber.

THE DOOR CLOSED BEHIND THE PAIR, and Hera sent the mental command, withdrawing the tension that her smart-metal mask had applied to deepen her barely formed crow's-feet and the strain in her face. She washed off her makeup in the stainless-steel basin, removing the eye shadow that had been applied to deepen the troughs beneath her eyes, only after thorough scrubbing.

The former archivist remembered all the material from the twentieth century referring to award-winning performances.

"Oh, darling, that little gold statue has nothing on you," Hera told her reflection in the mirror with a wry grin. She stood up, admiring her curves in the mirror. She closed her eyes in celebration of herself, imagining herself as perfect as the gleaming reflections created by mirrorskin and vanity.

After drinking in that thought, she opened her eyes, her wide lips curled up in a smile. "Poor Thurmond and Danton. Always the pawns, never the kings. Danton, going from being my lackey back to old, limp-dicked Baron Cobalt. And Thurmond, the sap."

She reapplied her makeup, primping herself for her appearance in command central, returning to her role as the leader of New Olympus. "Perhaps, when I'm finally queen of the world, and I've lashed these pathetic apes into some form of civilization, I'm going to have to restart the arts."

Hera straightened, checking various angles on her face to see if it was to her taste. It was. "I could be a one-woman show."

She folded her hands together under her chin, her voice pouring out bubbly and light. Oddly, she could still smell the sweet scent of the postcoital hybrid beside her. "Oh, Baron, *Oh, Baron!* Ohhhhhhhh, Baron."

She smirked, straightening. The olfactory memory disappeared in a flash, nervousness at her ploy to escape Cobaltville churning through her. "Yes, sire. According to my research, there is a stockpile of incomparable technology in Greece. If I could arrange an expedition, I could deliver unto you untold power."

Hera scrunched her shoulders, rubbing her arms against an unfelt chill. She leaned to her left. "Thurmond…hold me. It's so cold, so frightening…"

Then she leaned to her right. "Oh, Danton…he's kind to me, but there are times when I talk to him…he's not as brilliant as you are. You're the only one who has kept me sane this journey."

Hera spread her arms, turning in glee, going back to the one moment when she didn't have to act, the pure feeling of triumph that flooded her body when they'd finally reached the Tartarus Crack and encountered the endless vaults of secrets within. Somehow, the memories seemed richer, fuller now, a jolting high that threatened to send her off dancing madly, even as her brain switched closer to the present.

Her face grew serious and contemplative. "Think of how you'll be loved for your sacrifice, Thurmond. You gave up *your legs* for them. To become their champion and protector. The sheep will flock to you as their shepherd."

Now to condescension, reaching up as if to caress Danton's cheek. "He's no longer a whole man. You are healthy and strong. And you will be in command of thousands. You'll never be alone, while Thurmond will just be a pitied little freak in a chair."

A chuckle escaped her lips at that. She had divided the pair, and even though Z00s had been her personal messenger, they had that barrier. The cripple was tied to her by his mutilation, by the leash of sex, while Danton had been cowed with promises of power and true intellectual love, not the rutting of animals. It was a perfect balance.

A tittering laugh started to escape her lips, and she threw her hand over her mouth. Her eyes widened with realization. Danton had to have knocked something loose in the telepathic attack. She'd lost control of herself, emotions flooding to the surface. She glanced around her chamber, realizing her luck at suffering this momentary loss of self-control in her personal quarters.

Hera straightened, glaring at herself in the mirror. "Get your shit under control, dammit. Kill Marduk. Kill Danton. Reveal Thurmond's complicity with Danton, then have him killed. It will all go away in a single spray of blood, and I'll still be the queen."

She shuddered, adrenaline pulsing through her veins. Hera had the world ready for her, at her fingertips. The armor hummed around her, vibrating with power, and she took mental stock of herself. She could feel the drones within the hold of the scout ship. Danton had tried to sever her telepathic link with the lone Skybreaker, keying it through to whichever vat-spawned abomination that formed the psychic bridge between them.

Marduk had tried to play it dirty, sending his little toadie deep into her mind, not realizing that the very reason why Marduk needed Danton as his cat's-paw was because Hera's will was absolute and powerful. The overlord was simply out-matched. The attack on Hera's mind was not only an attempt to control Skybreaker, but also to render her a helpless opponent. The burbling to the surface of her memories would have left her crucified had any New Olympians heard it. They tried to destroy her by getting her to vomit her secrets in public.

As she brushed her fingertips over the pyramidal gem of the Threshold, she felt the crackling energy of the parallax point hum through her. The Threshold itself had been vital to the Skybreaker design. Its dimension portal power enabled the column to actually broadcast the electricity generated within the core through the nodes to the units, as well as transporting the drones.

It was with regret that Hera turned away from the power core. She wasn't able to teleport Marduk's drones. They didn't have a nearby Threshold, and were away from a parallax point, so she couldn't open a portal between Marduk's scout ship and her laboratory. The other drones wouldn't even respond, since they needed to be powered up, jump started, at range.

She'd have to rely on exploiting Kane and Grant.

It was a shame, too, Hera thought. Kane had potential as a lover.

"Oh, well." She sighed, heading to central command. Kane wasn't the only stud left on Earth.

DOMI DIDN'T LIKE DISTRACTING Kane and Grant while they were making their way to the coast, but their Commtact conference was necessary.

"Domi, you were there," Kane said. "Was she putting on a show for Diana?"

"It's hard to tell," Domi confessed. "She's been keeping her emotions so close to the vest that it's tough to figure out what she's really like. This was a different behavior, but it could just be an act."

Brigid chimed in, "I've been constructing a mental timeline, given the facts that we know, and everything seems to neatly fall into place."

Grant grunted. "Which could mean an airtight alibi, or Hera's been paying attention to whatever holes are in her story, and she's been slapping excuses into place for our sake."

"Given the fact that thousands have suffered because of the Tartarus mutants, Hera's got to have a great deal of deniability if she's involved with them," Kane noted. "So the construction of a cohesive, unbreakable story is right at the forefront of her thought processes."

Domi was quietly relaying the conversation to Diana, a soft undertone to the transmission, which also gave the amputee pilot input in the conference.

"The concept of being a victim of Thurmond and Danton's sexual violence seemed especially tailored for both Domi and me," Diana stated. "Domi's experiences in Cobaltville's Tartarus would make her sympathetic to Hera if it were real. And as for me…"

"You don't need to say any more," Domi said, resting her hand on Diana's.

"Thanks," the pilot replied. "Besides, I know Zoo, and right now, he's too busy concentrating on getting the job done against Marduk to engage in any intrigue. It's not evidence of a negative, but I also have the gut feeling that if push came to shove, Zoo would give it all up for New Olympus, even against Hera."

"I'm getting that same vibe from him, too," Grant admitted. "He's been asked to pull some heinous shit, just like we used to when we were Magistrates. But underneath, Thurmond always struck me as someone who was looking for more than just being the poor bastard stuck between the fucker in power and the people being shit upon."

"So we have two votes for getting in contact with Zoo," Kane said.

"What's your opinion?" Domi asked.

"You sound like you have your own," Kane countered.

Domi glanced to Diana. "I've only spent one night on rounds with him, but we spoke with a lot of Praetorians. It's easy to dismiss the ground troops as just a bunch of pawns, but there is a chemistry between them. Zoo actually treated them with respect, addressing them as equals and always greeting them with smiles. The Praetorians might seem like a grassroots campaign to earn loyalty, but it didn't smell like Zoo was shoveling manure toward them."

"I'm going to go with Domi's judgment," Brigid said. "But Kane, you're the one with the instincts here. Do we let Zoo in on the fact that Hera's trying to sell him out as the villain?"

"And even if we do let him know, do we keep his involvement in this a secret from the rest of New Olympus, and possibly threaten his life?" Diana asked.

"That decision is up to you, Diana," Kane offered. "Right now, I'm throwing in. It's unanimous. We've got to trust Zoo. He's always seemed the lesser of two evils."

"So much like the rest of mythology. Zeus, for all his flaws, always ultimately the benefactor while Hera remains the malefactor," Brigid pronounced.

"Domi, Diana, it's up to you two," Kane said. "We're at the waterline."

"Make sure you get back here," Domi replied.

"Make sure we have somewhere to come back to," Kane signed off.

Diana and Domi headed down to the hangar.

Chapter 18

Grant stretched out the high-tech hood, then tugged it over his head. He was amazed at how the high-tech material automatically self-adjusted, conforming like the shadow suit to the contours of his body. He'd expected to feel claustrophobic with the hood pulled into place, but instead of feeling like he'd stuffed his head into a sock, it felt as if he'd grown a second, comfortable skin. The mask fitted over his face, a gentle current activating at the edges of the cowl to create an airtight magnetic seal. There was no feeling of a charge, just the impression that he was plugged in. The opaque mask shuddered, then seemingly disappeared as if a strong breeze were blowing sand off a windshield.

Grant knew that the world outside wouldn't be able to see his face, but the optic camouflage technology enabled him to look through the black mask, akin to the one-way glass that had been used to isolate prisoners back in Cerberus or in Cobaltville. The optical enhancements built into the mask were odd and alien, compared to the far more conventional technology of the Magistrate helmets. He had to make certain not to concentrate on any one object too much, lest the sudden telescopic zoom of the smart mask engage. The effect was one that gave him not so much a headache but vertigo. Nausea underneath the sealed mask would ruin Grant's day.

He looked to Kane, who was also now clad head to toe in black. Kane tapped his forearm, and the shadow suit altered its coloration, absorbing ambient surrounding light and bending it through fiber-optic material to diffuse his appearance against the surrounding countryside.

"We're really getting the most out of these suits this trip," Grant said, following Kane's example by putting the shadow suit in stealth mode.

"We?" Kane asked. "How many times have you been smacked by musket balls in the past twenty-four hours?"

Grant suppressed a smile, even though he knew that Kane couldn't see through his mask. "Looking to add a little lifespan with your bitching?"

Kane chuckled. "Maybe. I'd also like a little cheese with my whine."

Grant winked. "Could have gotten that with the queen."

"Where were you when I needed that mental image to turn me off?" Kane griped. "Okay, let's see just how good the rebreathing units are on these hoods."

Grant looked at the waters thirty feet below them. Beyond, under the waves, Marduk's scout ship awaited. "How good? You mean you haven't tried diving with these?"

"Nope," Kane answered. "And Domi didn't even bother with her hood when checking the water filtration."

"Now you tell me," Grant groaned.

Kane stepped off the cliff, hitting the water feetfirst, keeping his body straight. The water sluiced around him, the disturbance on the surface the only indication for Grant that his friend had avoided the rocks and gone underwater. He followed, holding his breath as he dropped in after Kane.

The water enveloped Grant, though the shadow suit's environmental protections kept him from feeling any temperature change. Opening his eyes, he saw an indicator for ambient water temperature at sixty-four degrees Fahrenheit floating in his vision as if he could reach out and touch the numbers. Another indicator popped up, confirming that oxygen filtration was enabled. Grant breathed out, then inhaled.

"Looks like they work fine," a shimmering form noted, swimming next to Grant. The optics of the mask showed Kane as a shimmering outline in the water, a ghost of his former self. "Take a look."

Grant glanced to where Kane pointed and saw a distant shadow on the ocean floor. As he concentrated on the shape, the mask's optics kicked in and magnified the image. Though it was still a blurry mass resting on the sea bed, it was recognizable.

"Like a Marduk to water," Grant said. "Good. You going to object to me kicking his ass so hard, he'll wear it like a hat?"

"You're getting gentle in your old age," Kane commented. "I was hoping you'd try harder."

"Well, if you insist," Grant replied.

The partners kicked off, swimming toward the scout ship.

ZOO SAT BACK IN HIS WHEELCHAIR, watching Fast and Philboyd replacing the light machine guns in the shoulder gear mounts with heavier weapons. In front of him stood Domi, her arms crossed, red eyes gleaming so that he felt a surge of overwhelming guilt at being caught. His heart hammered, and he squeezed the armrests of the chair, absorbing Diana's tale of Hera's "confession."

Thurmond's lips drew tight, and he wanted to bury his head. The two women looked at him, and he knew that they wanted an answer.

"Tell us that she's pawning all of this off onto you," Domi said.

"The thing is, it is partly my fault," Thurmond answered. Bile boiled in his throat, but he swallowed it back down. His mouth tasted of acid, the sting reaching up into his nose. He wished that were a good enough excuse for the burn of tears forming in the corners of his eyes, but he would be lying to himself if he dismissed it. "I did buy into Hera's scheme. And I killed fellow pilots who had gotten too close."

In the hectic preparations for war with Marduk and Hades, the only ones in position to hear what Thurmond had to say were Diana and Domi, and he had to strain to speak loud enough for the women to hear. Each syllable was a knife into his heart, driven by the mounting pain in Diana's eyes.

"I did go, as Hera's personal messenger to the Tartarus Crack," he admitted. "And the patrols that were sent out to ambush me were merely cover so that the suspicious could be eliminated."

"Zoo?" Diana asked. "Will—"

Thurmond cut her off. "Please, I can't stomach that name now."

"Why not?" Domi asked, her voice as hard as stone.

Thurmond glanced at the wall where pilots were looking over their suit modifications with the ground crew. New armor plating covered the chests of the gear skeletons, and large-barreled cannons and launchers now adorned their massive shoulders. The Spartans were as magnificent as they'd ever seemed. Thurmond ground his teeth together, wishing that for once, he could lead them as the invulnerable defenders of freedom and life that he'd wanted them to be. "Zoo is the name of a friend who didn't really exist. He was as much a lie as everything Hera ever told me."

"No lie," Domi said.

Diana nodded in agreement. "If that were the case, we wouldn't have come to you. Right now, we're in need of some real friends. And you are the only one we could stand behind against Hera."

Thurmond locked his eyes with Diana's.

"Would we risk our lives by sharing this information with you?" Domi asked. "If you were as rotten as Hera said you were, you'd have us arrested and killed. Instead, you're sitting there, almost wishing for a bullet in your head, just so the pain stops."

Thurmond blinked, grinding his knuckle into the corner of one eye. "You can read minds, too?"

"It's all over your face," Domi answered. "I know people."

"So you'll trust the monster," Thurmond said. "Only because if you don't, the Praetorians and the Spartans wouldn't dream of following you."

"We're trusting you, period," Diana countered.

"Saving your life, too," Domi stated. "Just say the word, and you'll have a loyal army ready to back you up."

Thurmond returned his attention to the other pilots, readying for the next stage of war with Marduk. One Spartan flipped him a smart salute before hefting a rocket launcher. Thurmond buried his face in his hands. "It will still be her word against mine."

"Her word against your actions," Diana said.

"Do you honestly feel that Hera wouldn't be prepared?" Thurmond asked. "She's already dropped a load of bullshit in your laps and expected you to buy it."

"So you give up and let her railroad you," Domi replied. "You end up in front of a firing squad, and she rules unchecked."

"You'd stop her, and justice would be done," Thurmond admitted. "We'd both be dead…"

"Not without loss of good people, and not without shattering New Olympus," Diana pressed. "Dammit, Zoo, you're the ideal we've all lived up to. You are loved as a hero because you are one. You've fought tooth and nail to protect lives, and I've been relentless in drilling that responsibility into my Spartans. Everyone has."

"It's a fine time for you to come out of your shell," Thurmond said. "Especially since Hera wanted me to kill you for going close to the Crack."

Diana tensed. "Fine, then. Be the coward. Knuckle under and be Hera's fall guy. You don't want to be loved anymore? Then I'm done with you."

Diana pivoted her chair and rolled over to Artem15.

Thurmond glanced to Domi, who glared at him reproachfully. "You understand. You know the difference between right and wrong. The bad guys have to be punished."

Domi grimaced. "There's one thing I've learned as an albino. Things ain't always black and white."

She pressed her hand over his burly forearm. "Take a look. How much difference is there?"

Thurmond looked down at her flesh against his. Though she was painfully pale in comparison to him, she still had an inkling of color.

"Sure, you did wrong. I tried to murder Kane and Grant. Kane and Grant executed rebels without due process," Domi said. "It's not the wrong we've done. It's the right we've done to make up for it. You going to wallow in being a devil? Or are you going to make it all right by doing what needs to be done?"

Thurmond sighed. "What could I do?"

Domi shook her head in frustration. "If you really were a hero, you'd know what needs to be done."

Domi left Thurmond to his thoughts and doubts.

BRIGID RETURNED TO command central to find Hera standing tall and proud on her podium, checking out the screens.

"Welcome back, Brigid," Hera greeted. "It appears that the upgrades your people suggested are being completed handily."

"I recognized the similarities between the hinge mechanisms on the chest carapace were very similar to those that we have on our Sandcats," Brigid answered, standing off to her side. The archivist knew that the elevation increased Hera's self-importance, and the smugness in queen's features was due to the fact that she had thrown Z00s to the wolves.

"This is Z00s," a voice called over the radio. "All systems on-line."

The other pilots called in from the hangar as their clockwork war suits came to life.

The monitor showed the forty-nine mechanoid warriors assembled as one cohesive fighting force, sporting new armor plating and weaponry. While the arsenal wasn't as complete as the one Lakesh had assembled for Cerberus, it was impressive enough. Heavy machine guns and rocket and grenade launchers had replaced the lighter weaponry they had been fitted with. Since the secondary orichalcum skeletons had proved more than sufficient to survive twenty-yard jumps or plummeting free runs from cliff to cliff down a mile of crevasse, whatever recoil forces the new firepower would apply to the nigh invulnerable hydraulic frames would be negligible.

Z00s strode into the center of the floor to address the fighting gear skeletons and their pilots.

"We're fighting for the future today," he said. "The future is always seen as full of hope, at least by civilized societies. But it hasn't always been that way. After all, back in the late twentieth Century, the world lived in fear of global conflict that would lead to the extinction of humankind. And those fears came true on January 20, 2001. During the aftermath of the nuclear holocaust and the prolonged nuclear winter that followed, the future became the next day, the next hour, the next minute, and there wasn't much hope in that beyond finding a morsel of food that had been crammed in some tin."

The mechanoid flexed, mimicking the movements of the pilot as he took a deep breath. Brigid shot a glance toward Hera, whose face was an inscrutable mask.

"Civilization only succeeds when it has a future to strive for," Z00s continued. "The world tore itself to pieces because there were those in power who felt the future only brought about some inane religious prophecy about the ultimate battle between good and evil. They nattered about a mythic rapture that would cleanse the world, creating a utopian paradise."

He chuckled. "Over the past seven years, I learned that utopia doesn't come handed to you on a silver platter. It comes through hard work, and it comes from sacrifice. And New Olympus is hardly a utopia. It's besieged by monsters, it's in a state of war and it's not perfect. Nothing made by humans ever is."

Hera rested her hands on the railing around her dais. Fingers flexed.

"How is your hand?" Brigid asked, drawing Hera's attention.

Black eyes locked on her, anger boiling upward. "The armor is acting like a breathable cast. I also rigged a neural interrupter to minimize the pain, without need of drugs."

Brigid nodded. The answer was curt, and Hera seemed as if she wanted to pounce, to denounce, but Z00s hadn't said anything yet for her to act on.

"Humans are not perfect. No one is pure good, or pure evil—life doesn't work that way. Sure, you think that Hera and I are the greatest heroes in the world," he said. Brigid could feel the tension in the air like a choking cloud of smoke now. "But I was not always an angel. Our enemy today, Marduk, used to be a frail little frightened tyrant. He gave orders to me, his Magistrate, and when those orders were given, they were executed."

Z00s's shoulders sagged. "As a Magistrate, I was good at killing. Sometimes it was for the good of Cobaltville as a whole, chilling barbarians and mutants who would otherwise raid and murder the citizens who clung to the shadow of our giant city. But other times, I pulled the trigger, ending lives of men and women, the elderly and the children, whose only crime was protesting the absolute rule of that scaled piece of shit out there. You call me a hero, but I wasn't always so."

There was a hushed silence across all of New Olympus at that statement.

"Neither were our friends from Cerberus. Kane and Grant were Magistrates just like me. And Domi was one of the barbarians who did whatever she needed to survive in the Tartarus Pits," Z00s continued. "And a few years ago, all of that changed. They learned the truth. They saw that life had once been better. That the world was indeed a fine place, and worth fighting for."

Z00s extended his hands to the Spartans, the Praetorians and the hero suits before him. "They learned after I did that there are higher things to aspire to than merely being a good soldier. But the lessons we came to are the same."

ZOOs glanced toward Domi, who was listening to the speech at the head of the crowd. "The past isn't what we're fighting for. Nor the future. We're fighting for peace. We're fighting so that we don't have to fight, because we're sick of seeing people we love die. Today, I want to stop fighting. And I will. I'll either be dead and rotting, or the enemy we have been struggling against for nearly a decade will no longer attack us. To me, it doesn't matter, because I can see a future where violence isn't a day-to-day part of my life."

Hera's eyes narrowed when she saw Domi nod to ZOOs. Her gaze flicked to Brigid.

"Praetorians, Spartans, heroes, visitors from Cerberus, I bear my soul to you all," ZOOs proclaimed. Metal claws dug into his invulnerable chest armor, peeling the ancient steel carapace away, hinges and locks bursting into fragments. "For too long, I was separated from you by thick, good steel, while you were vulnerable in copper and brass shells. Today, you are as mighty as I once was…mightier."

Inside the cockpit, Thurmond was clad in his old Magistrate armor, the legs of his uniform tied off beneath the stumps. "My friends, I lived a lie in being a hero when I risked nothing and you risked all. Today, I beg your forgiveness, and ask you to stand at my side, not as those under my command, but as my equals, as my friends."

Artem15 bent over and lifted the torn carpace. She laid it on the ground, tore off the handle from a Cerberus trolley, then jammed it into the underside of the carpace, creating a steel D handle that she flattened in place. She handed ZOOs back the carpace, which he held like a shield.

"To hell and back," Artem15 said.

Z00s hefted the shield in one metal claw, then held up Artem15's hydraulic hand in a show of unity. New Olympus erupted with applause.

"Damn you, Baptiste," Hera whispered, loud enough for only the archivist to hear. "Damn you and your interfering thugs to hell."

Brigid grinned. "Cobalt exiled us to hell years ago, Helena. We've done our best to improve its conditions since, and if I say so myself, we've succeeded phenomenally. You think that you've pulled stuff we haven't seen before? You're the definition of tin-plated dictator, and we eat those for breakfast."

Hera's black eyes burned with impotent rage.

"You try blacklisting Z00s now, you'll be shooting yourself in the foot," Brigid added. "So my advice to you is shut up and let us do our job. Got it?"

An unnatural calm came over Hera Olympiad's face.

"Got it?" Brigid repeated.

Hera looked down at her and smiled gently. "Baptiste, how wonderful to see you again."

Almost as soon as the words fell from her lips, Hera clenched her fingers around the railing she leaned on. Metal squealed, crushed under tremendous pressure as the smart metal around her fingers thickened to become as fat as bananas.

The celebrating crowd in command central turned to look at Hera.

"My queen?" a Praetorian asked.

"I'm sorry. Residual trauma," Hera whispered. "Hades is not quite gone from my mind."

"Perhaps you should retire to your quarters," Brigid suggested.

"Perhaps you should mind your own goddamn business, you redheaded tart!" Hera snapped. Her fists, now massive hams enhanced by her armor, responding to her emotional trauma, clenched, knuckles whining as they ground against each other. "Oh God, Baptiste...I'm sorry. That was...that was Hades."

"Let me escort you," Brigid said. She reached up, realizing that she was leaving herself vulnerable. Hera winced, fighting against her emotions, her hands returning to the delicate silver-and-gold limbs that they usually were.

The Praetorians looked at the pair, concern masking their faces as Hera was led into the hall.

THE BRIDGE OF THE SCOUT SHIP was quiet, despite all of the activity, which was one thing that Marduk appreciated about his horde of Nephilim minions. The creatures, descended from one of the reptilian slave races that existed before the rise of humanity, had been reprogrammed on a genetic level to have only the barest of consciousness, and no will of their own. Each of the creatures possessed considerable problem-solving abilities, in order to prevent the need for Annunaki overlords to engage in micromanagement of their minions.

Silence equalled efficiency, and that was how Marduk liked it.

Then Hades entered the scene, grinning from ear to ear. "Sire..."

Marduk turned to the human. "What is it?"

"I managed to activate the communicator in Hera's quarters, to engage in some espionage," Hades stated. "Quite illuminating."

Hades set down a small tape recorder, playing a few

moments of Hera's prior gibbering. Marduk managed to contain his irritation at the insults thrown at "limp-dicked Baron Cobalt." That was another creature, a half-formed abortion no more viable for survival than the clone that Hades had created of Helena Garthwaite. Still, deep down, beneath the surface, there was a sting of pride flashing.

"You brought this to me?" Marduk asked as the tape finished.

"As I finished the replay for the second time, Hera was brought back to her quarters by Brigid Baptiste," Hades added. "She seemed to be suffering the aftereffects of my visit."

Marduk chuckled. "And she has Baptiste with her."

"And Hera was apologizing as they came in," Hades said. "She may not even have the mental strength to operate Skybreaker."

"Which leaves only those annoying robots," Marduk growled.

"The ranks of your Nephilim have been replenished, and rearmed from the stockpiles in the Crack," Hades offered. "Their soft-metal chest plates will render them vulnerable to the ASP blasters, and should ZOOs come against us, we have a skimmer ready for launch. Even secondary orichalcum cannot resist the main guns of a skimmer."

"Didn't you gather from Hera's thoughts that the gear skeletons would be upgraded?" Marduk asked.

"With weaponry available in the heart of the Crack," Hades replied. "Still, nothing more than you said Cerberus had when the Annunaki struck at them."

Marduk ran a thumb claw across his scaled chin. "We sent a strike force from *Tiamat*. It was an army, and they inflicted losses upon the Nephilim."

"Losses to the Nephilim," Hades repeated. "Who we can

recreate with ease. And if the Olympians do somehow manage to repel our forces, we raise the ship and use the really powerful guns against them. One shot, and the mountain housing New Olympus will collapse like a house of cards."

Marduk glanced to Hades. "You seem to be chomping at the bit for revenge more than I am. I didn't get to where I am by fighting to the last and risking my life."

Hades's nostrils flared. "You are an overlord. They dared to defy you!"

"One wave," Marduk said. "If that fails, then we raise the ship and fire a few salvos into this godforsaken set of rocks. I'm tiring of this place. There are prettier peaches to pluck, my little ape."

Hades nodded. "As you command."

Hades had turned to walk off the bridge when his head snapped back, blood and teeth bursting from his shredded lips. The former Magistrate launched into the air as if shot out of a cannon, sailing backward into two Nephilim who tumbled from their workstations.

Marduk sighed. "I was wondering when you would get here, Grant."

The massive Cerberus warrior turned off his fiber-optic camouflage. Hades's blood dripped from Grant's knuckles as his mask shimmered, showing off his face as if through a window in the black bodysuit. Grant's grin was apparent.

"I was wondering when Danton was going to shut the fuck up," Grant replied.

Marduk looked around at his Nephilim, who had spun in reaction to the intruder's sudden appearance. Though they hadn't been equipped with ASPs, they were clad in smart-metal armor, and each had considerable strength.

"So, where's Kane?" Marduk asked.

Grant shrugged, not in ignorance of the answer to the question, but flexing to loosen his muscles. He tilted his head, neck tendons popping like gunshots. "Making the most of my distraction."

Marduk nodded. "Very well. Kill this human. All hands! Be on the lookout for Kane! Kill every bloody human onboard!"

The Nephilim charged at Grant silently, but the silence of the bridge was cut with a war shout from the enraged Cerberus warrior.

Chapter 19

Kane heard Marduk's bellowed order of extermination as he planted the last of his half-dozen satchel charges in various compartments of the scout ship. As the Nephilim were roused from their autopilot mode of daily duties, Kane knew that Grant had to have made his move. He was proud that his huge partner had demonstrated considerable patience in waiting until his sabotage run had been completed.

Kane figured that he might as well make finding him easier, and do more damage to the Annunaki war craft. Pulling an implode grenade, he hurled it down a hallway where Nephilim reported to a duty station to retrieve their ASP blasters. The rattle of the canister bomb at their feet drew their attention. The soldiers looked down just in time to see the implosive cast out its initial burst, which vaporized atmosphere to create a sudden influx of matter and air. The subsequent void produced a body-crushing thunderclap. The Nephilim, despite their smart armor, were squashed into compact, pulpy masses, blood gushing from the crumpled neck holes in sprays of gore.

Mangled ASPs clattered around the implosion site, the armory cabinet wrecked beyond recovery as other Nephilim gawped in dismay at the sudden disappearance of their brothers.

"This way, boys," Kane said, dropping his cloaking. Two of the Nephilim warriors spotted the intruder and charged, while the remaining trio realized that they were helpless before the armed Cerberus warrior. Those three raced to a hatchway, presumably leading to another chamber of the scout ship where they'd have weaponry on hand.

The Sin Eater snapped out, and Kane caught one of the soldiers between the shoulder blades before he was through the door, a 240-grain bullet shattering the Nephilim's spine. Unfortunately, his body crashed through the open arch, alerting a more distant group of the overlord's warriors.

"So much for not drawing too much attention," Kane growled as he snapped a spin kick into the jaw of one of the charging crew members. The blow shattered the Nephilim's mandible in midstride, hurling him into the path of his fellow attacker. Both landed on the floor, skidding behind Kane as a tangled continuum of stunned humanoid.

It would take a few moments for the remaining, conscious attacker to disentangle himself from his unconscious partner, which allowed Kane to seek the cover of a ribbed section of wall. He'd made it barely in time as energy bolts ripped through the air from the archway, sparks flying as they tore into the armored material of the bulkhead. They didn't possess enough punch to spear through Kane's cover, giving him enough of a respite after the initial Nephilim volley to swing around with his Sin Eater and rip off a long burst.

Two of the overlord's soldiers jerked violently as powerful slugs smashed through their throats and skulls, decapitating the pair as their allies ducked back behind the arch.

Secure that the knot of Nephilim was staying put for a few moments, Kane unhooked another gren, this one an incendiary bomb, and whipped it underhanded. On the smooth, seamless floor, the grenade skidded swift and true, toward the soldier-packed doorway. The explosive device flared violently, flammable medium launched under the initial crack of the shell to saturate the air. A secondary spark ignited the slow-burning, airborne fuel to create a flaming inferno that licked over the armor-clad warriors. The humanoids screeched, dying reflexes spitting bolts of ASP energy into the floor as the blazing cloud darkened into a roiling canopy of choking smoke.

The stench of roasting reptilian flesh and the racket of grenades and blasterfire would draw the rest of the crew of the 250-foot scout craft. Flickering embers of charred hide fluttered as the ship's fire-control systems engaged, sealing off the scorched cabin behind impenetrable fireproof doors. Atmosphere vented from the room as the ship produced a localized vacuum in the area.

The sealed doors gave Kane some protection from the front of the ship, but the tripped Nephilim scrambled to his feet, his eyes glaring with feral rage at the human.

"Oh, you're looking for some of this?" Kane asked.

The creature didn't answer, lunging with all the power and ferocity of a jungle cat, taloned hands slicing through the air to rend Kane's flesh. The Sin Eater whipped around, roaring off its deadly message. Though the bullets didn't penetrate the Nephilim's chest armor, the high-powered slugs broke ribs and slowed the soldier's snarling advance. With a quick pivot, Kane slammed his forearm into the side of the Nephilim's skull, throwing enough weight behind the blow to shatter the creature's neck. The warrior crumpled into a lifeless heap at Kane's feet.

The Nephilim with the shattered jaw blinked, arms and legs twitching as the paralyzed limbs received faulty signals from the damaged spine. He sputtered, his eyes filled with agony. Kane couldn't bear to leave the creature to suffer, and fired a bullet through his nose, launching a spray of brains and blood out the top of his burst skull.

The thunder of Nephilim boots rumbled from the aft of the ship, and Kane reloaded the Sin Eater. With Marduk's reconstituted warrior legion aware and prepared to repel boarders, it was time to start shaking things up.

Besides, by now, the shore would be teeming with the robotic warriors of New Olympus.

Kane pulled the detonator for the satchel charges, and hoped that Grant left enough bridge crew alive to initiate surfacing procedures. The scout ship shuddered as powerful explosives ripped gaping wounds in its hull.

BY THE TIME THEY HAD reached Hera's quarters, Brigid had to support the queen, her strength drained by telepathic-induced trauma. Brigid listened as the queen sputtered, in a low voice, her random, inconclusive curses too soft to be discerned clearly.

Helping Hera through the doorway, Brigid dumped her on the bed. The smart-metal armor flexed and jerked, moving as if it were alive and independent of her own skin. Whatever Hades had done to her, Hera's thought processes were a shattered wasteland resembling the most devastated cities that Brigid had ever been through. The woman's black eyes stared helplessly, panic churning behind them as she sought some form of anchor.

"Hera? Hera! Listen to the sound of my voice!" Brigid called out, trying to reach through to the traumatized queen. "Focus on me!"

There was no response, and despite the darkness of Hera's eyes, Brigid was able to see that her pupils were wide, even though they were staring at a ceiling fixture that burned brightly. Brigid didn't know what could break Hera out of her trance, but she decided to take a page from Kane's book of brute force. With a good windup, Brigid brought the palm of her hand around in a slashing arc that would have cracked across Hera's cheek.

In the milliseconds before the slap landed, the goddess-queen came around and intercepted Brigid, seizing her wrist with all the power of a vise. For a moment, Brigid was terrified that Hera had broken her arm, so forceful was the grab, but luckily the shadow suit had absorbed some of the shock of deceleration and resisted the sudden crush of smart-metal-augmented digits.

"Hera?" Brigid asked.

"Shoot yourself in the foot," Hera mimicked.

Almost anything else would have been preferable at that moment. Brigid wished that Hera had awakened, cursing the days that the Cerberus warriors had been born. Instead, Brigid's taunt was picked up and hurled back in her face.

"I'm fucked, aren't I?" Brigid asked, still trying to tear free from the iron grip of the armored goddess.

Hera's eyes focused on the panicked archivist she had trapped by the wrist. "There hasn't been a word invented for how bad off you are now. Maybe, in your honor, when the world grovels at my feet, I'll name this situation 'Baptisted.' And all humanity will remember the day that your limbs were hung from my rafters by loops of your intestine—"

Brigid lunged forward in a head butt, her forehead impacting against Hera's nose with stunning force. Blood sprayed all over Brigid's face, but the grasp on her forearm had been broken, and the archivist stumbled away from the bed, scurrying as the silver-skinned queen screeched in outrage and agony, clutching the crimson faucet that used to be her nose.

"Oh, you sorry bitch!" Hera sputtered through the cascade of red pouring over her lips and chin. "You smashed my nose!"

Brigid shrugged. "Well, you were talking about dismembering me."

Hera stood, one hand clamping her nostrils shut, but the other swelled, expanding, forming into a spiked club similar to the one with which she had attacked Kane. Brigid had no doubt that even a glancing stroke would cripple her. The jolting memory of being struck in the head with a steel pipe flashed across her mind. She'd only barely survived that.

Brigid plucked her TP-9 from its holster and stiff-armed the pistol, cranking on the trigger as fast as she could. The front sight was leveled on Hera's unprotected face by the time she got to round number four, but at some instant between the time Brigid's trigger finger started to flex and the bullet erupted from the muzzle, a flash of quicksilver threw itself down across the queen's face. Brigid's bullet deformed against the smart metal, freezing against Hera's silver cheek, like some form of leaden birth mark before it plopped to the floor. Silvery eyes watched the spent 9 mm bullet bounce on the tiles at her feet, then rose to Brigid, slowly, surely, unflinching even as sparks burst on her armored skin.

"What a cute little toy, Baptiste," Hera said in a lilting, mocking tone. "Want to see mine?"

Brigid scrambled to her feet as the serpentine heads of the ASP pulsed and writhed around Hera's forearm. She'd lurched for the door, the floor boiling behind her as a gout of energy flew from the goddess's gesture. In another heartbeat, Brigid was through the doorway and out in the hall, racing for her life as Hera's metallic laughter rang in her ears.

BRIGID'S DISTRESS CALL reached Domi and Sela Sinclair at the same time, spurring both women into a charge toward Hera's quarters.

The activist's message was curt and direct. "I need a bigger gun!"

For Domi, that was enough imperative to charge down the halls, packing a Copperhead submachine gun, Sinclair on her heels wielding an M-16 with a grenade launcher. By all rights, Sinclair knew that she should have had enough firepower to take down a preimproved gear skeleton, but Kane's detailing of Marduk's invulnerability posed an unnerving question.

"What if these guns aren't big enough?" Sinclair asked.

Domi's charge pressed the cryogenically frozen twentieth-century military officer to keep up. "Improvise!"

Brigid scrambled around a corner at full gallop, not even slowing as she bounced off a wall and kept digging in. "She's coming! Get back!"

Domi skidded to a halt and dropped to one knee, leveling the Copperhead at the intersection that Brigid had just passed through. She held her fire, finger off the trigger until her friend had cleared the line of fire. Sinclair dropped to a prone position just beside her.

"Thought you said she was coming!" Domi said.

"Thought I'd asked for a bigger gun," Brigid grumbled.

"Holster's open," Domi returned.

Brigid grabbed the Detonics .45 out of the albino girl's holster and looked at it, weighing it against the empty TP-9 in her hand. "This isn't going to be enough."

"She's taking her sweet time," Sinclair interjected.

"Is that Domi I hear?" a voice called out from around the

corner. "Domi! Child! The snotty little freak bitch who fucking shot me in my fucking neck!"

"Pretty damn salty for a goddess," Sinclair muttered.

"Yup. It's me! Let's party, Hera!" Domi challenged.

Brigid had set up next to the other two Cerberus exiles, the .45 cocked and aimed at the corner. "She'll plow right through us with that ASP. She tore a chunk out of a wall with a blast."

"You're still alive," Domi argued. "And she's still slow."

It was only then that Domi saw that the normally long, flowing locks of red-flame hair that cascaded over Brigid's right shoulder were gone, blackened curls flaking away over one of Brigid's ears.

"She doesn't need to rush," Brigid said. "Get to cover…"

That's when Hera chose to make her appearance. The silver-and-gold-skinned goddess had been replaced with a horn-laden, eight-foot Amazon whose right hand was a Hydra-like slithering mass of bobbing dragon heads. Deranged chrome eyes regarded the trio standing the line in the hallway.

"Hi, girls," Hera greeted them. Two massive ram horns curling down in spirals framed her possessed face. "Do you think this look is too much? I can hardly tell anymore."

Domi pulled the trigger on the Copperhead, hosing the shimmering metallic demon, but the rifle-powered bullets bounced off of her armored hide. Sinclair's rifle and Brigid's borrowed .45 didn't do much better as Hera walked through the storm of bullets as if it were a light summer drizzle. Absently brushing flattened bullets off her torso, spilling them to the floor, Hera tilted her horned head, smirking.

"So, no comments on the new look?" the goddess asked as the trio's guns ran dry. Brigid grabbed a handful of Domi's collar and Sela Sinclair pulled the trigger on her grenade launcher, punching the shell into the ceiling over Hera's head. The missile detonated, belching a choking thick cloud of debris that crashed down around the armored queen's horned head and spiked shoulders.

Sinclair waited long enough to see a clawed silver limb wave through the smoke, then turned tail and ran. "We're going to need something bigger."

"I told you!" Brigid complained, reloading on the run. "Domi, pull the Praetorians out of her way. She'll slaughter them."

A belch of writhing fire snaked along the wall, unzipping the reinforced concrete in a blaze of power. Only the fact that Brigid had turned the corner immediately, yanking Domi to one side, saved the two women from being incinerated by the ASP cannon. Sinclair stumbled, ducking beneath the rocks blown out, her body armor protecting her from bone-cracking missiles.

As soon as the ASP bolt expended itself, Sela dived through the churning smoke, following Brigid and Domi back toward the hangar.

GRANT'S HUGE PAWS WRAPPED around the neck of a Nephilim flight deck member, ready to throttle the overlord's minion when the scout ship rocked under the detonation of the six satchel charges. The combined fury of sixty pounds of C-4 in various compartments ruptured the scout ship's atmospheric seals, tearing ragged, brutal wounds in its techno-organic hull.

Grant looked at the Nephilim, then shoved the flight crew member toward a control console. "Unless you want to drown, Duckie, you're gonna have to tell your boy to get this ship in the air!"

Marduk glared angrily at the lone surviving minion warrior on the bridge with him. Five corpses were strewed across the floor, one with his skull ruptured by a full-auto burst of Sin Eater slugs, another sporting the handle of a knife like a vestigial second head as the blade had been jammed through his neck. A third still smoked, his internal organs roasted by a bolt hurled by Marduk himself. The final two were fused together at the face, shattered skulls rendered inseparable by Grant's incredible strength.

The last survivor paused, indecisive.

"You heard the ape," Marduk snarled. "Lift off before we all drown!"

The Nephilim genuflected, then turned toward the helm, powering up the engines. The scout ship lurched as its thrusters fought against the suction of the ocean around them, as well as the added volume of water flooding through damaged compartments.

In the corner, Hades pulled himself to a sitting position. His mouth was a torn and mangled mass, broken teeth had clawed his lips asunder thanks to the power of Grant's punch catching him off guard. "Math-tuh!"

As Hades spoke, a chunk of tongue dribbled over his lower lip, bouncing spongily in his lap. "My mouf!"

Marduk glanced toward Hades, watching as the human mopped the waterfall of blood that spilled onto his chest armor. The overlord turned back to Grant. "Haven't I seen enough of that today?"

"Tell you what, snake-face," Grant challenged. "You won't have to look at anything else if you just stand still."

Marduk flicked his eyes toward Hades. "It's almost tempting, but no, thank you."

The overlord raised his forearm, but Grant was on him in a heartbeat, lapping aside the ASP. A spray of yellow fire snarled out of the forearm blaster as Grant shoved his Sin Eater under Marduk's sternum. Emptying the 20-round magazine at contact range didn't tear through the Annunaki's personal armor, but the combined effect was enough to cause Marduk's breath to explode in a fetid wind into Grant's face. With a shrug of his tall, powerful frame, the overlord hurled Grant against the bulkhead.

Marduk brought up his ASP-wreathed fist to return the favor from the Sin Eater in the gut, but Grant's stovepipe leg lashed up into his jaw, snapping back his head. Only the seven-foot Annunaki's superior strength kept the kick from breaking his neck like a twig, but even so, Marduk reeled from the power of Grant's strike, stumbling against the Nephilim pilot.

Water sluiced off the view screens, showing the Greek sky crystal clear over the Aegean waters, which had reclaimed vast areas of the shattered nation. The Nephilim pilot continued his task of raising the wounded scout ship out of the sea, thrusters powering the craft ever skyward.

Marduk winced as Grant slammed into his back, the ex-Magistrate's rock-hard shoulder nearly buckling his spine under a diving impact. With a pivot, Marduk spun Grant around with a wicked elbow to the jaw. The blow wasn't as solid as Marduk would have cared for, however, as Grant had rolled with the force of the punch, saving his cheekbone and mandible from being obliterated by Annunaki strength wrapped in nigh invulnerable smart metal.

Grant lurched back, grasping Marduk by the back of his head and spearing him face first against the view screen. As it was only a wall monitor, and not actual glass, Marduk's scale-armored face tore the digital plasma surface, and gel seeped from the gash scored in the pliable screen. Marduk dug his taloned fingers into the console and pushed back hard, hurling himself onto Grant, toppling both combatants to the floor.

Marduk raised his elbow, this time certain of a bone-snapping stroke when he spotted something on the screen. Along the shore, a bronze-colored armada of mecha stood, festooned with far more impressive weaponry than he had seen before.

Grant snaked his arm around Marduk's throat and squeezed harshly.

"Welcome to target practice, Duckie," Grant chuckled into his ear. "As much as I'd like to stick around and rip your head off your sorry shoulders—" the scout ship started rumbling, punished by withering fire that rose from the coast as if on cue "—I didn't sign on to have my ass shot out of the sky."

With a twist, Grant slammed Marduk headfirst into the floor with a resounding crack, blood flying from split Annunaki hide. A groan escaped the overlord's scaled lips, and Grant looked down on his stunned opponent. Leaving him to die was a cruel fate, but too many factors stilled any sense of mercy in Grant's soul. Foremost was the horrendous injuries he'd inflicted upon Shizuka and the grim memories of servitude to his previous incarnation. The threat he posed to New Olympus was icing on the cake.

"Goodbye, Marduk," Grant snarled.

Slithering to his feet, Grant glanced at the Nephilim trying to control the scout ship. The thrusters were failing, and the deck heaved to and fro. Further stability was hindered as rockets and grenades lanced along the flank of the scout ship, explosions rippling through its wounded sections.

Grant launched himself toward the door, seeking to escape the bridge. Hades lashed out, grabbing Grant's ankle and holding on with a death grip, twisting at his leg. "Ib we die, you, die doo!"

Grant looked at the pathetic clone master, his face smeared down his chin and dripping on the floor beneath him. Grant wrenched his foot free, then stomped down hard. The first kick folded Hades's nose flat into his face, popping more teeth loose from his lower jaw. A vicious, rage-fueled squeal escaped the torn lips, and fingers clawed out to catch Grant's foot before it came down again, but the second kick snagged at Hades's hairline and peeled flesh from bone all the way to the floor, crushing mandible with a gruesome crunch-pop accompanied by a flush of blood from the ripped face.

Hades's fingers sank into Grant's other calf, still tugging, though it could have just been a death reflex. Grant didn't care; he just wanted to extricate himself from the dying madman and hammered down his foot one last time, crushing Hades's skull.

Lifeless fingers slid down to the floor, but Grant was already in motion, heading toward one of the airlocks.

"Kane? You there?" Grant called.

"Just about to take a swim," Kane answered. "Care to join me?"

Grant stuffed a high-explosive grenade against the airlock, then tucked himself behind a rib in the bulkhead. "Be there in a moment. Save me a towel."

The grenade tore open the hatch, and Grant swung around the rib, hurling himself into open air, sailing to the water sixty feet below. The space around him rippled with the vengeful fire hurled by the New Olympian robot corps defending their home, but the racket disappeared as Grant sliced into the water, diving deep.

Above, the scout ship shook violently, dying as explosive shells ravaged her ruthlessly.

Chapter 20

Artem15 sidestepped, a tendril of ASP energy cracking the ground at her feet as she hurled another javelin at the hovering monstrosity that bled smoke into the sky. The warhead speared into a shorn bulkhead where Nephilim soldiers fired, hammering at the New Olympian robot horde. Behind them, rows of Praetorians fired disposable rocket launchers from the cover of boulders, turning the once blue noon skies into a crisscross of lightning and cottony smoke trails.

Z00s held up his secondary orichalcum chest shield, re-directing energy blasts away from a Praetorian position that had come under concentrated Nephilim fire. The Annunaki blasters crackled violently, but Z00s leaned into the barrage, protecting the Greek soldiers who fired around him, hammering relentlessly at the scout ship with their antitank missiles.

Artem15 lent a hand in the form of swiveling the .50-caliber heavy machine gun on her shoulder toward the Nephilim. The massive weapon belched out a stream of thunderous rounds, its muzzle-flash burning brightly even in the height of day, easily crossing the few hundred yards between the cliff and the overlord's ship. On the deck, Nephilim twisted under the heavyweight bullets that had been designed to punch through tanks and aircraft. The once invincible armored warriors burst apart under the relentless storm of lead she cut out. ASP bolts smashed against her, and while the mechanoid was pushed back, pain flaring through her cybernetic link to the towering robot warrior, Artem15 still stood, her armor boiling off molten slag here and there. Had she been protected only by the softer, easily manipulated copper and brass, Diana knew she would have fallen with the first impact. As it was, she could see through apple-sized gaps burned in the Sandcat armor door over her cockpit.

"Enough playing nice," she growled. Her left shoulder had only a machine gun, but it was time to bring out the big hammer against the deadly horde still fighting on the crippled scout ship. A 25 mm chain-driven cannon rested on her right shoulder, and Artem15 cut loose at 350 rounds per minute.

The rate of fire might have been only a fraction of the other machine guns that had been mounted on the fighting clockwork mobile armor, but what it lacked in volume, it made up in payload. The inch-thick shells were packed with high explosives, and when her first salvo struck the bulkhead, the shells created scars the size of dinner plates in the spaceworthy hull. Artem15 walked the stream of explosive shells into the smoldering wound in the side of the ship. A dozen 25 mm explosive rounds later, the last of the Nephilim hung like ragged laundry, shattered arms flapping bonelessly.

"Thank you," Z00s said, leaning against his shield. "This is the definition of good news and bad news. The good news is that Marduk was ignorant of your upgrades."

"The bad news being that you're number one with a bullet...or energy zap," Artem15 replied. "Got even better news."

"What's that?" Z00s asked, lurching upright again, hefting his charred shield.

"I doubt you'll want any more flagellation after that thing sinks back to the bottom of the Aegean." Artem15 chuckled.

Thurmond nodded, his robot mimicking his head bob. "The urge to have your ass kicked for doing wrong goes out the window when your ass is really being kicked."

"Good, because New Olympus needs a leader, and there's no way in hell that I want Hera still at the helm," Artem15 answered.

The air, filled with booms, pops and crackles, suddenly was cut by the screech of thousands of mutated throats issuing forth an agonizing wail. Mechanoid and Nephilim alike held their fire, the mournful cry lasting nearly a minute. Praetorian soldiers trembled at the unholy banshee song that knifed through the land.

"What the hell was that?" Are5 asked, lowering the M-61 Vulcan that he wielded like a rifle. "Oh, man…"

Artem15 glanced up and saw that the mountain ridge above them was lined with a wall of clones, their yellow eyes wild and feral. None of them carried weapons, but her telescopic cameras showed that they all cried tears of blood, nostrils frothing pink foam. She shuddered.

"Good news, bad news again," she stated.

"Gimme the good news," Z00s said.

"Hades is most likely dead," Artem15 explained.

"And the bad news is that now we have a couple of thousand wild things no longer on a psychic leash," Z00s concluded. "Praetorians! Fall back behind us! Warbots! Hold the line! No more Greeks will die today!"

"We used up most of our ammo on the scout ship, and it's still floating there," Artem15 countered. She drew a javelin from her quiver.

"We've got the advantage," Z00s answered. "They're too wild now to utilize any form of technology. The scout ship's too wrecked to be of any use to Marduk, even if he can get it higher in the air."

Artem15 glanced back, seeing shattered canisters rolling out of the ruptured belly of the craft, splashing into the turgid, muddied waters stirred up by the hover thrusters. "Zoo…"

"Those are the clone vats," Z00s explained. "Nobody's making any more of these things."

A boulder sailed through the air, arcing over the front line of mutants who were standing their ground. The rock bounced off the hillside and bowled over a Spartan warbot, popping the joints out of its shoulder and hip with the power of its impact. The pilot opened her carapace, trying to sit the robot up as Praetorians ignored Z00s's orders and rushed to her aid.

"Oh, hell," Z00s grumbled.

Humanoids lurched into view, shaggy, ape-limbed monstrosities that towered at twice the height of the original Tartarus clones. Artem15 could see huge, curved claws sweeping out like scythes on the ends of their massive arms. A furry, towering abomination hefted a massive rock over his head.

Are5 blew the boulder to pebbles with his grenade launcher, the creature bellowing as broken stone peppered his head and back. "Brigid, are you watching this on camera? Tell us you know what those things are!"

"This is central command. We're kind of occupied right now!" came a panicked cry. Over the radio, the mechanoid jockeys heard the roar of autofire and explosions back at New Olympus. "Just shoot the fucking things!"

The mutant mob roared in unison, then surged down the slope, a wall of cloned rage bearing down on the defenders of New Olympus.

KANE SLICED INTO THE WATERS of the Aegean. With powerful kicks, he plunged deeper below the surface as broken clone vat canisters splashed all around him. Their enormous mass would crush him like jelly if they hit him, so the ex-Magistrate decided that depth would be his best defense against crippling injury. The rebreathing unit on the high-tech hood engaged, allowing him to stay safely submerged.

He was glad that the mask allowed for use of the Commtact for instant communications, even beneath the surface. "Grant, where are you, man?"

"About two hundred feet to your north," Grant replied. "Looks like you'd better get out from under that shit."

"Yes, I'm trying," Kane griped. "Can you see anything?"

"The mask optics kicked in, but even so, you're stuck in the heart of a cloud," Grant answered.

"Don't swim this way, then," Kane ordered. "No telling when something's going to drop out of the hold and break your head open."

Kane cursed himself for tempting fate when the bottom of a broken vat bounced off his shoulder, rendering his left arm numb, even through the protective capabilities of the shadow suit material. He curled the stunned limb against his chest and kicked with all his might, homing in on Grant's position thanks to his mask interacting with the Commtact in his jaw. The adaptive electronics provided Kane a holographic indicator of his partner's place.

"This is central command to Kane and Grant," a voice

broke in on their Commtact line. Brigid had provided the Greeks with the frequency that the implanted transceivers worked on, helping to unify communications capabilities with the New Olympians.

"What is it?" Kane asked, his voice rough with the pain of being struck by three hundred pounds of wrecked Annunaki technology.

"CAT Beta is reporting casualties from a hard contact with Hera," the Greek reported. "Are you in any position for pickup? We need extra support here!"

"Casualties?" Grant asked, worry in his tone. "I'm halfway to shore."

"Negative! Stay away from the shore! We can't spare the manpower to get you two back to base," Z00s interjected. "There's too many mutants here!"

"And everything was going so smoothly," Kane moaned. He finally kicked to the surface. A hundred yards behind him, the scout ship lurched violently. A silvery object, twenty-five feet in diameter, fired out of its back, rocketing into the sky so fast that the air snapped around it. "Someone's hightailing it out of here!"

"Ain't Hades," Grant replied. "Fucking Marduk."

The scout ship crumbled in its center, the horrendous stresses of hundreds of high-explosive rounds and Kane's reign of sabotage ultimately proving too great a stress on the superstructure. As if its spine broke, the scout ship split in two, the front end plunging into the ocean, propelling a wall of water toward Kane.

There was no way that he could dive or swim out of the wave's path, so Kane went limp, relying on the life support systems of the shadow suit and sealed hood to keep him from drowning. If being scooped up by Artem15 had made him feel doll-like before, while being plucked from the angry talons of dozens of mutants, the force of the wave made him feel even tinier and lighter, a mere leaf riding the crest of a tidal wave that hurled him at the rocky beach two hundred yards away. Tossed head over heels in a helpless cartwheel, a chunk of bulkhead bounced violently off Kane's face, tearing his mask away.

Grant's voice bellowed over the Commtact, but suddenly deprived of breathable oxygen and thrown about like driftwood, Kane couldn't understand Grant. It was as if he were speaking an alien language. Breaching the face of the wave, he spotted the jagged boulders on the beach and realized that he needed to minimize his profile. He tucked his arms and legs against his chest, ducking his head down in an attempt to shield his skull with his shoulders. The cowl might have had some impressive life support and optical abilities, but offered little in terms of protection from blunt trauma. A bullet would scramble brains, and Kane desperately wished for his Mag helmet to magically appear before he dashed his skull against the rocky beach.

The wave collapsed, dragging Kane down hard onto the shore, but the ball he'd formed himself into had done its job. His back and shoulders absorbed a spine-jarring impact as he bounced off a boulder. The reactive fibers had absorbed some of the force, avoiding crippling injuries, though Kane realized that everything from the back of his neck down to his coccyx would be a massive purple-and-black bruise and he'd ache for weeks from the pounding he'd taken.

That was okay with Kane. Pain was a sign that he'd survived.

Smaller secondary waves lapped at Kane as he lifted his head above the surface.

Hands hooked under his armpits, hauling him to his feet as if he were a child. When Kane's vision cleared, he was glad to see Grant beside him again.

"You okay?" Grant asked.

Kane glared at him.

"All right, ask a stupid question," Grant rumbled. "Our buddies on the cliff are being hammered big time."

"What're the odds?" Kane asked, deploying his Sin Eater.

"You up for the fight?" Grant asked.

Kane shrugged. "Like we have a choice."

"Then let's go. Hades whipped up a ton of megatherium before he died," Grant answered.

"Megatherium?" Kane asked.

"The bastard love child of an allosaurus and a tree sloth," Grant explained. "Spending time in New Edo gives a lad a lot of time to study prehistoric monsters."

"Dinosaur sloths?" Kane asked again incredulously.

A giant, brown-furred monstrosity, ten feet in height, tumbled into view, fierce black eyes glaring at the two Cerberus warriors. It rose up on its hind legs, then raised one scythe-tipped arm to swing at them.

Both Kane and Grant fired their Sin Eaters, 9 mm slugs rattling against the creature's hide. The two men exhausted their magazines, only the final rounds finally bringing down the massive beast.

"Dinosaur sloths," Kane repeated, looking at the dead creature at their feet.

"They have bone nodules in their skin that makes their hide

tough enough to withstand a sabertooth tiger's fangs," Grant explained.

"Fascinating," Kane grumbled, slapping a fresh magazine into his Sin Eater. Muscles spasmed in his aching back as he climbed over the lumpy form of the dead prehistoric sloth. "Remind me to ask you more about it later."

The Cerberus warriors scrambled into a battlefield where cloned mutants and primordial creatures fought against mechanoid and Praetorian, talon and fang, sword and spike.

They charged into the melee.

SELA SINCLAIR APPLIED a dressing to her lacerated biceps, wincing as the blood ran down her sleeve, dripping to the floor. Central command shook violently, the roar of combat at the entrance threatening to burst her eardrums. Brigid Baptiste crawled back to Sinclair, reaching into her bandolier for more magazines to feed the borrowed M-16.

A Praetorian shrieked in agony as a pulse of energy vaporized his right arm and shoulder, blackened flesh flaking away. The wounded Greek collapsed to the floor, but others grabbed his ankles and dragged him away from the doorway. Brigid jammed the magazine into place on the rifle, watching the Praetorians rescue their own.

"How's your arm?" Brigid asked.

"I'm not going to be able to use it anymore today," Sinclair confessed.

Sten guns and bolt-action rifles sounded in the distance, breaking the pair's conversation. It was another flanking run by the defenders of New Olympus, opening fire on Hera's back to keep her from central command.

Hera's forearm cannon squealed, an audible shriek of energy surging down the hallway. Brigid swung around the doorjamb and cut loose with her M-16, firing at the silver-armored monstrosity as she turned on the flanking Praetorians.

"You insufferable ingrates!" Hera bellowed. "I made you! I made you all!"

"Bulletproof and humble—what a winning combination," Sinclair groaned. She plucked a Colt 1911 from her holster, thumbing off the safety. "Please tell me you know what we're going to do against her."

"Considering that her armor is absorbing operative mass from the wreckage she's striding through, I have a feeling that all these bullets we're pouring into her are only exacerbating the situation," Brigid stated, ducking back behind cover.

Yellow lightning danced through the doorway, turning tiles into airborne dust and debris. Sinclair could feel the shock wave coming off the erupting floor, even behind the shielding form of Brigid. The former archivist flipped the remaining scraggles of dangling, unscorched hair back over her shoulder, looking at Sinclair.

"Are you okay?" she asked.

"Am I okay?" Sinclair countered. She was tempted to mention that Brigid, with her hair burned away in several patches, with rips in her armored uniform, looked worse off. Instead, she nodded. "I'll live."

"Good," Brigid replied. She grabbed Sinclair's bandolier, plucking out a 40 mm grenade, feeding it into the launcher tube under the rifle. "You're out of these."

"I was expecting naked mutants, not her," the CAT Beta leader complained.

"What kind of round is this?" Brigid asked.

"It's a HESH," Sinclair replied. "If anything, that might do the trick."

Brigid leaned around the corner, then ducked back, another

bouncing tendril of high-powered energy spitting down the hall. Consoles along one wall detonated, sparks and shrapnel flying. Brigid swung out again and fired the grenade launcher.

Hera jerked under the impact, the high-explosive squash-headed shell puckering against her spiked and armored hide, then detonating, spewing a jet of superheated, metal-slicing, expanding gas through the smart metal. Pain ripped from Hera's lips, an agonized wail as her silvery flesh heated enough to burn the naked skin beneath, but still the insane goddess stood.

"Baptiste! Baptiste! I'm going to kill you by inches!" Hera threatened.

"I thought Domi had some cunning plan," Sinclair said, grimacing. She glanced around the doorjamb, watching Hera carve sections of wall away with gnarled talons. Steel rebar was grabbed by whipping tentacles of the goddess's hide, torn from the concrete before melting and flowing into the mass of the armor. More curved spines erupted from between Hera's shoulders, hanging over her head like the arched tail of a scorpion.

Brigid smiled. "She's on her way."

UNBRIDLED POWER HAD BROKEN through Hera's mind like a tidal wave shattering a dam, but the being that had once been Helena Garthwaite wouldn't have had it any other way. After all, why should she have been forced to settle for mere existence as a human sheathed in some pretty, shiny skin when the ancient Annunaki secrets bonded with her central nervous system gave her so much more? Her hand still ached where broken carpals were still mending, even under the acceleration of cellular activity inspired by the smart armor. Her back stung, despite the signals fired through the neural inhibitor neutralizing the majority of her pain.

Every few feet, she absorbed another pound of ambient metal, ripping it from the concrete or gathering up spent bullets and expended brass to blend in with her armor. The soup of nanomachines worked swiftly to reconfigure the additional mass into more articulated, responsive flat motors that flowed and flexed at the demands of her imagination. Boosted by the charged energy module in her ASP, Hera was able to motivate her armor, and the adaptive nature of the smart armor analyzed the modules to form more units. Each step closer to central command brought her past power conduits that her whiplike stingers stabbed at, draining nuclear-reactor-generated electricity to top off the imitation modules. With limitless access to additional mass and energy to fuel her ever growing and mutating body, Hera had literally transformed into a goddess. The rage at telepathic violation and the Ceberus warriors' interference in her royal designs were a spark that combined into an explosion that reached to the depths of Hera's soul, releasing her true nature.

Not a goddess, but a queen of hell. When she finished with Brigid Baptiste, she'd destroy the others and build up another New Olympus, this one reigned over by a pantheon of vengeance and spite.

Her goal was simple. Reach Brigid Baptiste and peel the skin off the snooty little red-haired nerd for every real and imagined wrong inflicted upon her over the past decade. The bullets and bombs she waded through were harmless, if not beneficial to her new juggernaut form. Invulnerable, immune to pain and possessed of strengths not seen even by the most talented of mechanoid pilots, Hera reveled in absolute power.

"Hey!" a voice shouted, cutting through Hera's reveries. She turned slowly, eyeing the tiny form of Domi perched behind a wheelchair. The albino girl's eyes were gleaming rubies dripping hatred expressly for her sake.

"Domi," Hera greeted. "Little animal girl. How did you know that I wasn't all sweetness and kindness? Was your mother a wolf? Did you smell the evil in me?"

"No. You were just like those other creepy sexual predators I had to bide my time with in the Tartarus Pits," Domi answered, leaning on the handles of the wheelchair. Hera looked at the seat, seeing it was packed with fat pouches.

"What's that?" Hera asked. "A booby-trapped wheel-chair?"

"Matter of fact, yes," Domi said. "Wanna taste?"

Hera threw her head back in laughter. "Bring it to me, child. Let's see what your little primate brain can come up with."

Domi shoved hard, rocketing the wheelchair forward. Hera lifted her arm and fired the ASP cannon, spitting a bolt into the packages in the seat when the chair hadn't traveled five feet. The tendril of destructive energy split the chair in two, shredding the packaging, flutters of papers filling the air.

Hera, confused, took three long strides forward, her improved gait carrying her to the wreckage of the wheelchair. One taloned hand scooped up the scorched pages of a yellowed old paperback.

"Cute. You lied to me, girl. Where's the bomb?" Hera asked.

"Who said the bomb had to be in the seat?" Domi asked from ten yards away. She jammed her thumb on the firing stud of her remote, and the C-4-packed tires of the wheelchair erupted, sheets of concussive force snapping spines and scales off Hera's bulked-up armor. Overpressure hammered both sides of Hera's head, battering her eardrums faster than the smart metal could flow into her ears to deaden the shock.

Her balance knocked out, Hera collapsed to one knee, the horned joint crushing tile and concrete beneath her.

Domi stood up, sneering at the fallen goddess. "Retard, huh?"

Hera glared at Domi hatefully, foot-long claws sinking into the walls on either side of her. From her throat to her navel, rows of nails and quills erupted, each one needle sharp and wicked. "Come here and give me a hug, you little whore."

Domi beckoned Hera closer with a waving finger. "I'm tired of coming to you, Hera. You come to me."

Surging with renewed fury, Hera pulled herself to her feet, articulated flat motors straining to get her back to her feet. Hinged spines that erupted from her back unfolded, smashing into the ground as a second set of stabilizing legs, moving in time to keep the equilibrium-impaired armored queen from stumbling and tripping.

Domi whirled and raced back down the smashed corridors toward Hera's quarters. As she ran, she spoke swiftly and loudly as if into her Commtact.

"Brigid! Fire up the Skybreaker! She's falling for it!" Domi shouted.

The Skybreaker! Hera's heart pounded like a trip-hammer, realizing that there was indeed a single weapon in all of New Olympus that could bring her low. Should Brigid have the resources to activate the ancient Annunaki weapon, its lightning would boil the smart metal and sear her flesh down to her blackened bones.

The two hinged spider legs jutting from Hera's back were joined by others, the long clawed limbs hefting her into the air, galloping through the hallways hot on Domi's heels.

She had to reach the Skybreaker, lest all was lost.

Chapter 21

Out of ammunition, Kane resorted to using the frame of his Sin Eater as a club, hammering the steel body of the machine pistol against mutant heads with enough force to shatter skulls. His knife was broken in two, the missing section of blade snapped off in the jugular of one of the megatherium that had been trying to pry Artem15 apart with huge sickle-shaped claws. The battle was ferocious, Hades's final legacy of clone rage proving to be a maniacal swarm that gave no quarter and required fanatical force to slay. Even the massive fists of the fifteen-foot mechanoids were only able to transform one or two at a time into a pulp.

Praetorians held a hillside, their Sten machine pistols and bolt-action rifles reducing the mutant crowd to half its original strength. The Tartarus horde still numbered close to a thousand, and the valiant Greeks were running out of bullets at this point.

Kane stumbled over one of dozens of dead Praetorians, tripping to the bloodied earth beneath him. Scaled humanoids saw the former Magistrate topple and launched themselves in wild abandon at him. Kane dug into the dirt to get out of their way when his fingertips brushed one of the Praetorian leaf-bladed swords. With a lunge, he dodged the two cloned mutates and scooped up the two foot long length of razor-sharp steel. A third mutant charged despite Kane's armed status, and its life ended with a powerful swing. Kane flicked the sword back from his decapitating stroke, plunging the point through the eye socket of another enraged hordeling, skewering him through the brain. A savage twist freed the blade and enabled him to continue his battle.

Grasping claws were severed, the attached limbs waving uselessly. When the flashing blade was snarled in rib or skull, Kane used his free fist or a wicked kick to fend off other attackers as he wrenched the sword loose.

A ten-foot shaggy form stomped the ground, lurching past his back. Kane whirled, expecting to fend off a megatherium armed with only two feet of steel. Instead, Kane felt pity for the prehistoric sloth as Grant held it in a headlock, beating its skull bloody with the broken stock of a bolt-action rifle.

"Die!" Grant bellowed, riding the toppling megatherium to the ground. Whether it was from incessant brain trauma or the strangling grip on its windpipe, the clone sloth was dead, its tongue rolling from between slackened lips, an eye punctured by a splinter of wood left behind when Grant snapped the rifle in two over its head.

Kane spun away, swinging the leaf-shaped blade point in a wide arc, powering the razor-sharp edge through throats, jaws and faces, inflicting lethal injuries on an encroaching swarm of replacements for dead hordelings. A swift reversal enabled Kane to slash another bloody swathe through those not immediately felled by his first swipe. Are5 and Her47les dropped on either side of Kane, their massive four-clawed feet crushing mutants into bloody pulps and taking pressure off the Cerberus hero.

"Get to the Praetorians, Kane! You need a gun!" Are5 demanded.

"We've got this mess," Herk added.

Kane seized a clone by the throat, then beat his head against Her47les's knee joint, crushing the clone's head. He tossed the limp corpse aside and hacked through another mutant's neck, the blade point coming out of the dead thing's crotch in advance of a flood of freed entrails.

"Or maybe you don't need a gun," Are5 noted, swatting at scrawny maniacs that crawled all over him.

"Dude's on autopilot!" Herk shouted, punting a pair of humanoids seventy yards with a single kick.

Kane wanted to say that there was something to that, but pure rage had constricted his throat to make speech impossible. His cognitive abilities were unaffected, but any pretense of civilization had been left behind as he chopped and slashed. Memories of sweaty African jungles and a flashing sword biting into apelike beings flickered into his mind, mixed with images of his savage blade chopping through the axes wielded by fomorii in prehistoric Ireland. Deep in his genetic memory, Kane was tapping reserves of strength to overcome his attackers.

And from the ancient, double-helix ladder of history, many rose to lend him their might and prowess. Kane didn't know their names, only vague identities. A puritan with the strength of a fanatic. The warrior consort of a witch queen. A barbarian from the Cimmerian highlands. A slave who battled his way to possession of a throne and a crown. A lone crusader in an urban wasteland. His muscle fibers screamed for rest, but the willpower of a line of champions denied those pleas.

And the mutant hordes toppled. When one leaf sword was bent beyond use, Kane scooped up another object, the gnarled barrel of a rifle, and he continued to beat and crush with it. The times that his hands were empty of weapons, he continued onward, punching windpipes, fingering out eyeballs and twisting necks until he seized up a rock or a length of driftwood to continue his pounding.

"Kane! Kane, dammit! Kane!" Grant bellowed.

The ex-Magistrate looked up. He was kneeling over a dead mutant whose face was punched into a frothy stew. The dead littered the ground in every direction. Dismembered clockwork warriors were strewed across the countryside around them, and mixed in with the countless mutants, Greek men lay. The hillside, though, was teeming with Praetorian soldiers too tired to cheer after the carnage wrought around them.

"They're dead," Grant panted. "The muties are all dead."

Kane couldn't talk. His arms hung limply at his sides. A broken megatherium claw jutted from a spot below his ribs, blood soaking down to his thighs.

"You've been punching that poor bastard for two minutes," Grant explained.

Kane nodded. Grant reached down and hauled his friend to his feet.

"It's over," Grant whispered, supporting Kane.

The bloody Magistrate tried to push Grant off him. "I can still fight…."

Grant didn't blame him for not wanting to quit, but he hoped that Kane would forgive him for the right cross that snapped him into unconsciousness. A pair of Praetorians accepted the burden of Kane as Z00s reached down for Grant. "This guy wouldn't stop until he bled dry. Get him some medical help."

"Hera's gone berserk," Thurmond told Grant. "They need everyone who can still fight."

"Count me in," Grant said, climbing onto Z00s's arm.

Leaving the twenty-three surviving Spartan units behind,

ZOOs and the six operating hero suits bounded off to deal with the last threat to the beleagured nation of New Olympus.

HERA SMASHED through the doors to her quarters, battering aside steel bulkheads and the reinforced-concrete door frame to get back to the laboratory. She'd lost track of Domi in the charge back. Her ancillary spider legs sank into the tile floor, gripping the ground beneath, seeking support as she searched through her bedroom.

"Baptiste! Domi! Come out to play!" she challenged, her voice hoarse. Charged energy modules all along her body pulsed, humming with stored electrical power. The undulating Hydra heads of her ASP waved, glowing with a prepared bolt of devastation ready to blast Domi or Brigid into her component atoms.

The laboratory door stood open, and Hera stomped through, riding the powerful hinged limbs that extended from her back. Wrathful gaze scanned for signs of the Cerberus women when she saw the Skybreaker core sitting off to one side of the lab. It was covered with cakes of plastic explosives hooked up to a central detonator. A walkie-talkie sat next to the detonator.

"How're you doing, Hera?" Domi called. "You know, for an uneducated retard, I played you like a harp."

"No. It's mine!" Hera screeched. "You can't take it away from me!"

The armor-clad queen lunged, snatching at blocks of explosive to pull them from the ancient column. "I found this!"

"Goodbye, Hera," Domi's voice came over the walkie-talkie.

The world turned white around Hera.

DOMI LET THE DETONATOR CLATTER to the floor as the final tremors faded. The tireless work of the Praetorian demolitions team had been instrumental. All she had to do was suggest traps, and the brilliant Greeks interpreted her plans, rapidly fixing up the wheelchair as a booby trap, and finally lacing the Skybreaker core with enough C-4 to insure that neither Hera nor her lightning weapon would ever threaten the world again.

Brigid gave Domi's shoulder a squeeze. "Good work, everybody."

Domi rested her hand on Brigid's, smiling. "Thank Grant for giving me the idea."

"What's that idea?" Brigid asked.

Domi chuckled. "There's no problem that can't be solved with the proper application of high explosives."

Brigid nodded and smiled. "It's worked well enough for us before."

"Hope you're not mad at me blowing the Skybreaker to hell," Domi mentioned.

Brigid shook her head. "It was just too dangerous. Leaving it in one piece would only inspire someone else to try to take it, and then we'd have to worry about it all over again."

"Central command to Domi and Baptiste. Z00s and Grant are in the hangar."

"Thank you, CC," Brigid responded.

Something shifted in the smoke-filled corridor. Brigid tensed, then dismissed the movement as settling wreckage. Hera's quarters, isolated from the rest of the installation, would never be accessed again, thanks to collapsed ceilings and caved-in walls. Hera's corpse would be sealed in the silent tomb forever. More rubble rumbled, rebar snapping.

Something was alive, and it was emitting a brilliant blue glow that was only partially diffused by the choking smoke.

Domi turned to look at Brigid, red eyes accusing. "You always gotta to go and tempt fate."

"Command, put out the alert to evacuate the facility," Brigid called, starting to run. "The bomb wasn't enough, and now I'm afraid she's integrated the Skybreaker into her mass."

"She what the what?" central command asked.

"She absorbed the big doomsday weapon capable of slaughtering hundreds of mutants in a single blast!" Brigid warned.

The mountain shifted as if it were experiencing an earthquake. Brigid and Domi suddenly found themselves walking against a bracing wind that lashed at them. The corridor behind them collapsed, walls and ceiling crumbling into a compressed barrier.

"What was that?" Domi asked, looking back at the rubble.

Brigid chewed her lip, green eyes flashing with a jolt of fear. "That was Hera making a back door to New Olympus."

Domi swallowed. It was bad enough when Hera had the power to blast holes through reinforced concrete and could bounce bullets off her hide. Given Brigid's explanation that Hera could absorb the strength of metal and devices through her smart-metal armor, that meant that Hera was made out of Annunaki alloys and possessed personal power that matched some of the worst threats they'd ever faced. "How the hell are we going to stop *that?*"

"I have no idea," Brigid whispered breathlessly.

GRANT WATCHED A SPEAR of blue lightning tear through the rear slope of the mountain that housed New Olympus, and his throat tightened, his jaw dropping in awe. "Brigid, Domi, are you okay?"

"We're fine," Brigid said. "Hera's not interested in us anymore. We're insects compared to her."

Grant focused his mask's optics on the mountainside and saw Hera, standing easily as tall as Z00s, striding through the massive hole blown in the side of the mountain. "Hera's big."

"How big?" Brigid inquired.

"Call it twelve to fifteen feet," Grant answered. "What the hell did she do, eat a Sandcat?"

"Worse, her armor ingested and absorbed the Skybreaker base unit," Brigid replied.

Grant's shoulders sagged. "Brigid, tell me you're joking. Because if she ate that…"

Hera shimmered, disappearing from the mountainside in a flash that was all too familiar to Grant.

"Where did she go?" Z00s asked.

"She's integrated a Threshold into her armor," Grant said. "Which means she can transmit herself to any parallax point in the world."

Z00s turned, looking toward the ruins of the oracle temple. His telescopic cameras detected a flare of plasma wave energy mist in the ancient node. "I know where she went."

The mechanoid commander whirled, and Grant held on tightly. Are5, P05eidon, Apo110, Artem15, Her47les and D10nysus were hot on his heels as they raced to the oracle where Hera stood.

"Where's Kane?" Brigid asked.

"He's out cold," Grant said.

"Hurt?" Brigid inquired.

"You mean aside from being slammed into a rocky shore

by a tidal wave, then having a prehistoric sloth break off a claw in his gut?" Grant asked. "If anyone's earned a nap, it's him."

"Sloths," Brigid repeated. "I'm officially through being surprised by anything for the rest of my life."

"Grant, I'm going to have to set you down," ZOOs said.

The big ex-Magistrate clambered down the robot's back as they stood at the base of the earthen ramp. Hera loomed over them, the air crackling with electricity around her. Grant had gathered up what weaponry he could from the Praetorians, and pulled a collapsible antitank rocket from his war bag. The other robot warriors had replenished a meager amount of ammunition from wrecked Spartan units, giving them something to use against the armored madwoman, but as lightning danced between her palms, the assembled warriors were uncertain if even that kind of firepower was enough to handle her.

"Helena, I'm going to have to ask you to surrender," ZOOs called out. "If you don't submit peacefully, we'll be forced to get rough."

"This is just too precious." Hera chuckled. "I'm to bow down to an assemblage of tin soldiers led by a scam artist?"

"Disengage your armor, and just walk away, Helena," ZOOs ordered.

"The name is Hera Olympiad," she countered. "And you would ally with this murderer?"

Artem15 hefted her last remaining javelin. "That's the thing. Sometimes when you ask for forgiveness, you actually get it."

Hera laughed, walking closer to the warrior force. Her eyes flitted down to Grant, and she snorted in derision. "Then forgive me if I don't roll over and allow you puny gnats to—"

Grant's antitank rocket erupted, enveloping the construct's head in a blossom of flame and smoke that bowled her backward. Artem15's javelin was hot behind it, lancing between the massive silver breasts of the insane goddess, warped metal folding away from a crater. Hera's head was a fused and mashed mockery of what she used to be, but it was apparent after the initial blast that Helena Garthwaite's body was cocooned in the thickest, most heavily armored portion of the giant's torso. Heavy machine-gun rounds rippled on skin like raindrops on a pond.

The combined firepower of the seven suits and Grant smashed into Hera, driving her backward, arms raised to ward off the incessant hammering of bullets and bombs. Where the Praetorians had only small arms designed for use against humans, the clockwork mobile war suits had weaponry meant for destroying armored vehicles and jet aircraft. For a brief moment, it appeared that the New Olympian warriors and Grant had defeated Hera.

A blue tongue of electrical fire lashed out from Hera's right arm, punching through the chest of Her47les, the Sandcat armor vaporizing under intense heat. Herk, the pilot, was nowhere to be seen as the armored tub he sat in had been scoured out of the chassis of the robot. The gear skeleton collapsed, useless and empty.

Grant, having used up his antitank rockets, grabbed a grenade launcher and a bandolier of shells and raced for cover, barely avoiding a searing energy bolt that scooped out a ten-foot crater behind him.

Hera ran toward the remaining six warbots, her fists forming into massive clubs. P05seidon stabbed at one of the queen's wrists with his signature trident, a massive steel affair that had been used to good effect. A powerful array of batteries in the shaft discharged, releasing an electrical current that shook Hera to her core.

"Shouldn't have made our toys so good, bitch," Donnie taunted.

Hera shrugged, swinging P05eidon off the ramp and down to the rocks below. "Shut up, you sanctimonious idiot," Hera growled.

Apo110's Greek flame, a lethally flammable chemical concoction, washed over her at murderous temperatures, spewed from the flamethrowers on his forearms. Even as spines and scales melted on Hera's armor, she gestured with her hand. A lightning bolt slammed into Apo110's gear skeleton obliquely, spinning him and hurling him dozens of yards. Only the nonconductive nature of the secondary orichalcum protected Pollie, the pilot, from electrocution, even though the cybernetic control systems shut down.

Another blast would be the death of the golden-maned warbot. Artem15 leaped, smashing her fist hard into Hera's chest, D10nysus striking her in the small of the back from the other side. Hydraulic muscles meted out punches capable of shattering steel, and they knocked Hera to her knees temporarily. Unfortunately, Hera had grabbed Artem15 and swung her like a club, batting D10nysus into the ocean.

"Little girl, you always were an ugly disappointment," Hera snarled.

As she braced herself to hurl Artem15 to her death by drowning, Hera was interrupted. A leaping Are5 collided with her feetfirst, dropping all three of them in an avalanche down the hard-packed dirt. Grant pumped grenades into Hera as fast as he could load them, but he might as well have been throwing pebbles as the silver goddess scrambled easily to her feet.

"You simpletons," Hera hissed. "Why do you fight? I am all-powerful. I am the one who can call down the lightning. I possess the power of Zeus's wrath!"

"Oh, trust me, you've got Zeus's wrath," Thurmond challenged.

Hera paused, quicksilver lips forming a malicious smile as she looked at the doorless gear skeleton standing before her. Thurmond, in his Magistrate armor, sat in the armored tub, holding the shield formed from his former chest piece. A thunderbolt warhead rested in his other hand. "After all of this, after all the other pilots you executed, after all the people you've murdered for Cobalt, you've grown a conscience."

Hera lashed out with a lightning bolt, but the secondary orichalcum chest plate absorbed the burst of electrical energy, dispersing the lethal voltage, despite the steel handle that held it to Z00s's forearm.

"It's hard to explain a sudden attack of conscience to a soulless bitch with delusions of godhood," Thurmond countered, circling the armored queen. "You know, I really liked the plan where all we did was retire from this war and be good guys until the end of our days. Why'd you give that up?"

"Because I'm not an imagination-impaired troll like you," Hera snapped. "What's the use of these weapons unless we can enjoy using them?"

"Fine, I'll build a fucking target range for you," Thurmond returned. "I love not the sword for its sharpness. I love that which it defends."

Hera's quicksilver eyes rolled in disbelief. "I should have never taught you how to read, Thurmond. It filled that empty cabbage you call a head with ideas."

ZOOs shrugged, then lunged, hurling his thunderbolt warhead at Hera. The bomb detonated, rocking Hera backward, but hinged spider legs extended from her back, balancing her upright. She raised both hands, gouts of lightning lashing at ZOOs, but the mechanoid leader bounded, soaring over the bolts. He crashed down into her, shield first, driving her deep into the soil under a ton and a half of hurtling warbot.

That was almost enough to stagger Hera, but the bracing spider legs whipped around, one stabbing into ZOOs' cockpit. A clawed point lodged through Thurmond's shoulder, pinning him to his armored couch, the other trembling as ZOOs's hydraulic grasp held it at bay.

Hera twisted, struggling to push out from beneath the secondary orichalcum shield, cursing up a storm as she had no leverage against the massive clockwork leader.

Lightning crackled at her fingertips, and Grant realized that it would take only a few moments for the telepathically scarred madwoman to realize that she could conduct lethal current through the spearing claw in Thurmond's shoulder, frying him to death in a single surge of energy. Grant seized one final weapon from his war bag, an implode grenade. Priming the destructive weapon, he hurled the egg-shaped bomb at the murderous spine-stabbing goddess-queen. The implode grenade struck the hinged knee of the spider limb and detonated. The convulsive shock wave severed the joint in a blow that elicited cries of pain from both Thurmond and Hera.

ZOOs wrenched free, grinding his shield into Hera's face, pinning her down. He transmitted on Grant's Commtact frequency. "We need something to stop her! What did Domi do to deactivate the armor?"

"She hit the cyberport between Hera's shoulder blades," Grant replied quickly. "But we don't have anything that can penetrate to her."

"I do," Are5 spoke up, drawing his thermal ax. "Zoo, you gotta hold her up for me."

"Do it," Thurmond said. "See you on the other side, Ari."

The amputee Magistrate hurled his shield aside, scooping up Hera in a bear hug, crushing the armored goddess with all the power in his massive hydraulic limbs. Hera squirmed, screeching at the violation.

"Go to hell, Thurmond!" Hera cursed. Her smart-metal armor ejected its lethal spines, murderous points spearing through the Magistrate armor.

"Mind if I bring you along?" Thurmond asked, coughing up blood. "Do it, Ari!"

Hera whipped her head around, seeing the shape of Are5 sailing through the air, thermal ax blazing in a deadly arc. "Damn you, Thurmond…I'm a goddess…"

Superheated secondary orichalcum split through the smart metal and its added mass, carving aside the lethal layers of armor plating and burying itself into Helena Garthwaite's torso, splitting the cybernetic nub between her shoulders.

Suddenly inert, without Hera's maddened brain to control it, the armor shut down. The lethal spines had already completed their task, having perforated Thurmond's heart and other organs. The stored electrical energy in Hera's armor discharged. A powerful lightning bolt shattered Are5's ax and hurling him onto his back. Blue bolts emitted from the fused pair of Z00s and Hera, and immense heat from the charged energy modules melted their armored bodies together into a single golden lump of wreckage.

Deafening silence fell, weighing upon Grant like a stifling blanket. Stunned, he glanced around at the surviving pilots. P05seidon was crawling up the cliff, battered and with broken shoulder weapons, but none the worse for wear. Grant turned to the melted slag that contained both hero and killer.

"It was an honor, Thurmond," Grant whispered. "Rest easy."

Epilogue

The temple of the oracle would never be the historical archive to ancient Greece that it once had been. Brigid Baptiste regretted that lost piece of lore, but the site was ground for new history. The molten puddle of secondary orichalcum and smart metal had become a mirror-polished pool of glimmering metal. Praetorian artisans had crafted a stone ring around the pool, honoring the final resting place of New Olympus's greatest hero, the ex-Magistrate once known as Thurmond.

Brigid held Kane's hand as they stood beside it, pausing on their trek back up to the parallax point. Domi was saying goodbye to Diana and Aristotle as neither relished the idea of pushing their wheelchairs up the long slope leading to the old ruins. As the two highest-ranking members of the New Olympian pantheon, they had the unenviable task of running the interim government for the Greeks, at least until they figured out some form of constitution.

"They're in good hands," Brigid noted.

"Yeah, for once we came to a place where the good folks outnumbered the crazy," Kane agreed.

"No. We're in Greece, which was the birthplace of democracy," Brigid said.

"Yeah, but it was the Romans who developed a representative republic," Kane countered. "And Americans who finally ironed everything out to be perfect."

Brigid elbowed Kane in his still sore ribs. "Then it's come full circle. We brought self-rule back to them."

Grant rested his hand on Domi's shoulder and guided her back to Kane and Brigid. "Philboyd's asking what's keeping us so long."

"Respect for our friends," Kane answered.

"Saying goodbye to my new sister," Domi added.

"Yeah," Grant said. "He probably is in a rush to get back and run his crooked card game."

"You know, has it ever occurred to you that I might be pretty good at cards," Brigid noted, slipping her arm around Grant's waist. "Eidetic memory is killer at helping you count the deck."

Grant raised an eyebrow. "That would be cheating."

"So? Philboyd cheats, too," Brigid answered.

Grant looked back to the New Olympian contingent seeing them off. The four of them turned and waved. "I'll think about it, Baptiste. Right now, I'm just glad we're heading back to Cerberus."

"Tired of this place already?" Kane asked, rubbing his sore jaw, glancing at Grant balefully.

"I just miss Shizuka, actually," Grant confessed. "But I don't think I'll ever be tired of Greece anymore."

Domi nodded, grinning. "Yeah. Especially now that we're practically family."

The four explorers walked up the ramp for the jump back to Cerberus.

ROOM 59

THE HARDEST CHOICES
ARE THE MOST PERSONAL....

New recruit Jason Siku is ex-CIA, a cold, calculating
agent with black ops skills and a brilliant mind—a
loner perfect for deep espionage work. Using his Inuit
heritage and a search for his lost family as cover, he
tracks intelligence reports of a new Russian Oscar-class
submarine capable of reigniting the Cold War. But when
Jason discovers weapons smugglers and an idealistic yet
dangerous brother he never knew existed, his mission
and a secret hope collide with deadly consequences.

Look for

THE ties THAT BIND

by

cliff RYDER

GOLD
EAGLE ®

Available October 2008
wherever books are sold.

TAKE 'EM FREE

2 action-packed novels plus a mystery bonus

NO RISK
NO OBLIGATION TO BUY

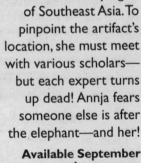

If you are looking for spine-tingling action and adventure, be sure to check out all that Gold Eagle books has to offer...

Rogue Angel by **Alex Archer**
Deathlands by **James Axler**
Outlanders by **James Axler**
The Executioner by **Don Pendleton**
Mack Bolan by **Don Pendleton**
Stony Man by **Don Pendleton**
NEW **Room 59** by **Cliff Ryder**

Journey to lost worlds, experience the heat of a fierce firefight, survive in a postapocalyptic future or go deep undercover with clandestine operatives.

Look for these books wherever books are sold.

GOLD EAGLE®

Fiction that surprises, gratifies and entertains. Real Heroes. Real Adventure.

www.readgoldeagle.blogspot.com